FALLING FOR JOHNNY

D1301851

Sale of this material benefits the Library.
Boston Public Library.
No longer the property of the
WITHDRAWN

ALISON MCLENNAN

A fictional story inspired by the Boston underworld and
the notorious Irish crime boss James "Whitey" Bulger.

"A doubtful friend is worse than a certain enemy. Let a man be one thing or the other, and we then know how to meet him."
— Aesop, Aesop's Fables

Published by Twisted Roots 2012
www.twistedrootspublishing.com
Ogden, UT
Copyright ©Alison McLennan 2011

This book is a work of fiction. Names, characters places and incidents may have been inspired by reality but have been fictionalized by the author and should not be misconstrued as factual.

All rights reserved, including the right to reproduce this book or portions thereof in any form whatsoever. For information on obtaining rights contact twistedrootspublishing.com

ISBN 978-0985394707
LCCN 2012946646
First Print Edition
Printed in the United States of America

Check with twistedrootspublishing.com to purchase audio and digital versions.

Thanks to all the faculty and students at the Solstice MFA program for guidance and support. Thanks to the "Old Guy" for letting me pick his brain about the Boston underworld. And to the one person truly dedicated to my success, whose energy and dedication I could not live without —my mother!

Sincerest gratitude to Sterling Watson who is an incredible writer, teacher, and mentor. I am eternally grateful for his dedication to mentoring, his encouragement, and feedback.

This book is dedicated to Mick, whose grounding in the real world allows me to create fictional ones. And to Finn, stay a kid as long as you can. Don't read this book too soon.

Preface

I MET a cagey old man on a mountain top. He seemed both out of place and like he belonged there, a Brooklyn Yoda—small, wrinkled, with a crooked nose. He was bundled up and shuffling people in and out of the Mount Allen ski tram. His words rang out with a hard Eastern edge, maybe New York or New Jersey. "You from Boston? What da ya think about Whitey Bulger? I heard he's hiding out in Huntsville."

"He's my uncle," I lied. It's almost expected in conversations like these. The Brooklyn Yoda's voice and that name, Whitey Bulger, haunted me. Of course I'd heard Whitey's name growing up, but I'd also heard a rumor about two guys dressed as clowns who drove around in a van and made shoes out of children. At the time of my encounter with the Brooklyn Yoda, I had just started a novel that took place in Quincy, Massachusetts, a city directly south of Boston. That's where I grew up—the source of my twisted roots.

I read everything I could find about Bulger and was surprised to find out that for a few years he lived directly across the street from me. From my reading, I formed a conglomerate image and created the fictional character, Johnny, in Falling for Johnny. Yet this novel isn't about the life and crimes of James "Whitey" Bulger. It's about falling—falling into crime, falling for drugs and the sweet numbing effects of libations, falling in love, and falling for people who aren't who they pretend to be.

At the time I began this novel, I thought Bulger was either dead or would never resurface. Literally, on my fortieth birthday, I awoke to the news that he had been arrested. I wrote him a letter and he wrote back. The voice that came through in that letter was similar to how I imagined he'd sound. Although the first part of this book may loosely resemble Bulger's life, this story is fiction and is not meant to accurately portray any real events or people.

Part I

Johnny

One

South Boston, 1949

THEY WERE about to break the law. Camel didn't see anything wrong with it, unless of course—they got caught. Hiding in the shadows of a metal trash can, sandwiched between Mugs and Scooter, he squatted on his haunches. He cast occasional glances down D Street, waited, and wished there was something more to do.

After a few minutes of silence, he pulled three pieces of Bazooka from his jacket pocket and offered a piece to Scooter and Mugs. Scooter took a piece, but Mugs scowled, shook a cigarette from a box of Lucky Strikes and placed it behind his ear. Camel and Scooter carefully unwrapped their comic strips from the hard, pink rectangles of gum. They huddled together and tried to read them by the filmy light shining from the streetlamp. Camel turned his scally cap around so the visor wouldn't shadow the words.

The truck's headlights illuminated the dark street. It rumbled up and stopped. The boys ran to it. Camel dropped his comic. The small paper skipped down the sidewalk before a whirling dervish of cold autumn air lifted and carried it away.

The boys off-loaded boxes from the back of the truck and stacked them onto another truck that had pulled up and was idling, filling the night with diesel fumes and a mechanical hum.

Spike O'Malley hoisted himself up and slung an arm around the side view mirror of the truck they were jacking. Camel noticed that even though Spike pointed a gun at the driver, they seemed to be carrying on a friendly conversation, as if they were old pals.

Widow Magee's curtains moved. The gang often sent Camel to deliver gift baskets to her. They knew she wouldn't talk. He liked Widow Magee. She always offered him candy and smiled, despite her knowledge of his criminal activities.

The boys finished off-loading the truck and ran down to the L Street bathhouse. They waited for Spike on a bench by Carson Beach. He finally drove up in a white Thunderbird and honked. Mugs ran over and came back with the cash. He handed a wad to Camel and Scooter. Scooter shoved the money into his back pocket without counting it. Camel watched the shiny Thunderbird glide down Columbia Avenue. He counted the bills in his hand—thirteen dollars.

"Hey Mugs, what's the total they take in from these jacks and what cut does everyone get?"

"Camel, ask any more questions like that and you'll be selling newspapers. You take what you get."

Camel's real name was John McPherson. He hated the name Camel. When he was a baby his older sister Mary had started calling him Camel because of his long eyelashes. His head had grown and the lashes were no longer prominent, but the name stuck.

The McPhersons lived in a blue-collar neighborhood, predominately Irish Catholic with pockets of Poles and Lithuanians. Three-story wooden houses, row houses, some five-story brick buildings and warehouses lined the streets. The tall buildings of Boston's financial district loomed on the northwest horizon, but in South Boston the steeples of the churches stood the highest, signifying the power of the parish. Large Catholic families populated South Boston and Dorchester. They were mostly working class and poor, but they voted, and their political power grew as they continued to take over the area. Huge semitrailers rumbled through quiet neighborhoods to get to the waterfront at all hours of the night. The men who had not gone to war worked on the docks, or if they were lucky at Boston Edison or Gillette.

When Johnny McPherson was ten his father Danny had an accident on the wharf that left him with one arm. Johnny's mother Dorothy had tried to make Danny's life easier by altering all the sleeves on his shirts and coats. Johnny's father fell into a deep depression anyway. He sat in the same armchair day after day—drinking. Three years after the accident, he died.

His mother did her best to provide for the family. She and his sister, Mary, scrubbed laundry and ironed clothes in their small government subsidized apartment at the Old Colony Housing Project. The twins, Catherine and Grace, were chubby lumps of pooping inconvenience. Even though they sucked on everything and left pudgy handprints all over the house, his mother still doted on them. His younger brother, Thomas, a studious altar boy, was the favorite—her pride and joy. She dreamed of the day he'd be a priest.

Despite his blond hair, Johnny was the black sheep. He ran everywhere. When scolded he'd stand still and solemn but his mother's words rang hollow. She tried his father's worn out strap, which still hung in the closet. Her blows tickled compared to the lickings his father had dished out.

8

When his mother confined him indoors and set him to scrubbing clothes, the energy spilled from his restless body. He knocked over washtubs and broke the quiet monotony of their domestic routine. "Go," his mother finally told him, "Just go."

ON THE STREET, Johnny found a place to thrive. He ran with a small gang of boys called the Lepers, an unfortunate shortening of Leprechauns. During rush hour, while the suits in Downtown Crossing piled on trains out of the city, Johnny and his friend, fast Eddie, picked pockets. At first, Johnny was motivated by a simple desire to purchase confections from O'Brien's Bakery and slowly lick off all the frosting. Then he discovered that his fast hands and even faster legs could earn him as much in an afternoon as his mother's laundry earned in an entire week.

The first time he brought food to the house, his mother was seated at the kitchen table with a weak cup of tea. One tea bag had to last an entire day. He placed a bag of groceries in front of her. A mixture of fear and relief crossed her face before she whisked the bag away. "Go to confession," she whispered harshly. He wanted his mother to look at him the same way she looked at Tommy when he was on the altar handing the host to Father Lynch. But he knew she never would.

Johnny's mother often had spells and disappeared into her bedroom for days at a time. Then his sister Mary became the mother. She took care of the brood making sure the work was finished and the family was fed. Mary kept them in line with the threat of no dinner or the promise of a sweet. Thomas prayed for his mother while Johnny snuck into her room and laid a few bills on the lace covered table beside her bed.

As Johnny grew into his teens, pleasures of the flesh replaced the desire to lick the frosting from a confection. He often wondered how the priests could forego these pleasures for life. He was certain they whacked off from time to time.

Johnny's blond hair and long eyelashes always made people look twice. But even though he attracted the attention of females from an early age he could never be described as cute. Sultry mischief glinted from his wolf-blue eyes hinting at a complex yet solitary sex life. Those wolf-eyes coupled with his pronounced canines that showed when he flashed his signature sideways grin— gave the impression that he just might eat you.

Some girls were drawn to his looks. He'd lead them to a secret place beyond the disapproving stares of dour women and the side long glances of restless men. Squeezed between a hedge and a fence that kept people safe from the electrifying force of the third rail, Johnny explored the ripe breasts and hardened nipples of girls who fell for his menacing good looks. Bird songs were intermittently silenced by passing subway trains, which rattled and vibrated the chain link fence in a way that never failed to excite him.

He would feel himself grow hard and hungry yet the girls always resisted his attempts to relieve his throbbing in the softness between their legs. Even the bad girls were still Catholic bad girls, not bad enough to go all the way. Johnny took his pent up energy into the boxing ring where he became a vicious fighter.

The trucks that rumbled through the streets of South Boston in the middle of the night provided perfect fodder for street gangs. No one in the neighborhood had sympathy for the big companies that were the victims of the heists. The city let commercial trucks endanger their young children by day and awaken them in the middle of the night. Trucks didn't rumble through Beacon Hill at all hours. When the police investigated, no one had ever seen or heard a thing.

The police finally set up a sting and staked out the streets in unmarked cars. The men were able to flee in cars but Johnny and a bunch of other boys were rounded up, thrown in a paddy wagon, brought down to the station and booked on charges. At Johnny's hearing his mother struck a deal with the judge and kept him out of juvenile detention by offering his custodial services free of charge at St. Mary's. He paid off his debt to society every weekday evening cleaning the hallways and scrubbing toilets.

Through his altar boy service and good grades, Johnny's brother Thomas had earned a scholarship to the school. Tommy hid bags of unblessed communion wafers for Johnny to snack on. They were tasteless pieces of cardboard but they filled the gnawing hole in his stomach since he couldn't get home for dinner till after eight.

Tommy assisted Father Lynch, who was the least strict of all the priests and nuns. He was not too old to play football with the boys and they looked up to him for his skill. Father Lynch often pulled a hard candy from his pocket and would surprise a sullen boy, tousling his hair and giving him a good-natured wink. He seemed to favor certain boys and they were envied by the others.

Johnny was one of those boys, and he in turn admired Father Lynch for his strength and the way he threw a ball. Most priests seemed like soft old women but Johnny knew Father Lynch could at least give a licking like a man and put the fear of God into you. Johnny was raised to fear God and the fires of hell, but he was a skeptic at heart. For all the things he'd done so far, he was probably going to hell or purgatory so it would benefit him if the whole thing turned out to be a sham. Johnny figured Tommy at least was praying for his soul.

ONE EVENING in late March, Johnny mopped the school's long second floor corridor. He watched the stark white fibers of the mop move across the shiny wood floor and wondered what was worse—this drawn out community service rap or the quick but painful and humiliating beatings the cops usually dished out because they were too lazy to fill out paperwork. He'd heard his mother plead with the judge and was ashamed yet touched at how low she'd stoop for him. For his mother, he'd try to stay out of trouble. He turned to wring the mop out in the metal bucket and jumped at the unexpected presence of Father Lynch.

"Father, you startled me. I thought I was alone."

"Oh you're never alone son. God is always with you."

"Well I better watch myself then."

"God forgives all those who trespass against him. You're doing a fine job here. I've been meaning to tell you that. You're paying your penance."

"Thank you, Father." Johnny didn't want to hear a sermon. He just wanted to finish his work and get home for dinner, if his sister had left him any.

"Are you hungry, Camel?"

"I'm always hungry. You can call me Johnny, Father."

"Oh, I thought they called you Camel."

"They do but I don't like it much."

"Well then Johnny, come into the rectory and we'll see what we can find. Your work is done for the evening. This floor will be treaded on first thing in the morning and no one will know the difference."

"Thank you Father. That's very kind of you."

Wide-legged and relaxed, Johnny splayed himself out at a table in the rectory. Father Lynch set a plate of corned beef and cabbage with carrots and potatoes in front of him. It was a cold plate of leftovers from the evening meal, but that didn't bother him. By now he was accustomed to a cold dinner. He shoveled in the food as fast as he could.

11

"Slow down son. You'll hurt yourself. Here, have some of this." Father Lynch poured some wine into a juice glass. "It aids digestion."

Johnny looked skeptically at the wine. After seeing what alcohol had done to his father, it was hard to believe it aided anything.

"Jesus turned water into wine, remember."

Johnny shrugged and gulped down the wine. He coughed a bit as he put the glass on the table.

"Most people sip it." Father Lynch refilled his cup.

"Do nuns drink wine too?" Johnny felt a little dizzy.

"Nuns?" Father Lynch laughed. "No. Nuns are…well nuns are nuns. But priests are allowed a few vices." He lit a cigarette. "I think God wants us to have a few vices. It helps us understand our flock. I understand you have a few vices Johnny."

"Well, that's why I'm here, isn't it? If it were my decision, believe me, I'd be doing something else."

Father Lynch blew smoke from his nostrils. "What would you be doing now? If you could be doing anything you wanted."

"Well now that I'm done eating, I might be… you know, trying to be with a girl. Or maybe I'd be boxing down at the ring."

"You take good care of your body. I can see that. You're strong and fit." Father Lynch squeezed his shoulder and sized him up. "Is that from boxing?"

"Mostly. You look fit yourself, Father. That's one thing I admire about you. The way you throw a ball—it's something. You don't see many priests able to do that."

"Most priests forsake the body for the spirit. I am different. I believe God gave us bodies to be strong, to do physical labor, to play sports, and to enjoy." Father Lynch leaned against the kitchen counter. He held his cigarette in one hand and sipped a glass of wine with the other. "How's the wine son?"

"It's okay. A bit sour—could use some sugar."

"It's an acquired taste. Let's move into my private quarters to have some more, just in case Mrs. Collins comes nosing around."

"Yeah, all right. I don't need any more trouble from her. She's had it in for me ever since I took her daughter out."

Father Lynch extinguished his cigarette and filled Johnny's glass again. With the bottle in one hand and a glass in the other, he walked out of the kitchen. From the hallway, he looked back at Johnny and cocked his head in the direction of his room. Johnny grinned and rose from the table. The wooden chair toppled onto the black and white checkered linoleum floor. Johnny set it right, picked up his glass, took a long gulp, and followed Father Lynch.

Father Lynch motioned Johnny toward two easy chairs and a table in a corner of his quarters. He placed the wine bottle on the table. "Take a seat and help yourself to as much of that as you want." He walked over to his bed, dresser, and closet. Johnny sat down and watched him slip off his black jacket, release the stiff white collar from around his neck, and place it under a small lamp on his bureau.

Johnny looked at the collar, which still seemed to contain the shape of Father Lynch's neck. It reminded him of a manacle. Father Lynch opened the closet and disappeared inside for a moment. He stepped out with a hanger and slid his coat onto it.

"You don't mind if I get comfortable, do you Johnny? You know underneath all this I'm just a man like you."

"Do what you like Father. It's your room."

Johnny placed his glass on the table. As he watched Father Lynch undress, he slid his tongue over his teeth and shifted his jaw from side to side. He noticed the strawberry blond hair that curled out over the top of Father Lynch's white tank undershirt and the muscles in his arms, which hardened even from the subtle effort of undressing.

"Where'd you get so many freckles, Father? I thought you priests weren't supposed to expose your holy flesh. But you look like you been taking some side trips to the Riviera." Johnny nodded at the thick masses of freckles on Father Lynch's shoulders that had joined to give his skin a golden hue. The wine had emboldened Johnny and loosened his tongue but the slight spinning in his head and the overly friendly way Father Lynch was acting warned him not to drink anymore. In an alleyway surrounded by cops with their hard boots and clubs searching for soft spots to kick, beat, and prod him, he had no choice but to curl up and take it. But here in the bedroom of a man only armed with a white collar and gold cross, Johnny knew he could win.

Father Lynch sank into the chair in front of him. He relaxed and rested his arm on its back. Johnny's eyes moved to the hair in his armpit then back to his face. He had some faded freckles and a normal sized nose. His grayish eyes were hooded by bushy blond brows, nothing ugly. But underneath that friendly demeanor was a faint look of disgust, like at any moment he might vomit. Father Lynch looked at him with the expression of a child who had only ever seen but never tasted candy.

Johnny flashed his sideways grin. "This is going to cost you, you know that Father?"

Father Lynch bolted upright in his chair. "What do you mean boy?"

"Whoa. I ain't your boy." Johnny laughed.

"Jesus. What kind of a monster are you?"

"Now, now. I'm no worse than you Father. At least I don't pretend to be a son of God. I love my mother, but we're all sons of bitches aren't we? Women, you gotta love them but they're hounds from hell, every one."

Father Lynch sank back in the chair trembling. "This talk it's—"

Johnny rose from his chair. "If you can't handle the fire then you better stay out of hell Father. I gotta go."

"No. Wait." Father Lynch grabbed Johnny's arm and swallowed. "How much?"

Johnny looked down at him. "You can look at me. See me naked. Flog your log if you want. But you gotta pay me two hundred dollars and no touching. I saw the way you were looking at me just then. I know you're going to picture me when I ain't here. Maybe you already have. Now I'm here. You got the real thing. But it's going to cost you."

JOHNNY SLID two hundred dollars worth of bills into his pocket and buttoned up his shirt. He'd thought briefly about oral sex. He had thought maybe he could close his eyes and just pretend it was Kathy Collins doing it. But he'd decided that was too much a stretch of the imagination.

Father Lynch sat in the easy chair with a look of revolted relief. Johnny realized Father Lynch often looked like he was about to vomit because his hypocrisy was an undigested carcass rotting in his stomach.

"Tell me one thing before I leave this town for good."

Father Lynch looked up but did not meet his gaze.

"Have you ever touched my brother?" Johnny felt the heat rise in his body as Father Lynch shifted nervously.

"No. Of course not."

Johnny leaned over and supported his weight on the arms of Father Lynch's chair. He leaned in close and whispered into his ear, "Good, because if you do, or I find out you ever did, I will come back and kill you."

Father Lynch snapped out of his daze and said through his teeth, "You wouldn't kill a man of God."

Johnny baited the dog, kicked him again, tried to get him to bite. "But you ain't one of them now, are you? What happened tonight makes you nothing more than a hypocrite."

Father Lynch lunged at him as Johnny had hoped he would. Johnny was that quick with the switchblade. It sprang from his pocket and he held it at the Father's defeated, quivering throat. "I bet they didn't teach you this in the seminary."

Johnny bounded out of the rectory disheveled and reeking of wine. He nearly knocked over Thomas who was looking for him.

"You won't believe what that queer pervert just tried on me," Johnny said as he charged down the street. Thomas followed him and righted the trash cans he kicked over. "Camel," he chased after him, "I'm sorry. I should have warned you."

"He didn't do nothin to me. I kicked him in the coolies! Did you know he was like that? Has he ever touched you?" Johnny turned on his brother, raised him by his jacket, and searched his eyes.

"No, but I had some suspicions. I couldn't really believe them though. I thought I was sinning for thinking such things about a priest."

"It's not your fault the guy's a three dollar bill, Tommy. You're perfect. You should know that." Johnny put Tommy in a headlock and knuckled his head till he wrenched free. He turned a corner down an alley. He leaned against a building and slid down to the sidewalk where he rested on his haunches. Tommy followed and squatted next to him.

"I'm not going back there, Camel. I'm never going to be a priest. It's over for me now. I'm quitting that school too."

Johnny looked into the distance. The energy had drained out of him but an idea had formed. He reached into his pocket and pulled out a thick wad of bills.

"No Tommy, you go back to that school. Don't be a priest though. Be a politician, and maybe one day you can save me from riding the thunderbolt."

"What? Camel, where did you get all that money?"

Johnny counted the money then looked at his brother.

"You go back to that school and pretend nothing happened, but every week you make sure to take some of the collection money and start picking up anything gold. Some of that stuff is real. Don't do it all at once, just a little at a time."

"I don't know if I can do that kind of thing."

"Listen, if Lynch catches you, tell him you know what he's up to. Tell him you got proof from me."

"What's the proof?"

"Doesn't matter— just make him think you have it."

"Camel I—"

"He didn't do nothin' to me. Tried though, and he found my knife at his throat." Johnny sprung the knife from his pocket and smiled at it. "You should have seen the look on his face."

"What are you going to do now?"

"I'm gonna skip. You take this." Johnny shoved the knife back into his pocket, retrieved the wad, peeled some bills off, and handed them to Tommy. "Give it to Ma. This is for you." He peeled off a few more bills. "I'll be back one day. Don't tell anyone about this. Not a soul. No one's going to believe it anyhow."

"What about Ma? What about your court order?"

"I can't do it anymore. I got to get out of here. I'm going to leave town for a while—figure out what I'm going to do with my life. Go some place no one calls me Camel. No more church. I'm not even going to pretend to be good. Because guess what? I ain't. Ma knows what I'm like. You be her pride and joy, but don't forget to get some of that collection money." Johnny hopped to his feet. "Let's smash some bottles, Tommy. Will you do that with me? I got to break something."

"I'll do anything for you brother. Anything."

Two

JOHNNY FOLLOWED the train tracks out of town. He wanted to get away from what had just happened. Using his body and good looks to get money made him feel powerful in a way but it also made him feel dirty, like a whore. He wouldn't do that again. Yet when he had held the knife at Lynch's throat and that lusty look of his changed to terror, something akin to pleasure had pulsed through his body making him feel alive and powerful, like he could do anything.

As soon as the next train came along he'd hop it, jump off somewhere and start over. He hadn't really believed in religion, but before tonight he'd at least believed in Father Lynch—believed he was a good guy. Now he knew Father Lynch was not only a creep but also a hypocrite. He wore robes and collars, acting haughty and holy when he was just as low as the people and acts he condemned. The whole thing was a con—the men in robes too good to be true. The way some men liked boys and other men—no one ever talked about that either, but it was there all right. He'd seen it more than once.

People would deny their true nature, wanting to be good, not wanting to want what they really wanted but wanting it more and more by denying it. He was finally free. He wasn't going to burn in hell for doing what he wanted. Bullshit. It was all bullshit. He locked the memory of Father Lynch away and focused on the future instead of the past.

Moonlight reflected off the rails. He kept his eyes on the gravel between the tracks that guided him forward. Each step was a step away. In the gravel between the rails he could just make out some little plants— fuzzy lamb's ear, parsley, and mint. Renegade seeds had blown from distant gardens and rooted in the rocky soil. He picked a mint leaf, smelled it, and popped it into his mouth. He had some money but he knew it wouldn't last long. He'd have to keep his eyes open for opportunities to make or take more before he got down to his last dime. He always socked some money away and pretended he didn't have it. Without at least a little bit of savings, he couldn't relax. He hated the hand-to-mouth way his family had to live.

The ground rumbled. The train's loud horn punctured the quiet night. The sound lingered and echoed like someone pounding on an organ. In that sound, he heard both warning and hope. The rails vibrated and pinged. Johnny snapped out of his rhythmic purposeful stride to nowhere and stepped out of the track. The train appeared. He jogged alongside it waiting for an opportunity to jump. Some of the cars were brightly painted with the words Carlos Bros. Circus on the side.

He couldn't believe his luck. The circus had been out in Abington, and although he had wanted to, he'd never managed to make it out to see a show. As he ran beside the train, he knew he was meant to be right where he was, like he'd already seen it happen. There was a crossing coming up and if he could just keep up with the train, it would slow and he'd be able to grab a rail.

When he was nearly out of breath and exhausted from running, the train finally slowed. With a sudden burst of energy, he jumped for the iron rung of the ladder. He had it with one arm and the rest of his body flailed for a moment until he summoned all his strength and swung his foot onto the ladder. Then it was easy to get stable. His timing was lucky. The car sped up and he felt the wind in his hair. A sliver of moon in the evening sky seemed to follow him. For a moment, he forgot what he was running from and only felt the refreshing night air cool his body. He clung to the ladder feeling free. Free to dream, with his future ahead and the past receding into the night as the factories, thickly settled houses, and tenements gave way to woods and forests.

When the exhilaration of the moment wore off, he realized he had no plan. He held on and wondered what to do next. He knew he couldn't cling to the ladder all night. But if it were possible to make it into one of the boxcars, he might get some rest. The door to the boxcar was closed. His only hope was to find an open door or roof vent he could squeeze through.

He climbed up the ladder onto the roof of the car and walked in a crouched manner to the end. He climbed down the ladder and up to the roof of the next car. On the third car, a door was partially open and he could see and smell horses. Maybe he could get some sleep in the horse car if they didn't step on him when the train stopped. They would shuffle to maintain balance— he'd have to be careful.

From the roof, he swung into the open boxcar door, falling onto his knees. He stood up and brushed some hay off his trousers. He was grateful to see the horses in makeshift stalls. They were spooked by his sudden dramatic entrance, and it took several minutes of shushing and sweet-talking to calm them down. Johnny retreated to the far corner of the car and sat against the wall. He closed his eyes and fell asleep sitting up.

When he awoke, the train was not moving. He stretched and peeked outside. The boxcars were being unloaded by gangs of scruffy looking unshaven men. He got out and joined them, drawing little attention, lending a hand when he could.

The fairgrounds were in a nearby field. Groups of men off-loaded heavy equipment from boxcars onto trucks. The trucks kicked up clouds of dust as they drove across the field. Other cars were being unloaded and the contents hand-carried to the fairgrounds. A man with a cowboy hat on horseback herded the horses Johnny had spent the night with across the dusty field. Gradually the boxcars emptied. In the distance, Johnny could see tents, poles, and makeshift structures starting to rise.

"Say, who does a fella see about getting some work with the show?" Johnny asked one of the men he'd been unloading with all morning.

The man looked at him surprised. "I thought you already worked for the show. You been unloading all morning."

"No, just trying to be helpful. I'd like to though."

"Well, go see Little John over there." He pointed to an enormous man in the distance who was busy directing people.

Johnny dusted himself off and walked over to the giant man. He had to wait some time till the giant finished barking orders to half a dozen men.

"Heard you might be looking for some help around here. I'm a hard worker. Can lift about 200 lbs. Won't let you down."

"Is that right? I saw you working this morning. Didn't think I'd hired you. How old are you kid?"

"Seventeen."

"You ain't wanted by the law for nothing are you?"

"No, Sir."

"All right then. We'll try you out. Go on over to that guy with the red plaid shirt. His name's Jack. Tell him I said you'll be on his crew."

The performers strutted like peacocks while the roustabouts and working men struggled to raise the tents and build the temporary structures that would house them. Even the midgets seemed to strut about with an air of self-importance. He laughed. What was a circus without midgets after all?

Johnny could hear his stomach rumble and was beginning to feel irritated. He had worked hard all morning without breakfast and was relieved that the mess tent was now set up. The first chow bell rang and the performers went to eat. On the second chow bell, his crew went to the mess tent. Scrambled eggs, bacon, sausages, and pancakes—Johnny couldn't believe he was allowed to take as much as he wanted.

"Only one rule, son," said the man in front of him. "Don't waste anything. Old Bessie and Floyd, the cooks, they been here right through the Depression back when they made soup out of stones, so don't ever let em see you throwing no food out."

"That's easy. I got a bottomless stomach. Waste not, want not, right?"

SOME PEOPLE lived in the boxcars. Others slept in tents. Some just laid out bedrolls and bunked down wherever they could. On the third morning, when nearly all the rigging was finally set up, Johnny noticed a ravishing woman strutting across the field from her own private boxcar wearing a bright red robe and high heels. A man wearing a cowboy hat with a handlebar mustache walked a few paces behind her with his head slightly bowed. He could be her servant, a body guard, or maybe her old man. Johnny guessed if there was a mud puddle in her path the man would lie down in front of her and let her walk over him, heels digging into his back and all.

They approached the ladder of the trapeze rig that Johnny had just been working on. The man held her robe from behind as she stepped out of it. She wore a one-piece sequined leotard, which caught the morning sun and sent flashes of light everywhere. As she climbed the ladder, Johnny could not take his eyes off her strong curvy body, believing he'd finally seen female perfection. She flew through the air with such effortless grace that he wanted to hang upside down by his knees and reach out to catch her. But it was another man who caught her and he wondered what it would take to be that man.

The man with the handle bar mustache stood next to Johnny. "That's our Eva. Ain't she something?" Neither man took their eyes off her curvy sequined figure, which glinted in the sun like a flying jewel. Johnny nodded, wondering what it would take to get her to even look in his general direction.

He did not have to wait long. In the heat of the next afternoon, sweaty and shirtless, swinging a hammer to drive a stake into the ground, he stopped to wipe his brow. Eva was there behind him.

"Roustabout, what's your name?" she asked with a thick French accent.

"Well hello. I didn't know you were there. Uh, my name's Johnny."

"Come here, Johnny. Let me see your teeth." She waited for him to come to her.

Feeling awkward, he took a few steps toward her and bared his teeth. She grabbed his mouth and said, "Open." He stretched his jaw and studied her eyes as she peered into his mouth. Her thick black lashes batted slowly and sensually as if at any moment she might just close her eyes entirely. But he felt no softness in her rough and calloused hand as she moved his head slightly to the side to get a better look at his molars.

"Very good," she said. "You come see me in my car tonight after dinner. Knock three times. I'll be waiting. Oh, in case you don't know, I'm Eva."

"I know," he said to himself as she walked away. He could not believe it. Now he had to wait the five long hours till after dinner. He was damn glad he had good teeth.

That evening he knocked three times on Eva's door.

"Come in, darling," she called. She sat on a daybed drinking wine. The man with the handlebar moustache sat in a chair drinking whiskey. His hat sat beside him on a table like a small companion. Damn. Johnny was disappointed to see the man. Somehow he had thought they were going to be alone. Somehow he had thought she was coming on to him, and now he wondered what she wanted and why she had been so interested in his teeth.

"Zees is my friend Charlie. He wants to throw knives at me," Eva said dismissively waving one hand in the air and sipping wine with the other.

Charlie stood up and shook Johnny's hand vigorously. "Nice to meet you son," he said in an easy Southern drawl. "Get you a whiskey?"

"Sure." Johnny had never drunk whiskey in his life, but he didn't want to seem as young as he was.

Charlie got up and poured him a glass. He handed it to Johnny and they settled stiffly into chairs.

"See, I'm a knife thrower, but I ain't got a lady right now so I'm trying to convince Miss Eva here to step in for me. I know she got the nerve by the way she hangs on them bars thirty feet in the air."

Johnny cleared his throat. "What happened to your last lady assistant?" He took a sip of the whiskey and tried to cover his cough as he felt it burn his throat.

21

"I see what you're thinking. No, no, no, it wasn't like that. She went off and got married, wanted to settle down and raise some babies. Oh no son, I've never so much as grazed a hair on any of my ladies' heads. Don't you worry about that."

"Okay Charlie," said Eva interrupting. "I will think about this. But right now you go practice. If you can throw straight after drinking that much whiskey, maybe I help you. You go. I want to talk to this boy alone now."

"I see how it is then." Charlie picked up his hat and placed it on his head. "But don't you forget about me, Eva."

"No, I will never forget about you, my love," she said rising from the daybed and walking toward him. She had one hand on the doorknob and lifted her face to kiss him. He leaned down and they kissed long and hard on the mouth. She ended the kiss and backed away from him. His eyes were still shut savoring it.

Charlie was in love with Eva, and yet he was leaving her there alone with him. What did he think he was, some harmless, naïve kid not worth his jealousy? Johnny wondered what he was doing there if Eva was Charlie's doll.

"Woo-eee!" Charlie yelped. "That kiss alone, Eva, will get me through many cold and lonely nights." The door shut and the sound of Charlie's footsteps faded into the night. He was probably heading off somewhere to throw knives at the silhouette of a woman and drink more whiskey.

Johnny was alone with Eva, one of the biggest stars of the show. He could get used to her comfortable boxcar. The soft looking bed was strewn with brightly colored pillows. He tried to keep cool. Eva looked at him boldly with desire, the way no other female ever had. The girls he chased had always averted their eyes, even when he knew they shared his longing. Her full lips were painted red and her mouth formed a sensual pout as if asking, "Why isn't someone kissing me?"

He tried to be confident, to sit straight, and drink his whiskey like a man, the way Charlie had, but he suppressed a cough as he took a drink and it burned his throat again.

"How old are you?"

"I'm nineteen ma'am, I mean Eva. How old are you?"

"So young and fresh and with such good teez." She inspected him the way you would produce. "Never ask a woman her age. That is her secret. She will never tell you the truth anyway. Age is not in your years. It is how you feel, how you move, and I feel young. But younger still when I look at you." She moved toward him.

22

"That's good." Johnny stood, relieved to find himself a head taller than her. He dared to slip his arms around her waist. "Young is good. We're both young and we both have good teeth." He bent to kiss her.

Three

SEX with a French trapeze artist. What more could he want? After the first night, he often slept in her car, fetched her morning coffee, and did a million other errands while trying not to neglect his duties as a roustabout. He could not complain about having regular sex with a gorgeous French woman. But he grimaced every time she called him Kitten, and since Kitten was her nickname for him he found himself grimacing a lot. He wouldn't have minded if she called him Tiger. That was manly, but Kitten made him feel like a baby, like a toy. It was almost worse than Camel. He juggled her needs with the demands of his own job and walked a fine line between the laborers and the performers. There was a clear boundary between the two groups, and when he started sleeping with Eva, he fit into neither category.

In the evenings after dinner when there was no show, he often found himself watching Charlie throw knives at Eva. Charlie showed him how to hold the knife, aim and throw it. Johnny practiced every chance he got till he could hit the outline of the body on the backboard.

One night, after knife throwing practice, they all went back to Eva's boxcar for drinks. Johnny sat on the daybed next to Eva. Charlie sat in his usual chair blending in with the décor like a floor lamp, his hat a faithful companion beside him. Johnny was anxious for him to leave so he could be alone with Eva. She kept kissing him and getting him all worked up. He was definitely not interested in any kind of a threesome with Charlie. He kept glancing over at Charlie hoping he might take the hint and get lost.

Eva sensed his distraction. "Don't mind if he stays, Kitten. He'd like to watch, that's all."

Johnny sat up straighter and looked from Eva to Charlie. "That seems kind of strange."

"You Americans with your Puritan heritage, so ashamed, so private about your sex, your bodies," she scolded. "I am a descendant of Louis the Fourteenth's favorite courtesan. Am I ashamed? No."

"She must have been good," said Johnny.

"Kitten, whatever you do with your life, just be the best you can be and don't ever be ashamed."

"Well, I for one ain't ashamed," said Charlie from the corner suddenly coming to life. "My mother was ashamed. She was

24

ashamed of being alone. She was ashamed of having me, ashamed of where we lived, of the clothes we wore. Lived her whole life being ashamed! Religious as all hell, always praying for a better go around in the afterlife. God rest her soul. I hope for her sake she found it." He shook his head and took a drink. "But I believe this is all there is. Ashes to ashes, dust to dust. So we better live each day as if it's our last."

That was the most he'd said all evening.

What the hell— if he wanted to watch, let him watch thought Johnny. After all, the guy had taught him all his knife throwing secrets. "Watchin's all he wants to do?"

"That's it, Kitten," Eva whispered into his ear and began kissing him again. She moved her hand down and caressed his hardness.

She pushed him back onto the daybed. His head sank into a silk tasseled pillow. He tried to decide if he should forget about Charlie or give him a show. He decided he'd show him what real men were made of. Ultimately, it wasn't the cowboy hat, or how good a shot you were, that made you a man. It was how you loved a woman. He'd been a boy, not too long ago, but after these months with Eva, he knew he was a man. He could make her moan and cry for more, and Charlie obviously couldn't.

He rolled Eva over onto her back, straddled her hips and took off his shirt, flinging it behind him, aiming for Charlie. He glanced at Charlie and smiled but the man's face was as immovable as the wall behind him. Eva squirmed with anticipation underneath him. He'd wait, draw it out, tease her till she begged. When he glanced over his shoulder again he saw Charlie's jaw shift subtly under the cloak of his moustache. He slid his trousers off, not caring what part of him he showed to Charlie.

Maybe Charlie had expected him to be shy. Maybe he wanted to get off on his awkwardness, but he'd soon see. The next time he glanced at Charlie, he was reaching for his hat, and the next time he was gone. But even though Johnny won in bed with Eva, it was Charlie who was always by her side.

JOHNNY watched the first show when Eva allowed Charlie to throw knives at her. As the balloons popped all around her sequined body, Johnny sensed something between Eva and Charlie that was deeper and more important than what he had with her. He knew he could never be part of it. After that show, when all the performers celebrated in exalted revelry, he found a secret card game in a dingy boxcar far from the after-show party.

"Say, ain't you Eva's new boy?" asked one of the players.

"I ain't no one's boy," he responded. Showing the tough, hard edged kid who ran away from South Boston.

"All right, kid. Whatever you say. Can you ante?"

He was down, then way up and holding steady when the boxcar door slid all the way open. The night breeze stirred the stale, smoky air of the illicit poker game. With the moonlight behind him, a caped man appeared as a silhouette. The card players groaned. "Gentleman, I've found you at last," he said and extended his arms in a grand gesture. Another groan arose from the card players. Some shook their heads and folded their hands.

"Ain't that the sideshow magician?" Johnny asked the man on his left.

"Yeah, and the only rule I have is: don't play cards with a magician."

"Why do you let him in?"

"If we don't, he'll tell the ringmasters about our game here and all the fun will be over. Don't worry. He'll pass out in about an hour or two, and we'll steal our money back. Just keep your bets low and watch his hands. If we catch him doing anything funny, he's out of here."

"Okay Count, disrobe," someone ordered, resigned to the fact that the magician wasn't going away. Starting with his cape, which he threw off with a flourish, the Count undressed down to his undershirt and pants.

"Pants too," someone yelled.

He cocked his head to the side and dropped his trousers revealing ladies' bloomers. The men broke into hysterics, followed by catcalls and whistles. The Count, a true showman, turned in a full circle and said, "Gentleman, get ready to lose your pants."

During the game, Johnny watched the Count's hands closely. The men were all weary, knowing he was up to his tricks but unable to catch him. Like clockwork, the Count won every other hand. At one point he raised the bet with the pocket watch of the man on his left. The man grabbed it and mocked a punch to his head. They continued to play, filling the Count's shot glass every chance they got, calling for toasts, watching him throw back shot after shot until finally he fell out of his chair. The card players took back their money, dragged him to the corner of the boxcar, threw his cape over him and returned to the game. Johnny decided that it would be worth his while to spend some time with the Count.

LATE one evening after a show, Johnny was practicing throwing knives at the empty backboard. He felt a strange power as if he had stepped into a zone of heightened awareness. His hand and mind were in perfect alignment. After hundreds of perfect throws, he was finally confident that it was safe for Eva to step in. He could feel her standing behind him silently watching.

She put a hand on the small of his back and nuzzled her nose into his neck. "You're doing very well, Kitten."

"I think I'm finally ready, Eva. How about stepping in there for a minute?"

She looked at him for a long time. He held her gaze and tried to steady his breathing as her hesitation burned his throat. "Well, how about it?"

She smiled apologetically. "Sorry." With her eyes fixed to the ground she strode past the backboard and out the back entrance of the tent.

He stood, stunned. Releasing all his rage he threw a knife as hard as he could at the center of the taped body. The knife hit the outlined body where the heart would be and vibrated for a minute from the force of his throw. Charlie entered the tent and stood behind him. He had that way of just appearing, and you'd never know exactly when or how he got there.

"Don't be sore at Eva, son. She's right you know."

"What do you mean? I haven't hit the body since about five hundred throws ago."

"Except that one."

Johnny looked at the knife stuck where the heart would be.

"That one was different. I meant it."

Charlie sighed and shook his head. "Well, when a human being steps into that space, everything changes. It's not just about your aim any more. You have to make sure your heart is pure and your head is clear. Any bad feeling, any jealousy or soreness you have toward that person will tighten the muscles in your hand without you even noticing it. Everything changes when there's a body in that spot, and the more involved you are with the person the harder it is. I don't usually get involved with my assistants."

"Yeah, so how do you stay so pure with Eva then? Especially when you see her with me?"

Charlie nodded his head and looked at the floor as if seeing something there, some scene from his life too painful to talk about. "It's complicated," he said looking into Johnny's eyes.

Johnny spent less time with them and more time playing cards with the Count, learning his tricks. The sleight of hand, he thought, could be very useful.

ONCE when he was alone with Eva he asked, "Aren't you ever afraid of Charlie? You know if he gets mad at you, he might just slip with one of those knives one day."

"Afraid of Charlie? No. Charlie loves me no matter what I do. I know he would never, never hurt me. You Kitten, you are very different. You have zee potential to be very dangerous."

Johnny opened his mouth to protest but Eva closed it with her hand and put her finger to his lips. "Shh. That's why I chose you."

"What about Charlie watching us? Don't you think that's a little off- center?"

"Oh Kitten," she said exasperated. "If you must know, he was injured in the war. Never say a word."

Johnny let it go but he always wondered what type of war injury prevented a man from having sex. Charlie didn't seem to have any trouble taking a leak.

Four

JOHNNY WAS TIRED. He was tired of setting up and breaking down the tents in an endless cycle. He was tired of working long hours for peanuts. The novelty and excitement of the circus had worn off and even his relationship with Eva had started to bore him. The way she had inspected his teeth, he could have been at the slave market. With their age difference and her being the star of the show, he'd never get the upper hand. He'd always be her boy toy. Although he messed around with acrobatics and knife throwing, he felt he could never rise to the status of a performer, and even if he could, it was not really what he wanted.

He wanted money, lots of money. In his mind, he was always imagining the details of different jobs—bank jobs, jewelry stores, anything with a large return. Petty crime didn't suit him. That was for desperados and hobos. When he lay down to sleep at night, he planned crimes the way an architect might plan a building. He missed the excitement of his gang, the threat of violence, and getting caught, which kept him on his toes and made him feel truly alive. When he was bored and irritated, he just wanted to knock a man's teeth out, to see him bleed, and smell his fear. Sometimes he just wanted a good fight.

Without saying goodbye to anyone, he left the circus in Pittsburg and enlisted in the Army. He soon discovered that was a mistake. Perhaps he would have had a great military career in another time, when invading armies plundered and pillaged. But these days, war lacked the spoils. It was just death and carnage. You were nothing more than a cog in the machine, and even if you survived warfare, what would you get? A medal? Honor? Glory? Then you were expected to go back and live in the run-down house, on the run-down street, in the crummy town where you grew up. Ancient warfare, with warriors and chieftains would have been more his style.

World War II was over and now the fight was against Communism. He didn't really understand what Communism was, but back home a lot of Union guys were labeled as Communists, and he wondered if it wasn't just something cooked up by the suits and big wigs to keep the working man down.

Johnny spent a lot of time in the stockade for insubordination and fighting. They told him he'd never amount to anything and would never get a job. They told him he was a good-for-nothing low-life and that he didn't deserve the chance to defend his own country. When boot camp was over they discharged him.

With limited choices, Johnny felt himself pulled toward what he knew in his heart was his calling. For the most part, honest working-class people stayed poor or at best became middle class. It seemed to him corruption was the only path that led to real wealth and power.

He saw two possibilities. The first was to play it straight on the surface and hide your corruption. All the cops on the take, the bribed judges, crooked politicians, and bosses taking kickbacks fell into this camp. There were problems with it. For one, you couldn't openly enjoy the spoils of your corruption and treat yourself to all the luxuries you wanted without raising suspicion. Also by taking that path, you became a hypocrite, and Johnny despised hypocrisy.

The second possibility was to choose crime as a vocation. Johnny knew if he was going to be bad, he could at least be honest about it. If he was going to be a criminal, he would dedicate himself to it and be on the top tier. Since he was a kid, he'd been fascinated by crime. When special news bulletins on the radio interrupted the regular programs to inform the good citizens that a public enemy had been apprehended, his heart always sank. He'd always rooted for the bad guys.

During his brief time as an enlisted man he had hooked up with a buddy who shared his desire to score big on a bank job. The fellow had some connections in Philly. They assembled a gang and planned to rob the Mid Atlantic bank in Scranton.

Like most men in the 1950s they wore fedora hats, suits with ties, and long trench coats. Hidden in the sleeves of Johnny's trench coat were submachine guns, one in each arm. They rushed into the bank, closed the front door and locked it. They slipped on Groucho Marx glasses. Johnny jumped on the counter. "Everyone down! If you want to live, don't move a muscle! We are just here for the money, so stay calm."

His partner cleared the tills and another waited outside with the getaway car. He felt like Machine Gun Kelly, John Dillinger, Baby Face Nelson, Al Capone— all his childhood heroes rolled into one. He was doing what he had imagined himself doing ever since he was a young boy watching gangster movies at the Saturday matinee and cheering for the bank robbers. He was living his dream. The robbery was successful. On top of the world and with great pride, Johnny mailed sixty thousand dollars to his brother, Tommy, in three installments.

June 7, 1957

Dear Tommy,

How are you? How are Mother and the girls? I'm well and in good health. Things are looking up here. Don't put this money in the bank. Give some to Ma and the girls, keep some for yourself and hide the rest. Go dig a hole in the woods somewhere, remember where you hide it but hide it good so no one else will find it. More to come. Will be home soon.

Your Brother,
Johnny

Five

THE BARS slammed shut. Johnny sat on the hard metal cot, stroked the itchy woolen blanket and realized the importance of strategy. Their second bank job had been reckless. He shook his head. If they had been more careful, the job would have been successful. They'd been cocky and hadn't even worn disguises. A witness had fingered him.

The predictable routine of prison life meant the days, as dreary and joyless as they were, at least passed quickly. The food was hard to tolerate. His little sisters could probably have cooked up something better than the slop they served in prison. He exercised, read, ate, and observed everything that went on around him. He looked for weaknesses in surveillance, doors that were left open, the longest times between head counts, possibilities for escape, and chances to pilfer contraband.

Using the sleight of hand he had learned from the Count, he managed to lift a razor blade from the barbershop. He tied it to a toothbrush and made a pretty good shiv. It was sharp enough to kill a man if he cut the right spot. With his good looks and fit compact body, he knew that some guy would soon try to make him his wife. He wanted to be ready.

He killed his first man with that shiv. Cut the guy's throat, right across the jugular—simple, effective, surprisingly fast—an underrated method, which he would remember. The bright red blood momentarily cheered him. He had a fleeting urge to dip his hands into the blood which pooled on the concrete floor, but he overcame his urge, wiped his hands on a towel and filed out of the shower.

Killing a man felt oddly familiar, yet he'd never done it before. He felt no remorse because the guy was coming for him. The reputation it earned him paid off. Finally, he could relax a little. He probably wouldn't have to kill again but he would if he had to.

The guards must have suspected him because they searched his cell. They found all the contraband he'd pilfered and hidden. He was considered a high security risk and they transferred him to Alcatraz.

"THE ROCK" was an island prison. No one had ever escaped from it. Many of the nation's most notorious criminals had served time there. Johnny felt dread mixed with pride that it would take Alcatraz to hold him. He would be among the baddest of the bad.

On the twelve minute boat ride, he enjoyed the ocean smell and the thick heavy air settling into his lungs. It reminded him of home. Alcatraz loomed on top of a small rocky island. It could have been a medieval castle. But his shackled hands and feet reminded him that not all guests at medieval castles were treated well, and he wondered what kind of modern torture was in store for him.

The guards checked every orifice of his body, hosed him down, and issued him a uniform. They escorted him to Broadway, a block of cells where all the fish landed. His cell was nine feet long, five feet wide, and seven feet high. It contained a cot, toilet, sink, metal table, and a shelf.

The mechanical bars closed shut, followed by a sickening thud, and then a final reverberating click. The noise seemed much louder and more final than the bars closing at Leavenworth. Each time that sound echoed through the tall chamber of cells above him, he felt a wild animal clawing inside him. He would never forget that sound.

As a gift from the prison, a book sat on his bed. It wasn't the Bible, but a thick book of prison rules and regulations. It didn't bother him that he didn't have a cell mate. But the jaundiced white walls, which were trimmed with pastel pink and mint green, nauseated him.

Escape from Alcatraz was impossible so he planned to play the system and shoot for a sentence reduction. His brother Tommy would pull every string and do everything that a state representative could to help him get released. Maybe Tommy could use some of the last bank job money to bribe the right officials. The prison would have a library so he could pass the time reading.

Johnny was proud that his brother had graduated from law school and even prouder that he had become a successful politician. Of course Tommy cared for the people. He'd vote for every piece of legislation and try to pass bills that would help the common man, the working class stiff who never got a break. Tommy, however, was not above reproach and would do whatever it took to help him. Johnny was like his brother in a way. He would never rob the elderly or the poor. He always focused on banks and big companies.

The prison library was limited. He wasn't allowed access to newspapers, magazines, or anything else that would allow him to keep up on current events. He ended up reading history, books on military strategy, true crime, and even behavioral psychology. Life outside his cell consisted of three twenty-minute meals, thirty minutes of "exercise" time on the yard, and a weekly shower. After a probationary period, he could earn the privilege of working.

Despite the high security, Alcatraz was a dangerous place. Johnny knew that the only way to survive was to find some kind of protection and he wasn't sure how to get it. Two cells down, there was a nineteen-year-old Cherokee who had to be at least six foot seven and over 250 pounds. No one would mess with that kid. If he'd been a little shorter, like six two or three, smaller guys would pick fights with him just to prove something. But this kid's size meant power.

During the endless dreary days, Johnny forced himself to exercise. He hoped movement would chase away his demons and make the time pass faster. It wasn't only size that made a guy powerful. Every morning he did sit-ups and push-ups in his cell. In the yard he kept to himself and read books. He tried to sit in a spot where the sun would break through and warm him. Yet the persistent fog and permanent ocean chill meant most of the year he had to wear his wool pea coat and pull the collar tight.

Every time he went into the yard, the Indian kid stared at him. The kid moved a little closer to him each day till finally he was almost behind him. His expressionless eyes and stony face made Johnny nervous. What the hell did he want?

ONE DAY, the kid was so close Johnny couldn't concentrate on his book. He turned and stared back.

"Good book?" The kid spoke with no inflection or emotion and it took Johnny a minute to realize the voice had come from him even though there was no one else around.

"Yeah, it's not bad. Passes the time. You read?"

The kid, who'd held his gaze the whole time, looked down briefly, then up and said, "Naw, never learned much."

Johnny nodded and looked around the yard. "How much time you got?"

"Life times three."

Johnny continued nodding. Several men caught his eye. It wouldn't be long till someone came for him. "Well, I can help you read better, if you like. There's a whole world in these books. It's a way to escape. All I need in return is for you to watch my back." The other inmates roamed around the yard like cut up potatoes boiling in a broth of their own malice.

The kid's face broke. Johnny held his breath. The sinister smile that erupted on the formerly expressionless face sent an excited chill through his body.

"Oh, I can do that." The kid looked around the yard, nodded with confidence and smiled like a hungry customer in an all-you-can-eat buffet.

This kid would relish the opportunity to tear apart anyone who messed with Johnny. His smile had revealed viciousness—an animal or a battle-crazed warrior who would never back down. Johnny felt the muscles in his body relax a little. He'd found his protection. Now all he had to do was teach the kid to read.

Six

ONE YEAR LATER, a guard led Johnny, his feet shackled, through the cell blocks. He did the shuffle-hop that had become his second gait all the way to the warden's office. Johnny had volunteered for a special research program that could lead to sentence reduction.

The warden's office was a different world. Johnny was overwhelmed by the array of colors and textures that were absent from the stark prison. As he sank into the velvet cushioned chair in front of the warden's desk he closed his eyes savoring the sensation of the plush fabric. He ached for freedom and all the commonplace things he'd taken for granted.

The warden dismissed the guards but kept Johnny's hands and feet shackled. He ran a doughy hand over his bald head as though searching for lost hair. His hand landed on a small patch of slicked hair over his ear. He seemed comforted that it was still there and smoothed it down protectively. Horn-rimmed glasses perched on the end of his nose. His fingers formed a steeple which rested on pursed lips. He sat back, stared at Johnny, and waited about four minutes before he spoke.

"I see you've volunteered for the research study. I'm sure your motivation is a sentence reduction rather than an interest in public service."

"Your insight into the prisoner's mind is amazing, sir." Shit. He had meant to kiss up but he sounded like a smart ass.

"If that was meant to be a wisecrack son, the guard will take you back to your cell because I don't tolerate disrespect. Is that clear?"

"Yes, sir."

"You qualified for this study because your IQ is above normal so don't play dumb with me. Now, before you agree, let me tell you what's involved because this study isn't about finding out if the food here's too salty, and we're not going to be asking you questions about your childhood. I'll tell you the particulars, then you can decide if you think you've got what it takes."

The program involved taking a drug called LSD and letting researchers study the effects on his mind. He remembered stumbling upon an orgy of circus people who had been smoking opium. They had been dazed, their bodies, mostly naked, had been sprawled all over each other—men, women and freaks of ambiguous gender with their sexual organs exposed, limp and raw from too much use. Even though he was far from a prude, he had been disgusted by that mass of flesh tangled in a shameless stupor. Drugs repelled him. He didn't even like to get drunk. But nine years was an incredible reduction from twenty.

"I'll do it on one condition," he told the warden. "I need to be away from the other prisoners when I'm under the influence of this stuff." He didn't want to show weakness to the other inmates.

"No problem with that request." A tiny smile formed at the corner of the warden's mouth. "You'll be in a special research setting which won't include the general prison population."

Johnny felt a tinge of fear. The warden pulled papers from a folder.

"I'll need you to sign an agreement and a waiver, and I'm also going to tell you a code word. The goal is to keep the word from the researchers. Imagine the nation will be invaded if you give up the word." The warden looked at Johnny in disgust and shook his head. "No. Self-centered men like you don't care about patriotism, do they? Imagine you won't get a sentence reduction if you tell them the word. Now the researchers will try every trick in the book to get you to tell them this word. The substance they give you will turn your mind to oatmeal. It may not be possible to retain any kind of self control. But if you can go the length of this experiment without ever telling them the word then your sentence will be reduced to nine years."

"What if I give up the word?"

"Twelve years."

He wondered if he could do it. He wanted to know the word. "So?"

"What?"

"So what's the word that I'm not supposed to tell them?"

"Oh yes. The word is—"the warden leaned in close to Johnny and looked toward the crack of the closed office door, "artichoke," he whispered nodding his head.

"Artichoke?" Johnny repeated. "What is that?"

The warden put his finger to his lips and looked around. "A vegetable—you peel off the leaves and dip them in butter? Never mind. Just keep that word secret and you could be a free man in nine years, maybe eight for good behavior. Now are you going to sign the papers?"

"Sir, I don't mean to be disrespectful but someone's going to have to take off these cuffs if you want me to sign any papers."

The warden pressed a button on his desk and a guard came in. He was uncuffed but the guard stood over him. Johnny started to read the papers.

"Uhh, uhh, uhh," interrupted the warden. "No need to read it. Just sign at the bottom or I'll find another volunteer."

THE PROGRAM, called MK-ULTRA, was an attempt by the CIA to study mind control techniques with the lofty goal of creating a programmable assassin. They were conducting secret studies in prisons and mental institutions across the country. Many of the subjects did not know they were participants. Several people lost their minds; others died or later committed suicide.

What the researchers failed to realize, was that to program a man, you had to break him, and broken men did not become assassins. They threw themselves out of sixteen-story buildings or wandered off naked into the desert never to be heard from again.

JOHNNY WAS STRIPPED naked and thrown into a dark, freezing, underground cell. There was nothing in the cell, not even a blanket. He received heavy doses of LSD through his water and food. When he was taken and questioned about the code word he laughed. Sometimes he couldn't stop laughing and they put him back in his cell. Besides the bone-chilling temperature, his cell was a sensory deprivation chamber. To pass the time, he often traced the lines of mortar between the bricks on the floor.

When the LSD took effect, it made up for the sensory deprivation by filling Johnny's head with terrifying hallucinations, which made him fear he'd lost his mind. Each day he battled insanity. The visual and sensory world spun out of his control. He knew he'd committed a crime, but it seemed they were committing a far worse crime against him.

In the darkness, he heard voices from his childhood. The faces of people he had grown up with appeared before him. They aged and became skeletons. He saw the armless shirtsleeve of his father hanging limply at his side and the naked stump that he always tried to hide. One minute his father was sitting in the same beat-up armchair where he drank himself to death and the next he was melting, liquefying, and becoming absorbed into the chair's faded fabric.

He saw his mother chained in the kitchen. His sisters tried to help her lie down, but a heavy shackle around her neck made it impossible. His sisters dissolved and swirled into circular snakes, lines of pulsating color with red, beady eyes and fangs.

His body chilled as flakes floated down from a steely sky. He ran with a wild group of boys, former Lepers. A large policeman chased after them scowling, with his billy club drawn. Johnny turned a corner down an alley, his feet glided on the ice as he slid under a parked car to hide. The policeman's shoes crunched the dry packed snow as he searched the alley. Johnny's nose rested a foot from his shiny black boots, his heart thumped and the blood pounded in his ears. He held his hands to his ears and attempted to block the unbearable pounding even though he knew it was coming from within him.

He took his hands down and held them out. Pudgy, short fingers wrapped around an ice cream cone. He stuck out his tongue to lick the sweet frozen cream but the scoop fell in the gutter and merged with the filthy trickle of water flowing into the sewer. His world collapsed, and he knew it had always been against him even from the start.

A broken child, he shivered in the darkness of his cell with the demons of the past and present swirling around him. He crouched on the floor, drew his legs into his chest and cried. Hot tears rolled down his cheeks, and he felt their warmth hit his thighs. His heart beat faster and ached as if expanding.

His hand burned. He looked down. His right hand held a crude blade over a flame. In his left he held a rock. He beat the blade with the rock; beat it as if his life depended on it, with purpose, all his concentration, all his effort on the blade.

Fanged creatures appeared around him, some half-men. A wolf leapt toward him. He lifted the sword and impaled the wolf through his throat. Hot fresh blood dripped from the wolf. His blue-gray furry chest still rose and fell but his panting slowed till he was still. The wolf's blood dripped onto Johnny's arm, which still held the sword. The wolf's blood smelled of iron, of energy without embodiment.

Out of the woods, men charged at him, hairy men with clubs looking and smelling like animals, then warriors and soldiers wearing uniforms and wielding weapons that spanned all of human history. They fell at the end of his blade as he rushed toward them in battle. Alone in his cell, he sliced the air with an invisible sword in a wild battle with invisible demons until they were all gone and he was at peace. He was alone again. He panted and sweated as the sweet exhaustion of a victorious battle washed over him.

After the memories and hallucinations dissipated, he saw a more subtle plane. Even in complete darkness he could tell the difference between steel and stone, one tight, the other porous, different compositions, different smells, each alive with its own vibration. He knew before the researchers were coming when they would come and who would come and what they would ask him. He saw into them, their fears, hopes, and unspoken desires. He did not analyze and he did not judge. He simply witnessed, without hope, without desire, without remorse.

DURING those strange months, he challenged himself physically with a series of poses, handstands and contortions. He squatted the ancient squat, which was once used to defecate, to give birth, to draw pictures in the dirt with a stick, to cook meals and eat, to fit into small spaces, to conserve energy and heat.

Many subtle changes happened in his body as he moved it in different ways. He created warmth through movement by radiating heat with his hands. In the absence of light, he felt the power of darkness. Without connection to tribe or teacher, with only the presence of the enemy who wanted to break him, he took the journey into the mind's dark mysteries and learned to direct the terrifying hallucinations so that he maintained a semblance of control.

The government researchers did not learn much about the effects of LSD from Johnny McPherson. He predicted their questions and actions with uncanny accuracy. They were the enemy and he gave them absolutely nothing, including the word. He believed he could read the minds of his questioners.

One of the researchers in the MK-ULTRA program had studied Siberian shamans after they were injured and exposed to cold and isolation. This researcher believed in enhanced perception. When he observed Johnny McPherson, he knew they had created a dangerous man. Not a controllable man, not a programmable man, but a bribable man, a man who would survive a version of hell to get out of prison, to be free. He was someone to watch. Six years later, before Johnny was released from prison, they called the Boston FBI office. An agent was assigned to watch Johnny McPherson should he return there upon release.

Seven

April 14, 1965

JOHNNY STOOD at the Greyhound station in San Francisco watching people and waiting for the first of several buses that would take him across the country all the way home to Boston. He had on the same clothes he had worn when he was incarcerated in 1956: blue jeans with the cuffs rolled up, penny loafers, a t-shirt, and a plaid wool parka. He blinked and stared as men with long hair passed by wearing colorful tight bell bottom pants. He smiled and shook his head. He was happy to be free but also sad as he thought of all those lost years behind bars and realized how much on the outside had changed.

As his eyes followed the legs of several women passing by, he was both surprised and pleased to find hemlines had risen. Watching those legs pass, he vowed to stay out of prison. It had been too long since he'd been with a woman. He'd spent all of his twenties with only men to keep him company. Watching women's legs go by made him want to make up for lost time. He had three hours to kill before his bus arrived and he wondered what his chances were.

Tommy had sent him a bus ticket and a little cash but not that much. He'd have to make it last on the long journey home. He knew it would be foolish to waste his money on sex. He hoped there would be more money waiting for him in Boston left over from the first bank job. But that was over ten years ago and it wouldn't surprise him if the money had already been spent. It would be hard to start over after being in the can so long, especially if he was going to go legit.

Johnny studied a woman loitering near a phone booth at the entrance to the bus station. She had long muscular legs. As his gaze made it up to her face, he was surprised to see such angular features. She caught his eye and walked awkwardly over to him balancing on high heel shoes.

"I saw you looking at me honey. What do you say?"

"Sorry sweetheart. I just got out of the slammer and I'm a bit short on coin."

"Oh yeah? Where you been locked up?"

"The Rock."

"Oooww, you must be bad."

41

"I am very bad, and I'm very horny. But like I said, I got no money."

"Well I got a soft-spot for ex-cons. So how about a free blow job? Where are you going anyway?"

"I'm shipping off to Boston. Got three hours till my bus comes."

"Well, considering where you been, this ain't going to take long. Come on. I'll give you a little something to remember San Francisco by, besides the inside of a cell."

"That would be nice." He followed her down an alley.

It was the best blow job of his entire life. But sometimes he would look back and wonder if she had actually been a he.

WHEN HE WALKED into his mother's modest house they jumped out from behind couches and doors all hugging him and talking at once. He choked back emotion as he took in the grown faces of his sisters. "Cathy, Gracie. Oh my God, no. The pudgy babies have grown into beauties." He hugged them, one with each arm.

His older sister, Mary, pushed a small boy toward him. "Mary is that you? My God, you're proper and sophisticated, just as I imagined. And who might this be?" Johnny looked down at the boy. He wore a tightly buttoned shirt and tie, which seemed to cut off circulation to his large head. Johnny felt mostly warmth from his older sister but there was also a slight twist of disapproval in her eye, which had been there ever since he could remember.

"This is Thomas. Thomas, say hello to your Uncle Johnny."

"Hello to your Uncle Johnny," the boy repeated as if someone were driving screws into his thumbs. "Can I go now?" he asked his mother.

"Run along. No rough play. Keep those Sunday clothes clean."

"Oh Mare, come on now. You didn't have to put the boy in his Sunday clothes for me."

"This is an important day. Welcome home," she said. He kissed her on the cheek and caught Tommy's eye from the doorway. His brother had been, what, fifteen, the last time he had seen him? Now he was a man, a handsome confident man who flashed a self-satisfied smile as he walked toward Johnny. Tommy was the hero of the family, of the whole town even, and he wore the glory like a fine fitted suit. A marble of resentment rolled in Johnny's chest.

They greeted each other with a manly half-hug pat on the shoulder mixed with a few soft punches. Tommy whispered in his ear, "It wouldn't have been possible without you and the money you sent. I know it. We all know it. But you know, no one's going to say it. So I'll say it. Thanks brother."

Johnny's resentment melted. "Tommmmyyy—what a politician, huh? You knew just what I needed to hear, didn't you kid? You must have read it on my face somehow before I even knew I'd thought it."

After so many years, it was strange to be with his family again. There was no judgment about the life he'd lived or where he'd spent the time because most everything they had, including his mother's house, and Tommy's high powered career, wouldn't have been possible without the money he'd sent. Although never spoken, the knowledge hung in the air like dust particles that are only illuminated by the sun.

HE MOVED in with his mother, and although she was the family's first homeowner in two generations of Irish immigrants, Johnny could see she lived an austere life. She saved and scraped and wasted nothing. He wanted to buy expensive cuts of meat and fill the house with luxury. He wanted to buy her a new dress and a washing machine so she would never have to scrub another garment over the tub. But his options for employment were severely limited. Sure, Tommy could get him some kind of government job but he couldn't bring himself to ask his baby brother for a handout, and even if he did, he would never make the kind of money he needed.

Johnny found a construction job in Quincy. They were building an apartment to accommodate the growing number of people who were moving out of Boston. He operated a jackhammer. At first he was fascinated by the tool's power, but that wore off quickly and he got sick of the noise and constant vibration.

ONE sunny spring afternoon he sat in a diner across from the construction site. As he reached for his coffee he noticed a slight tremor in his hand. When the waitress came over and poured him more coffee, he fought to steady his hand. "Thanks doll." He smiled and watched her walk away.

GLORIA. She was a beauty. The only thing he looked forward to when he came to work was seeing her on his break. He wanted to unbind her shiny black hair and take off the coffee stained apron and the sickly pink uniform she wore. She'd be perfect then, naked with her hair down. He'd pictured her naked at least half a dozen times already, focusing on the curve of her high and tight buttocks as she walked away, imagining how they would fit into his hands. Even though money was tight, he left her ridiculously big tips all week and then on Friday he asked her out.

Getting her to talk about herself was nearly impossible. "You must have some family?" he asked.

"No, they're all dead," she answered. He could only see the outline of his head in her black marble eyes.

"Well, where are you from?"

"Here, there, everywhere. We moved around a lot. My dad was in the Air Force."

She seemed to be hiding something as much as he was. With nothing to talk about, night after night they fell into bed. Her hunger and loneliness spoke to his flesh and revealed more about her desolation than words ever could. She was a timid, melancholy woman who became a tiger in bed and that suited him for the time being.

BY AUGUST the sun had burned his skin to dark apricot. His hands were calloused and cracked. He felt aches and tremors in his body from that goddamn jackhammer, which he'd come to despise. One afternoon at quitting time, dust-covered and irritated, he gathered his things and headed for the bus stop. A swank looking guy leaned against a black Chevy Chevelle SS. Johnny tried not to look too closely at the smug guy who seemed to be grinning at him because he already felt like punching someone, and he didn't want to do it in broad daylight right in front of his work place.

"Hey, Johnny," the guy called after him as he walked down the street. Johnny spun around and looked closer at him. It was Frank Egan. Johnny walked toward him. Frank wore a wide-collared button-up shirt with only three buttons done. A thick gold chain nestled in his dark curly chest hair. He folded his arms, leaned against his car and smiled. His teeth were whiter and straighter than Johnny remembered.

"Hey, Frankie. What are you doing around here?" Johnny squinted at him. The glare of the sun on the windshield behind him was like one huge diamond. Johnny's irritation softened because Frankie had not called him Camel.

"I came to see you, old pal. Hop in. I'll drive you home and we'll talk, maybe stop for a drink on the way, huh? You won't believe it. This car has even got air-conditioning. Come on—let's get out of the heat."

Johnny looked around. He felt a flutter in his stomach because he knew what Frank really wanted to talk to him about. "What the hell, why not." He opened the passenger door and jumped at the sight of a small body curled up on the back seat. "Jesus, what the hell is that?" Johnny pointed at a mass of tangled, pumpkin-colored hair. A thin white arm curled up to the face of a small girl. Her hand clutched a red crayon close to her mouth. It looked like she had been eating it before she fell asleep.

"Oh, yeah, sorry about that, she's my niece. My brother had to work and his wife is in the hospital. Cancer." Frankie whispered the word like saying it too loud would cause a sudden outbreak. "Hold on a minute. I need to get those crayons out before they ruin the seats." Frankie opened the back door and leaned over the girl's body. He removed the crayon from her hand as if he was diffusing a bomb. Then he handed the crayon to Johnny and exhaled relief. "Would you hold that while I get the rest?"

Johnny took the crayon and watched as Frankie gathered the others from the backseat. When he was done, Frankie quietly closed the rear door. They both got in the front seat. Frankie reached over beyond Johnny's knees and fumbled, with his hands full of crayons, to open the glove compartment. He threw the crayons next to a stainless steel colt, slammed the door shut and started the engine.

Johnny screwed up his face in disgust and looked at Frankie. "They're going to melt and ruin everything." Johnny fished a plastic bag out of his lunch pail. He turned the bag inside out, opened the glove box, took the crayons out, put them in the bag, twisted and tied off the end.

Frankie looked at him, smiled and nodded his head knowingly. "See, look at that. You're the man we need—a guy who thinks about details."

Frankie had come on behalf of Stevie Summer, the boss of an Irish gang out of Somerville. They'd established several successful business ventures with the Italians. But there was bad blood between them and a rival gang from Southie. Although they had coexisted for a long time, a few months back, someone had gotten killed over an argument about a woman. The retaliation killings

45

bounced back and forth like a ping pong ball until twenty bodies had piled up, an even ten on each side. "That's what happens when you get women involved," Johnny told Frankie.

Stevie Summer thought Johnny would be the perfect guy to make peace and end the bloodshed because he was on good terms with guys from both gangs. Stevie also needed someone with brains and an eye for detail. Johnny agreed. It was easy money and he missed it. He wanted a nice car and some threads. He was sick of being covered with dust at the end of each day, his body so sore he didn't even feel like moving. Some part of him had always known it was just a matter of time till he gave up the construction job and went back to the type of work that paid well, that he enjoyed, and was good at.

Gloria didn't ask much of him. She never talked about marriage, religion, family, or his future plans. But one October afternoon she told him she was pregnant. He suddenly saw his life close in on him. He worried that the LSD they'd given him while in prison might cause brain damage or birth defects in his child. Now that he was back in crime, he at least had enough money to support a family. But because of the dangerous nature of his work, if he had a family their lives would be at risk. He decided he'd hide them away in the country so no one knew they existed. He'd set them up, spend his free time with them but live at his mother's place or an apartment in the city. Gloria and his child would be safe from his criminal life. He'd follow his true calling and he'd have the money to keep everyone in style.

Eight

AROUND the time Gloria was due with his child, a strange hand printed envelope with no return address arrived in the mail at his mother's house. He took the letter and plopped down in the easy chair next to the phone. He turned it over a few times before opening it. The only particulars were a time, date, and location. There was no mention of who he was meeting or what the meeting was about.

He decided to ignore it, too dangerous. How stupid did they think he was? The day of the meeting, curiosity got the best of him. It was one in the morning, and as he sat in his car at Wollaston Beach staring out at the inky water he began to feel like a sitting duck. He drove down a side street and waited there for the other guy to pull up first. Finally, a dark blue Ford Thunderbird pulled up and a man got out. Even though it was the middle of the night, he wore a hat and dark glasses. The man looked around, stepped over the retaining wall, took a leak, and got back into his car.

Johnny crept up behind his car, snuck around the side and opened the passenger door, which, to his surprise, was unlocked. He pointed his gun at the man's face. It seemed familiar. As soon as the guy's tight lips broke into a frightened grin, Johnny recognized him.

"Jesus, baby-face Mulligan. I'd recognize those chubby cheeks anywhere." Johnny tucked the gun back inside his coat.

"Camel, it's good to see you. You're becoming quite a legend in Bean Town. How you doing?" They shook hands.

"You know Mully, I dropped that nickname. Just call me Johnny. I'm fine, but what the hell is this all about?"

"No small talk? All right. This is about you and me. What do you do for work these days, Johnny? Don't answer. I know what you do. You're in the Winter Hill Gang." Mulligan whispered even though no one could possibly hear them. "I know everything about you, cause guess what? I work for the Bureau! I'm a G-Man! Special Agent Mulligan, get a load of that." Mulligan laughed as if it were a joke. As if he had somehow fooled them all and infiltrated their organization. Mulligan had always been a goof, hungry for approval, and Johnny wondered what his angle was now.

"So, you're an agent and we're on different sides of the law. Do you really think we should be talking? If you're seen with me, or I'm seen with you for that matter, it could ruin our reputations."

Mulligan grinned. "Yeah, well, that's just the thing. I've been thinking about that lately. It's been keeping me up at night. Ever since they gave me this file and I opened it and saw you. I thought, yeah right, I'm gonna tell you Ivy League WASPS what my childhood hero is doing in his spare time so you can throw another one of us Micks in jail. You know what McPherson— I looked up to you. Then you disappeared and it was only rumors that kept me going."

Johnny never imagined that he'd been someone's childhood hero. "Have you been drinking Mully?"

Mully pulled a sleek metal flask out of his jacket pocket and handed it to Johnny. "Sorry, I should have offered you some."

"No thanks. Just explain to me what you're getting at because I'm not following you."

"Okay, listen. We create a secret alliance. You tell me everything you know about the Guineas and the other gangsters that you don't want to compete with, and I tell you whenever the feds are onto you. That way you know if you're going to do a job, you can do it without the heat. Your enemies and competitors will get caught while you rise to the top like the foam on a pint!"

"So what's in it for you then?"

"You rise, I rise. When your info leads to a conviction, then a lowly agent like me rises in the ranks of the bureau to become a star."

"So you want me to become a rat for the FBI?"

"C'mon, that's an oversimplification. I know you got a lot more upstairs than thinking like that. You can stay loyal to the men who are loyal to you. But you know and I know that even though all the talk is about loyalty, most guys would screw you if it would move them up an inch in the game."

"Yeah, so how do I know you're not one of those guys?"

"Well, for one, because we've got history, and maybe that doesn't mean much to you but it means a hell of a lot to me. Hell, I got more in common with you, Camel, than any of those Nancy boys prancing around the bureau buggering each other in the ass every time they get the chance. You know?"

"It's Johnny."

"Right, Johnny. I know you and you won't rest until you're on top. This is the surest, quickest way to get there. You will mysteriously evade the authorities while all of your enemies have the misfortune of falling into our hands."

"I got to chew on this."

"I understand. It's no small thing."

INSTEAD of smoothing things out between the Killeans and the Winter Hill Gang he simply turned over anyone he didn't like to Special Agent Mulligan. Guys were not only killing each other but they were also getting pinched left, right, and center. Of course, any job Johnny was involved in came off like clockwork. The guys thought he had a lucky charm so they gravitated toward him. When poor Stevie had the misfortune of getting indicted for horse fixing, Johnny stepped in to fill the void. The Killeans had been reduced to a skeleton crew. Members who Johnny deemed too rebellious to absorb and control were either murdered or pinched. Johnny also ratted on the Italians. Before long he controlled most of the rackets.

Nine

DAMN. It had to be a girl. His hands were more accustomed to violence than tenderness. Yet he held her tiny fragile body as though she was made of hand blown glass. She was in perfect health—no brain damage or third eyeball. At first he worried that her innocence could be sullied by his sins. He still couldn't escape thoughts of good and evil, the religion he'd grown up with. He'd never been a believer, but holding a miracle of life in his hands softened him. After his daughter was born, he went to confession—a lot.

His little daughter, Katie, was even better than his first puppy, Baxter. That son of a gun had looked just like Pete the Pup from Our Gang. Johnny had saved him from a garbage can when he was about seven weeks old. He'd raised that little guy, hidden him in his room, smuggled him in and out of their apartment at Old Harbor, his mother always saying, "One day someone's going to find out about that dog. Then you'll be sorry you ever got attached."

She was right. Some asshole in the building must have reported him because the dog catcher came and took him. By the time Johnny scraped up enough money to spring Baxter from the pound, it was too late. But Katie was even better than a puppy, and he'd see to it that no one took her away. Dada was her first and favorite word.

Gloria, while submissive and beautiful, would not sustain him for long. It didn't matter. He felt a fierce protectiveness toward her and his daughter. He'd look after them forever, even if he found another woman. Yet his strong attachment made him weak and he feared this weakness. Dread and fear gnawed at him for no apparent reason other than his happiness.

HE KEPT THEM in Lakeville, a sleepy town filled with summer cottages. Lakeville only came to life for a short time each summer when sunburned people gathered at the burger shack. In summer, milky streams dribbled from ice cream cones onto children's downy arms, while men emerged from the general store across the road with brown bags of night crawlers and loaves of overpriced bread. Besides all this action, there was a bar and grill where you might find a little trouble but that was about it.

After Labor Day, the summer residents vanished. Wind and cracking ice replaced the whine of motor boats, the calls of children, and the nighttime chorus of frogs and crickets. One Sunday in January, Johnny sat in the winterized cottage with Gloria and Katie. Gloria didn't have the gift of gab like most of the other women he knew. He found himself talking more to fill the silence. She had taken up knitting and sat quietly for hours with needles and yarn on her lap. He worried Katie would never learn to speak well because she and Gloria seemed to have a silent way of communicating that did not involve words.

He'd already chopped a month's supply of wood. A high pile sat by the wood burning stove. The smell of earthy smoke filled the small living room. Outside, sun glinted off black ice on the long frozen lake, which stretched for miles. Wind rattled the windows. Katie sat on the floor playing with dolls. He sipped some tea and watched as her head, laden with long black curls, dropped to her chest. He scooped her up from the floor, carried her into the bedroom, placed her in the crib and tucked a blanket around her.

He went back into the living room, stood by the wood burning stove for a minute and let the heat soak into his jeans before he moved to the window. A skater carved blade tracks across the frozen lake. Gloria sat silently. The only noise came from the clicking of her needles and the crackling and popping of the fire. Johnny visited as much as he could, but the intense stillness stirred his restless spirit and put him on edge. This time he brought a trunk full of guns and ammunition to keep him amused.

"I'm going to do a little target practice out by the lake."

Gloria nodded and smiled. She was so peaceful yet so sad. Sometimes he wished she had just a little more life in her.

He set up cans all over the property and laid out a variety of firearms on a picnic table—a classic .22 semi-automatic, a revolver, a new Glock that was so popular now but seemed a little futuristic and gimmicky to him. The cracks from his gun broke the frozen silence and echoed in the stillness.

He turned. Gloria stood behind him staring. She had pulled on a coat, some boots and a red knit hat. Her long black hair poked out of the hat and fell over her shoulders giving her a girlish look.

"Want me to teach you?"

"I know how." She picked up the .22 and inspected it. She released the safety, aimed it at a can about sixty feet away and fired.

Johnny watched the can jump back. "Nice shot."

"Thanks."

"Where'd you learn how to shoot?"

"I lived in the country for a while when I was a girl. There was nothing else to do."

"Pick out any one of these guns and it's yours sweetheart. You should probably have a piece living out here all alone."

She looked at the guns on the table, picked a few up and set them down. "Why do you have so many guns Johnny?"

He smiled and nuzzled behind her as she examined the guns on the table. He slipped his arms around her waist, put his nose in the crook of her neck and whispered into her ear, "I just love em, that's all. Let's go on inside to bed before Katie wakes up."

SINCE ANY NUMBER of people might want to kill him, he became preoccupied with safety. When he visited Katie and Gloria, he drove miles in the opposite direction and made sure he wasn't being tailed before he circled around. Sometimes the trip took two or three times longer than needed.

He often got late calls from guys in the gang while he was staying in Quincy. But when he answered the phone at two o'clock one morning and a polite woman's voice asked, "Is this Mr. McPherson?" Dread spread through his body.

Ignoring traffic lights and speed limits he drove to the hospital wondering who among his enemies had discovered and dragged his woman and four-year-old daughter into the slaughter of the gang war. Katie, with her small soft hands and the beautiful black curls she'd inherited from her mother, always pointed at everything. She'd look up at him with his own sky blue eyes and ask, "Whas that Dada? Whas that? Whas that?"

He drove out of the city past the thick woods imagining how he would torture whoever dared to hurt his family. When he got to the hospital, he found it wasn't a heavy handed gangster who had taken the life from his innocent four-year-old daughter. It was the invisible hand of God.

Aspirin had killed his daughter. The tiny panacea pill had taken her from the world in the midst of feverish dreams. They called it Reye's syndrome. But Johnny called it the bullshit of a cowardly God who didn't have the balls to face him. What kind of twisted God would take the life of an innocent child to punish a guilty man?

At the hospital, they offered him something to calm his nerves. He refused it. He'd never let any kind of drugs poison his mind again. Whatever they'd given Gloria had knocked her out cold. She was lying in the waiting room with her mouth wide open, her body splayed across three seats, and her dress, which upon closer inspection was actually a nightgown, rode high exposing her thigh. A man in the waiting room was staring at her bare legs. As Johnny approached, the man averted his eyes. Johnny marched over to the nurse's station and tried to control his anger as he asked why they gave her so much goddamn tranquilizer.

She'd been hysterical the nurse said. He had a hard time imagining Gloria hysterical. He went into a hospital room and ripped a blanket from an empty bed. In the waiting area he placed it over her and covered her bare legs.

When it was time to say goodbye, he removed the last tube from Katie's small perfect nose and lowered himself for a final kiss on her rosy lips, which would soon turn blue. He picked her up and walked out of the hospital room painted the same sickening pink as the trim in his cell at Alcatraz. He walked down the long corridor with his daughter's body draped across his arms like used linen. He believed if he could get her away from industrial linoleum and beeping machines with their plastic, snakelike tubes she would come back to life. The country air would revive her.

Nurses and the doctor followed him cautiously. They stayed a few paces behind until he reached the exit. He smelled antiseptic. The doctor's sterile womanish hand rested on his shoulder. Johnny turned, placed Katie in the doctor's outstretched arms, and walked into the dark night alone. Outside, his whole body shook with loss and anger. He sobbed for the first and last time in many years as he swore off God and hospitals.

MONTHS WENT BY and Johnny feared Gloria would never speak again. Her sadness was heavy and seemed to swallow her tongue. He bought two Patterdale Terrier puppies—brothers. They had soft black hair, white spots, deep blue eyes, and a smell that was better than warm laundry. At least a smile formed in the corner of Gloria's mouth as the puppy sat on her lap and licked her hand. Something that had been dead finally seemed to awaken from her dark, haunted eyes.

He had asked her if she wanted to move and if she wanted him to find her another place. She'd said no. She liked it there even with the ghost and memories of Katie all around. She didn't want to forget her. She said she'd found another job waitressing. She wanted to get out and do something to take her mind off Katie's death and help her pass the days. He'd told her he probably couldn't visit much, especially there, but he'd keep sending her money. She said she knew and she understood and she thanked him for the puppy. He took the other puppy, kissed her on the cheek and told her they'd stay in touch.

Part II

Riley

Ten

ON A GRAY September day, ten years later, Johnny's men waited for him around a table in Hangman's Tavern. Ever since he bought Hangman's in 1980, he had been meaning to change the ridiculous name and class the place up a bit. He got Hangman's at a rock bottom price because the previous owner had believed it was haunted. To reinforce his belief, Johnny had sent some men over to bang things and flicker lights in the middle of the night.

He had always meant to replace the dark paneling and neon signs, which advertised low end beers like Narragansett and Pabst Blue Ribbon. Dry wall, nice oak stools instead of the torn vinyl ones, and track lighting was all it would take. But he hadn't gotten around to it yet. Truth was, he didn't like hanging around in bars much. The smoke and the boozing were unhealthy and depressing. He did his business there and then left it to the barflies and battlers.

AN OVERDRESSED BOOKIE had requested a sit down. The guy would be begging for a loan. He'd probably gambled his whole book on a sure thing and was shitting himself because he'd lost it all. Johnny had heard all the sob stories before. If people would just learn a little impulse control, they'd get themselves into a lot less trouble.

Paul Marks straddled his chair backward like it was a broad, and Kenny Savoy cleaned his fingernails with a knife like some Mick potato farmer. Jesus, some of these boys, you couldn't take them anywhere. Johnny resisted the urge to ask if they'd patted down the bookie. By now it should be second nature—he shouldn't have to ask.

The guy wore a gray double-breasted suit with a skinny pink tie and sat straight with his legs crossed. He didn't look like a bookie; he looked like a fairy. For Christ sake, his salt and pepper hair puffed almost as high as a woman's. Who the hell was this clown? Wearing a pink tie in Southie? He looked like an exotic bird. Oh yeah, right, it was little Mikey-fucking-Donavan, all uppity now because he went to law school and rubbed elbows with Wasps and Jews. They'd never met, but Johnny knew about him. He made it his business to know about anyone who made a dime on his turf.

"What do you want Donavan?" Johnny called from the bar. He sprayed some seltzer into a glass and squeezed a lemon quarter over the top. "I'd offer you a drink but you owe me so much money I'm not feeling that hospitable." Johnny walked over to the table, sat down, and looked straight into Donavan's eyes for an answer.

Donavan shifted and re-crossed his legs. "Funny you should mention that. I don't know who told you I was back in business, but I'd love to find out. You see, I'm not operating over this side of town anymore. I've got a discreet client base downtown, and I operate out of a classy little joint on Tremont Street. Not really your territory Camel so I was surprised when the boys came to collect."

Chairs screeched backward. Johnny pulled out a revolver. He grabbed Donavan by the back of his head, wrenched it back and shoved the revolver into his mouth. "Don't ever call me Camel. My name is Johnny." He released Donavan's head, sank into his chair, and took a long swallow of seltzer. Even Donavan's aftershave smelled hoity-toity. "Jesus! That pisses me off. I can't even see straight." He shook his head and took another sip of seltzer. "You say that name and all I want to do is blow your head off. The same guy that tipped me off about your business must have told you to call me that. Makes me think somebody really doesn't like you."

The men laughed and grunted, relieved that they didn't have to clean up. Donavan moved his jaw around as if trying to adjust it from the sudden obtrusive presence of the revolver. Johnny was impressed by, yet hated his calmness. "I didn't hear what you were saying before that. Were you trying to tell me you're out of my league now?"

"I was just saying I have a more upscale client base, and I don't operate around here anymore." He waved his hand around the place like it was a toilet he'd managed to climb out of.

Johnny nodded and peered at Donavan knowingly. "Mikey Donavan all the way from Lace Curtain Dorchester descends down to Southie to grace us with his presence and tell us he's too good to pay us. Donavan, I don't care if you're taking bets from the fucking Japanese. Because you came from this town, you belong to me. In fact, I think I'll charge you a little extra because I don't like your snotty attitude. Tuesday, Donavan. You better get a loan from one of your rich Jew clients because my boys are coming to collect Tuesday."

Eleven

BELOW THE MANSIONS and high hedged lawns on Adams Avenue, smaller houses rubbed shutters on crowded, narrow streets. Michael Donavan lived on the side of Hilltop Street, in a house that strove to be much grander than it was. His wife had wanted a home in the historic Adams District but they couldn't afford it, so they settled for a small Cape house a few blocks away.

Soon after he graduated from law school, Michael had come to realize that a legal career would not automatically bring him wealth and status. Normally reserved, after a few drinks, he had been up for just about anything. But even in moments of advanced inebriation he could recite legal statutes or quotes by Greek philosophers, Existentialists, even Confucius. He could spew verbatim just about anything that tickled his pickled fancy because he had been gifted with an encyclopedic brain.

Yet when his wife asked him to hang some curtains or look into a clunking noise in their car, he was at a complete loss. The mechanical world—the concrete world with all of its valves, axels, rear differentials, cross-threaded bolts and different sized screw drivers—totally confounded him and reduced him to a fumbling idiot. Even though he passed the bar exam two sheets to the wind and sailed through academic life with relative ease, the real world proved a challenge.

Unfortunately, most of the tasks involved in being a public defender proved to be either extremely irritating or sleep inducing. Financially, he'd been better off before law school when he was working as a P.R. man and running a bookmaking business. Even old ladies played the numbers, and to him, bookmaking was more a profitable community service than a criminal venture.

He had fallen hard for his wife. She was beautiful and elegant and in public she had an unshakable poise. But once they were married she had become an incredible nag, and she lusted for the kind of wealth and luxury he feared he would never be able to provide.

He quit drinking, attended AA religiously, kept his day job and restarted his bookmaking business hoping to make up for his crazy drinking years and get the monkey off his back. He was a good father to his only daughter, even though he longed for a son. A slob by nature, he let his wife pick out his clothes, tell him how to comb his hair, and even buy his aftershave, until he felt not like himself, but like a version of her if she had been a man. Even though he left the house each morning well dressed with a nice leather briefcase, stuffed inside were only a few legal files mixed with Kung Fu magazines and weapons catalogues.

Twelve

RILEY DONAVAN woke Tuesday morning to the smell of her father's aftershave. He'd worn Old Spice for years till Riley's mother had made him upgrade. Her mother had complained that Old Spice gave her headaches. She said it was too cheap. But Riley had kind of liked it. The stuff he used now, her mother picked up at a department store, Filene's or Lord and Taylor. Maybe it was expensive, but it made him smell like someone else.

Each morning, Riley stared up at a poster of a leather clad Jim Morrison who hung on the slanted ceiling over her bed. The poster covered over Holly Hobby wallpaper, which Riley had once chosen but now found childish and annoying. Sporting a homey bonnet and patchwork dress, Holly Hobby managed to break through the spaces between rock posters. Her wholesome smile emerged just six inches and parallel to Jim Morrison's bulging crotch.

Riley remembered that she needed to catch her dad before he left for work so she jumped out of bed and poked her head into the bathroom. He was brushing his teeth. She rested her head on the door frame and watched him.

He looked into the mirror, saw her reflection, spit, rinsed and smiled. "Mornin, Rye. What're you doing up so early?" He tousled her hair and went into his room.

She followed and watched as he buttoned his shirt. A holster hung limp over his shoulder. Just before he'd leave the house, he'd slide a gun into it. He always made a half-hearted attempt to hide it.

"Dad, why do you need a gun at work? Do you ever use it?"

"Huh? Oh, no. When I get to work I lock it in a drawer. Most of the time, I just sit at my desk and do paperwork. The gun is for personal protection because I got this great parking spot near my building, but I have to walk through the Combat Zone. I just carry it to let people know not to mess with me. All I gotta do is move my jacket and show them I'm carrying. They back off right away." He finished buttoning his shirt, reached over and grabbed his keychain from a wooden bowl on his dresser. "You know, even if someone comes from behind, I always have this in my hand." Attached to his keychain was a thick black stick about the length of a pencil.

"Watch this." He grabbed her wrist and mocked striking several points on her body with the stick. "Ya, ya, ya!" He pointed to the spots. "These are all pressure points. One strike on a

60

pressure point with the old Kubaton will bring a man to his knees. You should memorize the pressure points—they're very effective against attackers." He dropped her arm, opened the top drawer of his bureau, grabbed a ball of socks and tossed them onto the bed.

"Okay Dad." She rubbed her wrist and raised her eyebrows. "Can I just ask a favor?"

He selected a tie from his closet, whipped it around his neck, tucked it under his shirt collar, crossed the room to look in the mirror and started tying it.

"Whatcha need?"

"I— uh, need some money."

"Okay. What for and how much?"

"Well, when I went to gymnastics on Monday, they said my account was way past due and if I don't pay at least fifty dollars I can't go to practice anymore or register for the next meet."

He stopped straightening his tie and looked at her. His gaze turned to the side of the unmade bed where her mother had slept. The sheets were wrinkled and twisted but her mother was gone. Her father looked back at her. "Why didn't your mother pay it?" He shook his head and resumed straightening his tie.

"I don't know, Dad. She's been trying to get me to quit because of what happened to Julie Flaherty."

He expelled air through his nostrils and clenched his jaw. "Don't worry honey. I'll give you the money."

He crossed back to his bureau and opened the middle drawer. A smiling wooden Buddha sat on his bureau top next to a small pewter statue of Saint Anthony and a framed copy of The Serenity Prayer. Its golden embossed letters read: God grant me the Serenity to accept the things I cannot change... Courage to change the things I can and Wisdom to know the difference...

Scattered on the bureau around the framed prayer were tokens of her father's sobriety. She had not been alive during what her mother called "the drinking years, the crazy years," the years her mother said that she had waited each morning for a call from the morgue. But Riley had heard enough about them. She knew her father had drunk a lot around the time he took the bar exam, so for a long time she had thought the bar exam had something to do with alcohol. She was glad she hadn't seen him like that. Some of her friend's dads had gone to Vietnam. Her dad had been a little too old for the draft but from the sounds of it, he'd come through some other battle, and these special coins scattered on the bureau were his medals.

He fished through his drawer with an increasing agitation that turned to panic. He looked at the wrinkled sheets on the bed again and then opened the bottom drawer. He rifled through it then slammed it shut and started on the top drawer. He came up empty. His hands went to his head and he was suddenly transformed from a man with neat hair in a business suit ready for work to a crazed maniac. Riley wished she hadn't asked him for the money.

"Ann!" he yelled at the top of his lungs opening the middle drawer again and throwing everything out. "Ann!" he screamed.

Riley followed his gaze to some shiny department store bags on the floor near her mother's closet. His Adam's apple enlarged as he swallowed. His chest rose and fell as he tried to control his anger.

"Don't worry about it Dad. It's not important. I can—" She heard her mother coming up the stairs.

"For crying out loud, Michael. It is too early to be yelling like that." Her mother stopped in the doorway. She saw the overturned drawer and raised a coffee cup to her lips.

"Ann, did you take a huge roll of bills from a sock in this drawer?"

"Maybe."

"Yes or no, goddamn it! There was a lot of money here and I need to know where it is."

"Well, I did find some money in that drawer but it's gone now."

"Gone? What do you mean gone? How could you spend—where did it go? Where's the money? Ann I need that money!"

"Well you shouldn't be hiding money in your sock drawer. Who do you think does your laundry, your fairy Godmother? I can't believe you were hiding that much money from me. Michael, are you gambling again?"

Riley didn't say a word. This was not good. She had a feeling not only that she wasn't going to get the money for gymnastics but also that she had just opened a huge can of worms. Her mother looked at her accusingly.

"Riley, what is this all about? What's going on?"

"Oh, don't look at her like that Ann. She asked me for money for gymnastics because you haven't paid her fees."

"That's right. I haven't paid her fees because I don't want her to do gymnastics. I'd happily pay fees for ballet or Irish Step."

"Mom, I hate that stuff. Would you rather have me do drugs after school? That's what most kids do."

"Don't be fresh."

God her mom was such a bitch.

Her father spoke with his hands cutting the air. "Listen. This is not the issue right now. The issue right now is that I need the money back. You may have spent some of it," he gestured at the shopping bags, "but there's no way you could have spent all of it. So just give the rest of it back and we'll discuss this later."

Her father's tone sounded fake-calm now as if her mother was a toddler holding a gun.

"Michael, I don't have the money. But let me assure you. Let me assure you both." She looked at Riley and smiled. She spoke with the same talking-a-kindergartener-off-a-ledge voice that her dad had just used. "What I did with the money is for the good of the family and soon enough you will both thank me." She smiled triumphantly at her secret and raised her eyebrows to add mystery.

Oh goody. Matching Polo running suits? Or maybe she's signed us up for family tennis lessons? A cruise, perhaps? That would be great. Her dad would probably throw her mom overboard.

"Goddamn it!" Her dad slammed his dresser drawer so hard the Serenity Prayer toppled and shattered on the floor. He stared at the shards of glass on the wood floor surrounding the broken frame.

"That wasn't my money." His voice was guttural but Riley heard fear in it.

Her mother wore that fake, prudish, too good face.

"Then whose money was it?" she asked.

Thirteen

TUESDAY EVENING Paul Marks strutted down Tremont Street with Kenny Savoy. They couldn't find a parking spot so they had to walk six blocks. They'd checked several bars along the way but there'd been no sign of Donavan. The Camel had said some high rollers frequented Dee Dee's place.

Usually Markie didn't mind a good stroll, especially on a cool fall evening. But his feet were killing him from the new Italian shoes he'd just bought.

He looked over at Savoy. The guy was wearing enough Irish bling to sink a small fishing vessel. Yeah, maybe that look would get you somewhere in Southie. But in this part of town it was ridiculous, not to mention conspicuous. Savoy? That name didn't even sound Irish. But everyone in Southie claimed to be Irish even if it was only one eighth of their heritage or there had once been an Irish Setter in the family.

Savoy was not a professional. A professional would know the neighborhood where he was doing business and he'd try to fit in. People came to this area for nightcaps after a show over in the theatre district. Markie had been to the theatre once. He'd taken some college chick to see Cats. He'd liked the show enough, but he didn't get lucky after. Jesus, over a hundred bucks for those tickets and no sex.

Savoy had probably never been to a show. He didn't blend around here. He looked like a thug. Markie was almost embarrassed to be seen with him. He unzipped his leather jacket and walked a little behind and to the side of Savoy.

But Savoy kept stopping and turning to him like an overexcited dog. "Come on, man. You think this guy's gonna cough up or are we gonna get to kick some ass?"

For Christ's sake he'd almost shouted it. Markie forced himself to be patient. He had been a rookie once, not too long ago, just an overexcited street soldier like Savoy.

They stopped. Above them glowed a pink neon martini glass half tipped with a little neon olive on a tooth-pick. Underneath the neon martini glass, "Dee Dee's" was written in cursive. It was a classy joint, a far cry from Hangman's. Markie stood outside the entrance and took some mint gum from his pocket. He'd been trying to quit smoking, mainly to impress the Camel. The Camel looked down on people who smoked and Markie feared he'd smell cigarette smoke on his clothes and really lay into him. But quitting the cancer sticks was killing him, especially in situations like this.

He didn't want to walk in the front door with Savoy. The guy was a fish out of water. He turned to Savoy. "Listen, let's see if there's a back entrance to this place. You know, you might as well blow a fucking warning bugle the way you're dressed."

"What's wrong with what I'm wearing? You're the one who looks like a fucking Guido all Guicci'd up. Why don't you go work for that Guinea, Aguliano, huh?"

"You got a lot to learn kid. It's called being inconspicuous. If we got to get into it with this guy, someone around here might finger you. They don't know how it is. This ain't Southie."

They walked down an alley around the back, a few parking spaces led to a narrow side street. What luck, they wouldn't even have to go into the bar. Donavan stood in front of his car turning a giant key ring in his hand as if he were the jailor of a medieval dungeon. The guy had a lot of keys. He was so busy trying to find the right one he didn't even see them coming.

MICHAEL DONAVAN had just stepped out the back door of Dee Dee's place, the bar where he conducted most of his business. He stood by his car and turned a crowded key ring in his hand. He pretended not to notice the two men coming from behind yet he could see they moved with the wide-legged swagger of thugs. He felt a tightening in his groin as if his balls were scurrying to protect themselves. A tingling rose up to his belly and then radiated out until every muscle in his body twitched.

He took a deep breath and rested his eyes in a Zen-like gaze on the Kubotan hanging from his key chain. It could inflict excruciating pain if you struck with force at the right places. He had memorized all the ways he could take a man down with this simple device. Each work day, as he shuffled through documents and sat in boring meetings, he mentally rehearsed defending himself against an attack. This was his chance.

What could he do? He didn't have the money. There was no way he could get that much cash in such a short period of time. He had swallowed his pride and called everyone he knew, even people he didn't really know, until finally he just said, screw it. Let them come.

He knew the men coming toward him would be armed. He felt the pressure of his own gun against his side and kept his attention focused on unlocking the door. But when they were near enough behind him to reach, he spun around and struck the Kubotan hard to the closest guy's throat. The man sank to his knees gasping for air and his gum, still fresh and green, rolled to the ground.

The second guy reached for his gun. Michael grabbed the man's wrist with his free arm and thrust the Kubotan into his shoulder.

"Mother Fucker!" The guy screamed and hugged his arm, which hung useless at his side.

Michael took the thug's gun from the back of his pants and pointed it at the two men while he got into his car.

"Tell McPherson I need another week. I'll pay the interest but you guys need to back off. You know, this business used to be somewhat civilized." Michael jumped into his car, locked the doors and backed out of the small parking lot. As he was driving home, his hands trembled and he pined for the drink he knew he couldn't have. Jesus, what had he just done?

Fourteen

RILEY couldn't go to gymnastics after school on Tuesday because she didn't have the fifty dollars she owed. But she didn't want to go home because she was pissed off at her mother. She decided to hang out with some kids from school.

Billy MacDonald took a long hit from a joint. Riley watched him hold in the smoke until it tickled its way out of his nose. He blew the smoke toward her and handed her the joint. He smiled. "To what do we owe the pleasure of your company, Riley Donavan? I thought you were always busy after school. Aren't you on a gymnastics team or something?"

"I quit." Riley took a short token puff. She exhaled as soon as the skunky weed hit her tongue.

Billy watched her, shook his head, took the joint back from her and laughed. "No, no, no. You got to inhale deep and hold it in, see." He demonstrated. "Don't worry you'll get the hang of it."

Riley wasn't sure she wanted to get the hang of getting stoned and spending all her afternoons in this crummy alley.

"Welcome to the Spa." Billy gestured around at the rundown alcove at the convergence of two apartment buildings. Graffiti covered the brick walls. She recognized several of the names of the kids who hung out there. Some had been spray painted more artfully than others.

Her friend Jackie was making out with her latest boyfriend on a beat-up plaid couch. Its fabric was torn and the stuffing sprouted out like cauliflower heads. Riley looked up. The couch was sheltered by a platform that jutted out from the building.

"Pretty good, huh?" said Billy. "Don't even get wet when it rains."

Kids filtered in. Mostly Wolly boys and a few girls she knew from school but had never really hung out with. They all noticed her presence. "Hey, Riley. What're you doing here?"

"Nothing. Just hanging out."

The pot kicked in and she felt weird. People's words started to take on double meanings. Billy kept grinning at her and she wondered if he expected something in exchange for the joint. She couldn't just up and leave because they'd think she was snubbing them and this broken down palace they called the Spa. When no one was looking, she slipped away.

AT HOME, she sat in front of the TV totally immersed in a rerun of Happy Days. She'd been watching TV for a while. Shows she normally thought were stupid took on layers of complexity. Why was the Fonz still hanging around with high school kids? Maybe he had a thing for Richie. What a creep. These days they'd say he had some kind of disability, or maybe call him a pedophile, but back then it must have been cool to act like that.

When Riley had entered the house, her mother was on the phone so she avoided speaking to her. Now it seemed to Riley that her mother had been gossiping on the phone with her tennis friends for an hour or two. Riley went into the kitchen and got a snack. Her mother was still sitting at the kitchen table with her legs tucked under her. The phone was wedged in the crook of her neck so she could file and paint her nails. Riley glared at her but she didn't even notice.

She went back into the living room and plopped back down on the couch. The front door opened and her father came in. From the living room she watched him close the door behind him and turn the dead bolt. He looked out the door's top window like a kid who had just been chased home by bullies. He came into the living room and pulled the shades. Was it her imagination or was he acting weird? She'd never seen him pull the shades.

"Riley, come on over and watch TV in this chair." He pointed to his Lazy Boy, which was off to the side of the TV.

"I'm fine Dad."

"There's supposed to be a lightning storm, Riley. I don't want you to sit near the window."

"What lightning storm? It's not even raining." She crossed the room and slumped into his chair. Her parents were nuts.

"You're still upset about this morning, aren't you?"

Riley looked at her dad. His hands were shaking. "You seem more upset than me. I had to quit gymnastics. That kind of sucks you know. I've worked my ass off for nothing. "

"No, don't quit. You shouldn't quit. I don't have the fifty dollars today but I can get it to you in a couple of days. That won't be a problem."

"Dad, are we really so broke that we don't have fifty dollars? Did you ask mom what she did with all your money?"

"No, I'm going to talk to her about that right now."

"Okay. We'll I'm going out then."

"No! Don't go out."

"I don't want to listen to you guys fight again. I'm just going over to Jill's house. We'll do homework or something." Riley stood and moved toward the door.

"Riley, please. Don't go out. We won't fight. We'll just discuss."

"Right." She turned off the TV and started up the stairs. "I'm going to my room." She called back to her father, "When mom gets off the phone, tell her I don't feel good and I'm not having dinner."

"Rye—" he called behind her as she closed her bedroom door.

Fifteen

IT WAS TOO EARLY in the morning to be up. Markie raised a sagging coffee cup to his lips. He took a sip. As the tepid liquid pooled in his mouth, he rolled down the car window. He was about to spit the vile fluid onto the sidewalk when he remembered that he was supposed to keep a low profile. So he swallowed it. A stream of cool air awakened the craggy pores on his face. He debated driving back to Dunkin Donuts for fresh coffee but decided he'd better keep watching the Donavan house.

People on the block left their houses. One guy started his car and backed out of his driveway. Another hurried down the street to catch the bus or maybe the T. He watched a man in dress shoes carrying a briefcase and another with unlaced work boots swinging a thermos. A woman in a business suit clutching a tote bag passed his car. His gaze traced the length of her body down her skirt and landed in disappointment on her sneakers.

It seemed to him that everyone did time, if not in prison then at a desk, on an assembly line or behind the wheel of a bus or a truck. All of these people hurried to be on time for work only to count the hours until they could leave. As the sun broke through the clouds promising another perfect autumn day, Markie longed for freedom.

His claustrophobia began each morning when he tried to force his large body into clothes that never seemed to fit right. The collars of his shirts dug into his neck and his wide, hairy legs pushed against the denim of his jeans longing to be free. He shaved so close, yet his dark, thick beard insisted on growing back by lunch.

Then there was the hair, which grew so fast that he had to get it cut every three weeks. When he was a kid, all of his trouble had started with his hair. Dark wiry curls had sprouted suspiciously above his freckled face and caused rumors to spread around his neighborhood about the race of his unknown father.

"Hey Fro," some boy would call taunting him in the schoolyard and before Markie could think about it, blood was spraying from the boy's nose. He would look down at the offending fist and shake his head at it, reprimanding the hand as if it had a life of its own. After the hand had broken a dozen noses, the kids stopped calling him "Fro" and started calling him "The Hand."

70

But it was too late. His fate was tangled in the hair that sprang from his head like an oil soaked sea sponge. If his mother had kept his hair short, he might not have had to break all those noses in the schoolyard. Then she wouldn't have been called to meet with the principal who might never have noticed that she was "unfit." After Markie landed in Massachusetts State custody, there was no hope for him. He committed a series of petty crimes and ended up doing a stint in the can.

After prison, he had found he just couldn't punch a clock. A workday imprisoned him as if his workplace were his cell. Luckily, his reputation as "The Hand" combined with his imposing size meant he'd always have work as a bouncer.

The Camel had discovered him while he was working the door at Triple E's. The Camel had ruled the South Boston underworld ever since Markie could remember. But you couldn't call him the Camel or he'd kill you. You called him John or Johnny to his face and the Camel behind his back otherwise no one would know who you were talking about.

Markie knew that the Camel would be disgusted if he could see him sitting in the car smoking and shoving fast food into his face. He hesitated to eat a bag of chips around the guy because his judging eyes would bore holes right into Markie's expanding waist line. He looked down at his growing gut and rubbed it with a bit of tenderness mixed with disgust. Prison had at least kept him trim and fit. The Camel didn't smoke or do drugs. He hardly even drank. The guy could've been an angel if he didn't happen to like killing people and taking their money. The Camel had said the goal of this job was to "send a message" so no one was to be hurt and it couldn't be rushed.

Donavan left for work early. As soon as Markie saw his car pull out of the driveway, he'd drive up the street a little so he could watch the house better. After what had happened, Donavan must be shitting himself. He'd have to know it wasn't over. Donavan didn't look tough but he sure knew where to hit a guy. Markie was looking forward to getting revenge for the incident in the ally. Damn, his throat still hurt when he swallowed.

Donavan went to work and his daughter went to school at regular times but his wife was in and out of the house all day on random errands. Last Thursday, she had left the house at 1:40 wearing a tennis skirt and carrying a racquet. She had returned

71

about ten minutes before the girl came home from school. But she didn't go out for long on Friday or Monday. He'd taken the weekend off. There'd be too many people buzzing around the neighborhood raking their leaves and going in and out of their houses all day and he didn't want to risk being seen.

Maybe the tennis was a Tuesday-Thursday gig. Maybe she'd go again today. Markie had to move soon, both for his own sanity and because if the Camel thought he was screwing around, he'd end up back where he started, breaking the fingers of low life drug dealers who hadn't paid up.

BY the next Tuesday, her father had come up with the fifty dollars so she could return to gymnastics after school. Riley bounded down the stairs and into the kitchen to grab some breakfast before school. She couldn't wait to go back to gymnastics. There was a meet coming up and she'd missed almost a week of practice.

Her mother turned from the sink and shot her a look of pure disapproval. Riley braced for the criticism that came each morning no matter how much care she put into getting dressed.

"Riley, your hair! Did you even brush it?" Her mother looked at her hair and wrinkled her nose.

"Yes. Of course I did."

"Well go back upstairs and brush it again. It looks like a bird's nest. And that skirt is too short."

"It's no shorter than the tennis skirt you wear."

Her mother turned from the sink. "What did you say, young lady?"

"Nothing." Riley sighed loudly and watched her mother cross the kitchen and settle at the table in front of a halved grapefruit and a single Pall Mall. A thin line of smoke rose from the cigarette and every so often curled in on itself in response to some invisible disturbance. Riley turned and started back up the stairs to her bedroom.

"Get a move on. You're going to be late!"

Now that she was out of sight, Riley stopped in the middle of the stairs to roll her eyes dramatically.

"Don't roll your eyes at me young lady."

Riley shook her head and continued up the stairs to re-brush her hair and change her clothes. She had fluffed up her hair and put on a short skirt to impress Eric Silvers, whose locker was next to hers. But after her mother's tirade she chose Levis and a t-shirt. She went back downstairs.

Her mother let out a guttural sigh of exasperation. "I don't want you to look like a boy, Riley. I just want you to have some class."

When she finally stepped out her front door to go to school, the crisp air refreshed her spirits. She was grateful for the walk to school that gave her some freedom. A scent triggered some vague memory that she couldn't place. She inhaled deeper and looked around. She shuffled in the gutter and gathered a pile of leaves with her feet as she walked. The only thing that would please her mother was if Riley dressed like a preppy and she couldn't bear that image of herself.

What if she had no mother? What if it were just her and her father? What would life be like then? Paradise, she thought. Without her mother to nitpick and henpeck, they'd do whatever they wanted.

Riley entered Central Junior High School. She was overwhelmed by too many competing odors, most of which weren't pleasant. She wondered in what world her overly sensitive nose could be useful. At her locker she detected a faint smell of skunk mixed with Polo cologne.

"Ugh, I smell skunk," she muttered half to herself and half to Eric Silvers who stood at the locker next to her with his pink Izod shirt collar tucked in and his hair slicked back. A small green glob of Dippity-Doo hair gel was plastered against his white blond hair but Riley decided it was best not to point it out.

"That's me," whispered Eric. "I got sprayed by a skunk when I was wearing these sneakers but that was like two weeks ago and I soaked them in tomato juice."

Riley looked down at his shoes. "Are those the ones made out of kangaroo?"

"Yeah, they cost a hundred bucks so I'm not throwing them out." He moved closer to her. He looked up and down the hall making sure no one could hear them. "You can still smell that? I can't smell it anymore."

"I have a really sensitive nose. Sometimes I wonder if I was supposed to have been born a dog."

Eric shook his head. "You're no dog." The bell rang.

Mr. Crow, the science teacher, came into the hallway wearing oversized glasses and a coffee stained lab coat. "Get to class people." He shouted and waved his arms. "You're all late! The

73

party starts without you." Riley moved quickly before he got too close with his awful coffee breath.

Sixteen

AFTER the wave of morning workers passed, teens and children stumbled out of their houses toward schools across the city. Two girls connected at the shoulders walked by Markie's car. They pushed against each other and zigzagged down the sidewalk. A boy squatted in the gutter holding something on the end of his finger up to his face.

Within half an hour, bells would ring and all the kids would be swallowed up by those schools with their brick walls and their industrial linoleum floors. From his car he could hear the recess bell of the elementary school down the street. It was always followed by kids screaming. They sounded like a pack of wild hyenas set free by a bell. The next bell would silence them, till the next bell rang and released them. On and on it would go. Constriction and release, it reminded him of sex, almost.

In the afternoon, the kids would stumble back home again but slower and defeated. It was getting too predictable, the routine in which he had no part. Even the long fleeting shadows and grouchy calls of geese came at the same time each day.

Everything was regular but the movement of that damned woman who floated in and out of her house without a care in the world. The sunlight lifted her long, red-blond hair like a halo and it seemed she could just fly away if she wanted. Yet Donavan left the house early and looked like he was on the verge of a nervous breakdown. He had to know they were coming, that the Camel was not a patient or forgiving man who would wait around an extra week for his money. They hadn't mentioned to Camel what had happened in the alley with Donavan. That would have made them look bad. They just told him they couldn't get him alone so he'd escaped a beating. The Camel had looked at Markie and Savoy, looked at them with those scary eyes. Oh God, he'd do anything to avoid that look. It made him feel like a goddamn kid again.

Markie peered from behind his newspaper as the Donavan girl came out of the house. She sniffed the air like some lost animal. Her dark curly hair tumbled down her back like the soft tendrils of a grape vine—if only his hair had grown downward, instead of sprouting toward the sky like a mass of sun-starved seedlings.

He caught a glimpse of her face then hid behind his paper till she passed. He folded the paper down a little. His eyes automatically drifted to her ass. He caught himself. Jesus, he shouldn't be checking out a girl this young. His daughters were her age. He'd punch a guy in the face if he caught him checking out one of his girls. He shook his head. There was something unsettling about that girl's eyes. It made him wish he had never seen her face.

THE SUN had heated up the car. Markie rolled the window down, lit another cigarette, rested his head back, took three long drags, and stubbed it out. He shook his head and massaged his brow. Fast food wrappers, old coffee cups and newspapers littered the floor, and he fought the weird feeling that the whole mess might come alive and suffocate him. Sitting in the car for hours doing nothing gave him the same stir crazy feeling he'd had in the slammer. The light blue work-shirt that he had squeezed himself into didn't help. Except for the name, "Gus," embroidered in red over his chest pocket, it reminded him of the shirt he'd worn every day in prison.

He hated wearing someone else's clothes. He looked down at the name and wondered for the hundredth time what had happened to Gus. Maybe Gus had died wearing the shirt. Maybe he'd had a heart attack while unscrewing some old lady's clogged pipe.

He looked at the toolbox on the passenger seat. The power of the explosives in that box made him restless in the same way the certainty of screwing a woman did. The Camel knew that he was more than just muscle and had already trusted him to plant the explosives on another job. On that job, he had watched the explosion in his rearview mirror and felt higher than when he snorted blow. It was as if he had created a great work of art.

He hoped Mrs. Donovan would go to tennis again today so he could get on with it. He glanced at his watch to check the time. It was 1:45. Thursday she'd left at 1:45. A few seconds later he checked his watch again. It was still 1:45. Markie stared at the house and checked his watch about every thirty seconds.

At 1:50 she finally ran out looking flustered. He focused on her legs. A short white tennis skirt revealed slender thighs. He was glad she wouldn't be hurt. It didn't seem right to kill such a fine looking woman and since this was the last time he would see her, he took one last good look. He might use her image later in his fantasies.

Her car passed his and he knew immediately from her preoccupied look that she hadn't noticed him. He could have made lewd gestures at her out the window and she probably wouldn't have seen him. As he got out of his car and hurried down the street he chuckled about it. Women like her avoided looking at men like him. He entered the Donavan house carrying the toolbox.

He emerged from the house a few moments later walking toward his car with a casual speed in case anyone happened to be watching. He was about to drive away when the woman's shiny blue Ford sped back down the street and pulled up in front of the house. He froze. "Shit," he mumbled under his breath. He'd been so focused on her legs he didn't realize she wasn't carrying her racquet. She leapt out of her car and strode up the stairs to her house. It was too late to stop her.

This time as he drove away he flipped down the mirror so he wouldn't see. He braced for the explosion trying not to picture what that foxy redhead would look like if she didn't get out of the house on time.

Seventeen

ANN DONAVAN reached for her tennis racquet on the kitchen chair and noticed Riley's gym shoes by the back door. It wouldn't take long to run them by the school for her. What would it matter? Ann would miss some stretches and drills; but if Riley forgot her shoes again they'd give her after school detention. She crossed the kitchen, bent over, and grabbed Riley's sneakers. A thunderous boom shook the house. She dropped the racquet and clung to the soft white and red Nike sneakers. A hot violent force ripped across the room like a demon. Her body was lifted and thrown. She lay on the floor crying from agony and the painful knowledge that she'd been plucked from this world too soon. "My baby," she cried as she cradled the sneakers in her arms.

"YOU'RE NO DOG." Riley turned those words over in her head as she sat in last period history. Eric had moved in closer and smiled down at her when he'd said that and she wondered what it meant. Mr. Bailey's lecture about how King Henry VIII beheaded his wives wafted in and out of her awareness. He seemed to relish the gory details in a creepy way that made her wonder if he fantasized about beheading his own wife.

When the first hint of smoke hit her nostrils, Riley stopped thinking about Eric and sniffed in different directions trying to detect where the smoke was coming from. She was not surprised that no one else noticed the smell. She was constantly barraged by odors that didn't seem to exist for most people. She could walk down the street on any given day and know who was doing laundry, who'd had bacon for breakfast and who chain smoked cigarettes. Maybe in another time, her nose would have been useful. She could have sat on the hillside sniffing for invading armies. She'd smell their fires, their strange foods and even their foreign excrement. Then she'd run down and warn the villagers who would worship her as their savior. Mr. Bailey stopped talking and waited for the loud whine of sirens to pass the school.

The big hand of the clock, the same government issued clock that graced every public school and government office across the country, was at 3:25. Logically, only five more minutes till the final bell. But Riley and all the clock-watching students in seventh-period history knew that the small hand of the defective clock would jump back three minutes before it moved forward. Every school day they watched and shook their heads when it happened, releasing sighs of collective exasperation as if there was a cosmic conspiracy to keep them in school for three minutes longer.

Just after the clock made its jump back, Ms. Van Dyke, the school counselor popped her head in the door. "Riley, do you think you could accompany me to my office for a moment?" The other students made an "ooooo" sound.

"Quiet," said Mr. Bailey, "or that's five minutes after." The class settled. Riley rose from her chair, collected her books, and schlepped toward the door.

She protested as soon as they were in the hall and the classroom door was shut. "I didn't do anything."

"You're not in trouble. I just need to talk to you."

The counselor seemed nervous, a departure from her usual self-assured, condescending manner. She didn't like the woman much. Oh brother, what now? Riley always managed to get into some kind trouble with the threat of calling her mother constantly looming over head.

She followed the school counselor down the hall toward the office. The bell rang and adolescent bodies spilled into the hallway with an enthusiasm that could only signal the end of the day. After-school plans were being made and several of Riley's friends gestured to her. But Riley sullenly followed Ms. Van Dyke whose large hips cleared a path, knocking students out of the way without her even noticing.

"What you in trouble for, Riley?" a friend yelled.

"I don't even know," Riley yelled back smiling. At least there was some glamour in being called to the office. Once inside the counselor's office, Riley panicked and wondered if she'd been seen smoking the pot.

"Sit down please," said Ms. Van Dyke

Riley sat on the edge of her chair. She did not want to relax or indicate that she intended to stay any longer than necessary.

"What's wrong?" Her free time was being taken, and she wondered why Van Dyke had waited till after school instead of getting her out of class. Ms. Van Dyke hesitated. Riley eyed her and wondered if she really was a dyke or if people just said that because it was part of her name. It would be pretty strange to be a dyke and have the name Dyke but maybe she had become a dyke after being called one for so long.

"There's been an accident," Ms. Van Dyke began reluctantly.

"What accident? Would you just tell me what's going on?"

"There's a fire at your house."

Riley remembered the smoke and the sirens. She stared directly at Ms. Van Dyke whose eyes jumped to almost everything in her office except Riley. "Is my mom okay?"

"Well your mother might have been in the house. Her car was parked in front."

"Is she okay?"

Ms. Van Dyke hesitated. "I don't know."

"So what? What are you saying? Is my mother hurt?"

"Nothing is certain just yet, Riley."

Riley stared at Ms. Van Dyke who still could not meet her gaze. She felt her pulse rate increase with each second of silence that filled the small office. Her eyes wandered to the wall behind Ms. Van Dyke and rested on a bizarre poster of Garfield warning against the dangers of marijuana. Her impatience mounted as she took in the poster next to it of cute puppies peddling advice about how to deal with adversity. She gathered up her things and rushed out of the office.

"Riley, stop. You should wait here for your father."

Riley started running through the school. When she reached the exit, she pushed open the heavy doors with her shoulder and bolted toward her house. As she ran the long stretch of sidewalk, she looked up. Black smoke billowed into the sky right over the hill from where her house stood. She threw her books to the ground and ran faster. Most of the students had scattered but small groups still lingered here and there watching the puffy smoke mushroom into the light blue sky. Riley sprinted as if her arrival might stop the tragedy that had already happened.

Without looking, she dashed across the four-way intersection. A car swerved to miss her. The screech of its brakes punctured the steady cry of sirens in the distance. The car stopped just inches from her hip. She kept running as the driver emerged from the car and screamed hollow obscenities, which faded behind her.

When she turned the corner to her street, the acrid smell of smoke burned her nostrils and made her eyes water. She had to push past a crowd of onlookers. A few reached out to grab her but she brushed them off, pushed her way through the crowd, squeezed between the fire engines and ran toward the yellow tape around her house like a runner toward the finish line. A fireman grabbed her and pulled her back. She thrashed but he held her tightly and pressed her face into the stiff thick canvas of his coat, which smelled like her father's old Docksiders. The fireman carried her over and gave her to a young female paramedic with curly hair.

Riley's whole body heaved as her lungs tried to recover from her breathless sprint across town. The paramedic's hand guided her down to a gurney. The woman placed an oxygen mask on her but it was the last thing she wanted or needed.

Riley finally calmed down and brought herself to look at the charred house. At first she assumed her mother must be dead. But then she saw her mother's car parked carelessly on the street with the door left open. No, Riley thought, my mother wouldn't have parked like that.

When she saw her father talking to a policeman, she ripped off the oxygen mask and started toward him.

"Where you going?" asked the female paramedic who was assigned to stay with her.

Riley pointed to a flustered man in a business suit who ran both hands through his short, thick hair as if he'd find an answer there. "That's my dad."

"Okay honey."

Riley hurried toward her father. "Dad!" she yelled.

He spun around, rushed over and embraced her. In her father's arms she finally broke down sobbing. He held her for a very long time. There was nothing to say.

When Riley's sobbing eased, he released his embrace and walked her over to their car. He opened the front door and she got in. "I'll be right back. Will you be okay for a few minutes?"

Riley nodded. Her father spoke to an old policeman for a while, came back to the car and slid onto the seat next to her. His hands trembled as he fumbled for the keys. At the end of this crisp fall day, the fading sun made one last attempt to shine. Red, yellow, and orange leaves momentarily became brighter in the last rays of light. One bright golden leaf fell in a slow spiral down onto the car. Riley and her father stared at the leaf which had pasted itself defiantly to the middle of the windshield.

"Dad?"

"Yuh?

"Is Mom—"she asked through tears gasping for enough breath to form the dreaded question. "Is Mom really dead?"

"Yes," was all that he could manage without breaking down.

Eighteen

THEY sat in the car. Mikey Donavan focused on his hands, folded tightly in his lap. He needed the cohesion of his fingers to keep himself together. He had no idea what to do next or where to go. He only felt the overwhelming desire for a drink.

For the past six years he had taken "one day at a time" and had found that most days weren't so bad. Some days, when major and minor irritations mounted, he found himself craving a drink so badly that he could not free the thought from his mind. On those days, he went to a meeting—listened to people's gruesome stories, shameful confessionals about hurt children, estranged spouses, things and people they had lost, sometimes forever. Remembering what he could have become and what he could have lost if he continued down that winding road to hell, usually curbed his craving. But now it seemed he had lost it all anyway. They drove silently. Darkness fell. Streetlights, headlights and the neon signs of stores replaced the daylight.

"Where we going Dad?"

"Uh, you hungry?"

"No."

"Let's go to Giraud's....get some coffee and hot food. You have to eat. We'll try and make a plan." He couldn't think of anywhere else to go or anyone he could turn to lest they read his rising guilt.

"Riley, we will get through this. Your mother was a good woman. She went straight to heaven." He finally broke down. His face contorted. The stoplight and road ahead blurred into a wash of colors. His anguish released in staccato waves. He did not believe the words he had just spoken, not the part about heaven anyway, and yet he hoped his daughter might believe, find comfort. He knew only that his wife was a good woman. She had wanted the best for them all, and it was his fault she was dead.

THE FADED red vinyl seats in the dark paneled booth at Giraud's absorbed the shocked and vacant shells of their bodies. They sat staring at menus unable to read a single word. Giraud's had seen them through every major and minor crisis in their lives that had occurred around meal time. They had once found comfort in the familiarity of the dimly lit diner because it had remained the same even when you couldn't count on anything else. But nothing was the same now. Without her mother, nothing would ever be the same.

The waitress came to their table. Riley knew she could not eat—not now, maybe never.

"What would you like, dear?"

"I'm not really hung—" Riley looked at her father. She decided it would be easier if she just ordered something. It would make him feel better if she at least tried to eat. "I'll just have some soup."

"Minestrone or clam chowder?"

"I don't care—uh, clam chowder."

"Cup or a bowl?"

"Cup."

"To drink?"

"Sprite."

The waitress looked at her dad.

"I'll have a bowl of clam chowder and a Guinness please."

She collected their menus and walked away. Riley thought her father had ordered a Guinness. Normally he would order an O'Doul's, a non-alcoholic beer. The waitress came back with a tray and set their drinks down. Riley and her dad both stared at the beer in front of him.

"Dad, is that a regular beer?" Riley asked softly. He was staring at it mesmerized.

"What's that? Oh, yuh. I don't know if I have the strength to handle this day, Riley."

"Well, are you going to turn into an alcoholic again if you drink that?"

"Once you're an alcoholic, you're always an alcoholic, sweetheart."

"Oh."

"But it's been a hell of a day." He shook his head and looked at the beer. He hadn't taken his eyes off it since the waitress had set it down and neither had Riley.

"I know but—"

Her father picked up the glass and took a long drink. He set it down and let out a heavy sigh. "There's an old saying that goes, 'A man takes a drink, then a drink takes a drink, then a drink takes a man.' There's a lot of truth in that, a lot of truth, but I promise you Rye, I will stop after this one drink." He nodded and looked around the restaurant, focused on every detail as if some answer were waiting to reveal itself. Riley waited for him to make eye

83

contact, but he avoided looking at her. There had to be something more— something he wasn't telling her.

"Dad, what just happened? Why did our house blow up?"

"It was a terrible accident, honey. It was probably a gas leak or something. Maybe your mother left the stove on. It's too soon to say for sure just yet."

"Did it have anything to do with the money Mom stole from your dresser last week?"

"What? No. Not at all. What would make you think something like that?"

"I don't know. Do you think someone you've prosecuted would do something like this for revenge?"

"I doubt it. Most of them are petty thieves with addiction problems. Anything's possible, but, most likely it was an accident."

"Why did mom steal all your money?"

"Look, I know you've been angry with your mother, but my money is her money, and she thought I was hiding it from her. This is going to be very hard for you to hear." Her father nodded and looked away from her. "It would be easier if you could stay mad at her now that she's gone. It would be easier if you could convince yourself that she hadn't been a good mother." He stopped talking, swallowed, put his head down, closed his eyes, and pinched the bridge of his nose. "But your mother was a good woman. She wanted the best for us. Do you know…" He stopped talking again.

Riley looked around the restaurant. It was practically empty but she didn't want to fall apart, not here. She swallowed and tried to keep the feelings in her stomach from rising up to her face where she knew she couldn't control them.

"Do you know—" Her father tried to continue again but his voice broke. "Do you know what your mother did with that money?"

Riley shook her head. She couldn't risk saying anything.

"There was this place on Grand Street in Falmouth—a beautiful, old, weathered shingle house overlooking Falmouth Height's beach. One summer when you were three maybe four years old, we scraped up enough money to stay there for a week. I'll never forget that week—the sunsets, watching you swim in the ocean for the first time, picking up seaweed and throwing it at your mom, and her screaming but laughing too because she was so happy. We were so happy then." Her father put his head back down and shielded his face while he cried.

It took everything Riley had not to cry too. She held it in till her stomach hurt. She looked around the restaurant, looked at everything but her father and waited for her him to collect himself so he could continue.

"After that your mother always wanted to 'summer' on the cape." He shook his head. "As if summer were a verb and not a season. With everything else, we could never find the money or the time. Well, your mother, she took that money from my drawer and rented that same house for the whole month of July. She was going to surprise us at the end of the school year. She said it was going to be like a sweet sixteen thing for you. You know, she just wanted the best for us, Rye. She really was a good mother and a good wife."

Riley folded her arms on the table and put her head down.

"Come on, Rye. Let's go. It was a bad idea coming here. We'll sit in the car till it passes." He came over to her side of the booth and guided her up and out of the restaurant. She kept her head down so she did not have to see anybody looking at her.

HER father drove to CVS to pick up toothbrushes. Riley stayed in the car. Her eyes would look like giant pink clams for hours, maybe days. She had the kind of complexion that waved sadness like a bright red flag. She'd hated it ever since she was a kid and everyone made fun of her for crying even hours after she'd stopped.

He came out of the store and they drove out to her great-aunt's house on the border of Mattapan and Dorchester.

"Do we have to stay at Aunt Gert's, Dad?"

"Just one night. I have to check on her anyway. Tomorrow I'll find us a place."

Codman Hill had once been a grand, old neighborhood until a mass exodus to the suburbs left it crime ridden and depressed. A small population of elderly people had lived there since after World War II, and had stayed due to either stubbornness or lack of money. Great-aunt Gert's house sat on the side of a hill at the top of a long, steep, concrete staircase that was now nearly impossible for her to climb.

Riley and her father slowly climbed the stairs. Riley dreaded the odor of ancient leather shoes and week-old fish. They stood in front of the door. Her father hesitated a moment, took a deep breath, then rang the bell. Before even entering the house, Riley felt as if they had gone back in time. The doorbell alone sounded fifty years old. They waited for a while and her father rang the bell again pressing it harder as if that would somehow make it louder. Finally, the door opened a crack and a small figure appeared.

"Why, Mikey. Hello. Just a minute. Let me get the dog." Gert closed the door and then reopened it. "Come on in."

A statue of a medium-sized bulldog sat in the corner of the entryway. "Good Boy," Gert said to the statue. She led them into the living room and gestured to a chair and couch that were in immaculate condition but had been there since the late 1940s. "Come have a seat."

Riley sat down uneasily—her stomach turned from the smell. She smiled tightly as her great aunt grabbed her cheeks.

"Oh, let me look at you. You're getting so big. God love ya."

"Gert." Her father pointed at an empty TV stand. "Where's your TV?" he asked loudly.

"They came and took it to the repair shop."

"Who?"

"Two colored men. They came in and took it to be repaired. Do you think it's ready yet?"

"They came in the house and took your TV? Did you let them in?"

"Yes. They were from the television repair shop. The volume needs to be adjusted. I can't hear a thing from that box anymore."

"That's because you're deaf, Gert," he explained. "Did they take anything else? Did they hurt you?"

"Why no. They were very well mannered. They sat there on the couch, and I got them a tonic. Then they picked up the TV. I watched them carry it all the way down the stairs. God love them. They said they'd have it repaired."

Her father sighed, put his head down in his cupped hands and massaged his temples. Riley watched him and hoped he wouldn't break down again.

"From now on, don't open the door for anyone but me, okay? I'll get your TV back."

"Sure Mikey. Can I get you a tonic?"

"Gert, something really bad has happened at our house."

86

Nineteen

RILEY WOKE the next morning unsure where she was. The nightmare of the previous day came back to her. She didn't want to get out of bed but she was afraid her father would leave her there alone with Aunt Gert if he thought she was still sleeping. She could hear the boom of his voice from downstairs, talking to Gert in a slow, loud way so she could understand him better.

Riley descended the creaky, wooden stairs. She paused at the statue of the bulldog and looked into its eyes. It did look sort of real but it hadn't kept away burglars. The fact that two men had come into the house and waltzed off with the TV scared her, and she hoped she did not have to stay here another night.

Her father sat at the kitchen table with a pile of papers in front of him. "How did you sleep? Want some breakfast? There's some Rice Crispies here." He waved the cereal box in the air as if it could magically eradicate their problems. His blue blood-shot eyes rested on puffy maroon pillows. He wore his suit from the day before but now it had a shabby-lived in look. Riley shuddered.

"No thanks, Dad. What's all that?"

"Riley, I've got a lot of difficult things to take care of today. Maybe you should stay here."

Her aunt had just shuffled out of the room.

"Dad," Riley whispered. "Don't leave me here, please. Whatever you do, don't leave me here. Let me go with you. I can wait in the car and read a book or something. Or I'll go to the library."

His tired eyes raced around the room and finally came to rest on the back of the cereal box. "Okay, I understand."

Riley also wore the same clothes she'd had on the day before because she didn't have anything to change into. Her father drove back into Quincy, gave her $100 and dropped her off in front of Learner's Department store while he went to the police station.

"I'll pick you up right out front here in about an hour."

Riley had never been clothes shopping without her mother controlling everything she bought. Now she had one hundred dollars and free range at her favorite store. But her mother was dead and she felt no joy in it. As she walked through the store, she felt her mother's presence, following her to each rack. She stopped to look at a paisley miniskirt.

"Too short." She heard her mother's voice from behind her. She spun around but no one was there. One of the last things her mother had said to her was that her skirt was too short.

She moved to the pants section. She realized she would need something to wear to her mother's funeral. Her mother had placed great emphasis on proper funeral attire. As a child, Riley had attended many funerals and wakes with her mother when the generations of "greats," her great-grandparents, great-aunts and uncles had died in succession. Riley had never imagined she would attend her mother's funeral. Death was supposed to happen at the end of life, not in the middle.

Riley knew you weren't supposed to wear red to a funeral and children didn't have to wear black, but at fifteen she was no longer a child so she should wear black. Her mother would have wanted her to wear a skirt or a dress. Riley hated skirts and dresses because of the scratchy nylons you were supposed to wear under them. She had always worn skirts without nylons and it had driven her mother nuts.

She searched through all the black clothing in the store trying to find something that would have met her mother's approval. The choices were overwhelming. Her mother had always narrowed the selection. She had disapproved of stylish clothing for Riley, claiming it made her look like a streetwalker. Riley knew she could dress anyway she wanted to now. Her father wouldn't notice. She would probably just keep wearing Levis and t-shirts, but if she wanted she could dress like a streetwalker one day and the Tooth Fairy the next.

Twenty

AT THE QUINCY POLICE headquarters, Michael Donavan sat in a wooden chair across from Detective O'Brien who half sat on his desk looking down at him with his arms folded across his chest.

"Coffee, Mr. Donavan?"

"No. Thank you."

"Okay, I'll cut to the chase. This doesn't look like an accident, and as you probably know, the husband is always the prime suspect." The detective stared at him.

"I know." Michael stared back unflinching.

"You know?" said O'Brien surprised and sarcastic.

"Yes, and I'm not responsible. But I know who is."

"Yeah, well why you don't let me in on that."

"I'm going to be up front with you."

"I'd appreciate that," O'Brien interrupted.

"Can I continue?"

"Be my guest." O'Brien cupped his jaw in his hand and looked down at Michael with feigned patience.

"I was taking some bets, you know, making some money on the side. My wife wanted a summer house on the Cape."

"Aren't you an attorney, Mr. Donavan?"

"Ahh, this again." Michael sighed. "It doesn't pay as well as you'd think. I work for the government, you know."

"Yeah, well so do I, but I'm not taking bets on the side."

"I'm sure you're clean as a whistle, Detective O'Brien."

"Got that right." O'Brien put his hands on his thighs, bent toward him and spoke low. "Wow, you must have been taking in some juice to risk being disbarred?"

Michael nodded. "Let's just say I was doing better than my day job." He shook his head. "But John McPherson shook me down, and I made the mistake of trying to negotiate."

"Who's John McPherson?"

"You know—the Camel?"

"Oh shit, the Camel did this?"

Michael nodded. "Yeah, and I found out the hard way you don't call him the Camel to his face."

"You didn't pay him? Oh, that was dumb. You know we've tried, but there's nothing we can do about that guy. Either he's got a lucky charm or someone's tipping him off." O'Brien whistled through his teeth, shook his head, moved behind his desk and started to look through some files as if the case were closed. "Nothing's too big or too small for him. He's brutal—got his fingers in everything. Not just Southie anymore either."

"So, what can be done?" Michael asked.

"Done?" O'Brien stroked his chin and looked off at some unfixed point in the distance as though he were contemplating the nature of the universe. "Done?" he repeated. "Probably nothing. If it's any consolation, I don't think he meant to kill your wife, just torch the house. It looks like she went out then forgot something and ran back in."

"It's no consolation."

"Well maybe I can put you in touch with some guys from the Bureau. You cooperate, tell them what you know and this whole bookmaking affair might stay off the record."

"I'd cooperate anyway. I want to see this guy behind bars if it's the last thing I do." They shook hands. Michael nodded sadly and headed out of the police station.

"Sorry about your wife," O'Brien called after him.

Twenty-one

HER MOTHER'S COFFIN was closed and draped with flowers. Too many flowers mixing with women's perfume gave the funeral home a stifling atmosphere, which nauseated Riley. She sat next to her father on an ornate, old-fashioned couch that forced her spine into an upright position. The painted eyes of creepy statues stared at her from every corner of the room. They were cheap imitations of the Royal Daltons and Hummel figurines her grandmother had collected. Burying old people in an old-fashioned atmosphere surrounded by old things had seemed natural at her grandparents' funerals, but for her mother, it was so wrong.

Every few minutes Riley's father rose to greet someone. He kept his head at a downward angle, nodding, shaking hands, receiving condolences and sympathetic kisses planted superficially on his cheek. Riley was excused from this ritual. She was fifteen and her mother was dead. No one expected much of her.

She thought of her mother lying in the coffin and wondered if her auburn hair was down like she had worn it during the day, or up like when she was going out for the evening. All the women Riley had ever seen lying in caskets had worn bright red lipstick. But they had all been old women.

She remembered why the casket was closed. Had her mother felt unbearable pain as she had burned to death? She'd never seen her dead body. What, if anything, was actually in the casket? She looked at her father and knew she could never ask him and so would probably never know what was left of her mother after the fire. Her mother's beautiful body, her elegant clothes, and the perfect nails she was constantly painting and filing, all gone, every bit of her burnt to ash. Riley's lip quivered. She tried to push back the tears—to wipe them away before anyone noticed and tried to console her because she wanted to be left alone.

By remembering her mother's quick temper, Riley managed to compose herself. Riley's mother had attempted to mold her into the perfect daughter by trying to tame her unruly hair, make her take ballet, and force her into clothes that were too stiff and frilly. Riley bit her quivering lip and stopped her tears before her skin got all red and blotchy. There was some relief in her mother's death because Riley knew that however hard she tried she could never have pleased her. She pictured her mother's pursed lips, the slightly aquiline nose, her impeccable appearance, and her unwavering certainty that she was always right.

Suddenly, she felt hollow but free, as though she had just been un-tethered for the first time. Ever since her mother's death, a small tremor of anxiety had coursed through her body. It wasn't entirely unpleasant because it made her feel somehow alive—on the cusp of a great adventure—like anything was possible. But her poor mother, she would never see her again, hug her, or feel her approval on those rare but cherished occasions when she made her proud.

Fear overshadowed her grief. Her father was drinking again and had become withdrawn. He was starting to let his appearance go and he avoided looking at her. Riley had been closer to him than anyone else on earth. She had inherited his raven hair and intense blue eyes. It hurt to lose her mother. Yet it hurt even more that her dad was slipping away too. She wondered what would become of them now that her mother was gone.

Twenty-two

AFTER TWO long weeks at Aunt Gert's, they moved into their own apartment. At night Riley lay in bed listening to the claw-footed radiator clang and hiss while distant subway trains rattled intermittently. She rarely saw her father. When she did he seemed like a remnant of his former self. He reminded her of a nice clean shirt that had been hung out to dry, but had blown away and become a mangled piece of faded fabric stuck in a chain-link fence.

With five or ten dollar bills, he left notes on the table that said, "Riley, had some business to take care of. Use this for dinner. Love, Dad." They were written in continuous scrawl. If they hadn't always said exactly the same thing she wouldn't have been able to decipher them.

She had trouble getting to sleep and then the clanging, clunking, hissing sound of the heater would wake her in the middle of the night. Eerie minutes would pass when her identity and circumstances completely escaped her. The meow of her tiger cat always brought her back to the sad state of her life. Her father had rescued their cat, Chairman Meow, from the ruins of their house. That was his last meaningful act before he faded into the background like some insignificant stage prop. As the October nights grew colder, her cat and the cantankerous heater were her only companions.

The cat had always lived outdoors. Her mother had not been an animal person and had protested the very existence of the cat, so he was relegated to the garage with the door cracked six inches for his convenience. He had never been allowed in the house lest he disturb her mother's domestic perfection with a paw print, tuft of hair, puked up grass, or any of the other disgusting things cats left in their wake. Although their apartment was on the fourth floor, the Chairman adjusted to apartment living, making his way up the fire escape and squeezing under the cracked window.

Exasperated, Riley wiped his muddy footprints from the toilet seat for the third day in a row and wondered if maybe her mother was right about keeping him outside. Her life had been so normal before her mother died. Now she realized how many things she'd been sheltered from. All the rules her mother had imposed, the order, insistence on timeliness, cleanliness, manners, mealtimes, curfews and dress codes, had seemed so intolerable to Riley, but now she was beginning to see how they were meant to protect her.

Riley didn't know if the Chairman found mice in their apartment or if he somehow ascended the fire escape with them in his jaws, but several times she had awakened to the sound of crunching bones. She cringed as he broke the hind legs of a mouse or pierced its body with his fangs.

It was always a slow death, a death Chairman Meow seemed to prolong for his own pleasure. At first she was disgusted and appalled by the Chairman's cruel ways. But then she wondered what she had expected. Could she really expect a cat to kill a mouse with sympathetic efficiency and then take him out and give him a good Christian burial? Once she awoke to the mangled body of a mouse lying on her chest. She screamed but no one answered. She had to face her cat's predatory instincts alone in the middle of the night because her father was not there.

Although they lived near the T, most of the time Riley rode her bike. Every time she went out, she dragged it up and down the apartment stairwell trying not to inhale too deeply. Without light and air to diffuse them, a century of odors had been trapped in the cracked, filthy tiles and the dingy walls. In that stairwell, Riley could smell the heavy Sunday dinners of families dead and gone, cigarettes and cigars and vestiges of perfume always with undertones of something rotting.

There were more cars to watch out for than in her old neighborhood, but her deep misery gave her a detached fearlessness. She dared them to hit her. Without fear or thought she made her bike an extension of her body. The only moments of something that resembled happiness now happened on her bike as she weaved in and out of traffic reaching destinations in record time. The annoyed expressions of drivers—the fists, middle fingers, and honking—didn't even faze her.

The money her father left on the table didn't go far. At least he stocked the freezer with TV dinners and had cereal on hand, but he never thought of buying things that girls need— like tampons, mascara, and hair conditioner. When Riley had felt like putting on makeup, she'd always used her mother's. She had slipped things out of her mother's closet or jewelry box and slipped them back without her knowing. Now Riley had to acquire all these things herself.

She didn't want to trouble her father for the money, so she started delivering a weekly newspaper called the Southie Sun. On Wednesday afternoons, she went door to door collecting. At first she had just said "collecting" when people answered the door, but after being paid for the daily paper instead of the weekly she started to say, "Collecting for the Sun." Some people still paid her for the daily paper, but she didn't feel as guilty taking the extra money.

Not many people were home on Wednesday afternoons, and the people who answered the doors always seemed a little sketchy, but collecting on the weekends was worse because a lot of people were either drunk or hung over.

RILEY rang the bell of a house on E Street. The shades were drawn and she was about to leave when a young woman opened the door and peered out at her.

"It's just the paper girl," the woman called over her shoulder before opening the door wider. She took the time to light a cigarette and exhaled a huge cloud of smoke before asking, "What do I owe you?"

A shirtless man came out and stood behind the woman.

"Just the paper girl," repeated Riley.

The man smiled and slipped his arms around the woman's waist bending to kiss her neck.

"Fifty cents," said Riley.

"What?" The woman handed her a fin. "For Christ's sakes, just take this."

"Thanks." Riley turned to go before the woman changed her mind. She walked down the street five dollars happier. She squirreled away the profits from her newspaper route in an old Folgers coffee can under her bed. It didn't take long before she filled one can then started on the next.

The people in her new neighborhood knew each other but they didn't know her and only a few of them knew her father. After all the gossip and rumors over her mother's death and the fire in Quincy, Riley was glad no one knew her. She kept to herself. She made the hard decision to go to school in South Boston rather than Quincy because she was tired of hearing her name whispered when she walked by. She preferred the anonymity of a place where no one knew or seemed to be interested in her.

ONE afternoon Riley was riding her bike with her only friend, Kathy Walsh, perched on the back rack where Riley usually carried her newspapers. Kathy's family couldn't afford a bike and Riley sometimes wondered if they could even afford food because Kathy Walsh was nothing but a bag of bones. She had even earned the nickname "Bones." Since she didn't weigh much, Riley didn't mind doubling her everywhere. They had scraped together a couple of dollars and were on their way to buy some fries. She rarely spent the money in her coffee can because it was for an emergency.

She was swinging her bike from side to side trying to gain momentum up a steep hill when a boy appeared. He stepped out from the yard of a rundown house, grabbed her handlebars and straddled the front tire of her bike nearly knocking them both off. Riley put her feet down and Bones repositioned herself. Riley recognized the boy from the street. One day he had called something out to her but she hadn't paid any attention and she wondered if she'd dropped something.

He leaned toward her and stared down. "Nice tits," he said.

Her body, which had always served her well in gymnastics and sports, was now becoming a major source of trouble because of her tits. Riley hated all the attention they attracted and wished she could push them back into her body. Girls were jealous of her, boys harassed her, and even old men gave her a second look. Fuckin pervs.

"Sully, just let her alone," begged Bones.

"Hey you, monkey arms." He looked at Bones and commanded, "Fuck off."

Bones sat frozen in the seat. Riley's eyes fell to the dark thick hair on Bones's forearms.

"Now!" he yelled.

Bones jumped off the bike and ran at breakneck speed. Riley watched her disappear down the hill. She looked at the boy in front of her who was still straddling her bike. "That was mean," she said.

He smirked. "Let's go inside." He gestured to the run-down triple-decker behind him. "No one's home. I'll give you a smoke."

"No thanks."

His eyes narrowed and hardened. "C'mon."

"No. I have to go." If she jumped off her bike and ran she'd never get it back. Sand colored curls fell over his ears and brushed the collar of his denim coat, which was covered with patches, skulls, and tongues—rock band insignia. He stared at her with intense green eyes that both dared her to resist or give in. He was only a boy—much bigger than she—but still—a boy and it was only a house—maybe on the verge of being condemned—but still a house.

She swung her leg over her bike and leaned it against a chain-link fence. She followed him up the creaky porch stairs. Gray paint peeled from the house in long strips and lay in the overgrown bushes like faded party streamers. There was a crashing sound and she turned to discover that her bike had fallen over.

Inside, it looked like a bunch of teenagers lived there with no parents. There was actually graffiti on the walls. Her apartment was shabby but at least there was no graffiti. Empty beer cans, old pizza boxes, cigarette butts, and an assortment of TVs and car stereos were scattered on the floor.

Some sort of line had been crossed and she looked around in awe. She had entered a different world. Sully plopped himself down on a worn-out couch without legs. The faded floral pattern on it seemed oddly feminine amidst everything else in the room. Riley noticed his WHO concert shirt and the song Teenage Wasteland came into her head. "You like The Who?" she asked. "Me too."

"Oh yeah," he scoffed. "Then name the members of the band."

Her mind went blank. She thought too hard, afraid of embarrassing herself. His disdain was a challenge and she suddenly and desperately wanted his approval.

"See," he said, "that's what I thought."

Riley glanced at the door and silently calculated her chances of bolting to her bike and riding away. She felt him watching her and wondered if maybe he liked her. He had told Bones to fuck off but wanted her to come into this place that was almost glamorous in its squalor.

"Sit down," he commanded. Riley sat as far away from him as possible.

He motioned next to him on the beat up couch. "I meant over here. What's the matter? Don't you like me?"

Confused by his aggressive affection, she had no idea what to do. She wondered if she might get off easier if she just played along a little. She stood up and inched across the cluttered room toward him. Up close she could see liquid stains shadowing the couch's faded flowers. The smell of stale beer and cigarette smoke slowed her decent toward a seat on the couch two feet from him.

He let out a disgusted, impatient sigh and lunged toward her, leaning his weight against her body and forcing her back on the couch. There was a time, not too long ago, when Riley could fight a boy and win. She reckoned there were probably a few boys in her class she could still beat or at least hold her own with, but Sully was at least a year older and much bigger than the scrawny boys in her class. His hands struggled to grab her flailing arms and at the same time reach under her shirt. On his clothes she could smell cooking grease from the local sub shop mixed with cigarette smoke. When the bare skin of his neck was close to her, she couldn't help but try to smell his actual flesh.

He spent most of his energy attempting to control her arms and pin them next to her head. He whispered in her ear, "What are you sniffing for? Are you a dog or something? Stop fighting. You know you want me." They wrestled on the couch. Finally he let up, reached inside his denim jacket and pulled out a pack of Marlboro Reds. Riley bolted as fast as she could out the door.

She crept up the stairs to her apartment quietly maneuvering her bike. If she told her father about this, he would kill that kid. One time he had said to her very clearly and very intensely in a low steady tone, "If anyone ever hurts you, I'll kill them."

Her father would take that gun of his, which he tried to slide in and out of his coat without her seeing—he'd take it and kill him, probably in daylight. Then he'd go to jail and she'd be an orphan. Where would she go and who would take care of her? Maybe they'd put her in the Home for Little Wanderers, that old creepy brick building in Jamaica Plain that they often drove by on the way to Brookline. She'd seen her dad explode, and she knew that all his intelligence and the magic way he had with people went out the window when he lost his temper. She couldn't tell him what had happened. She had to protect him and herself from his angry foolishness.

The cuts and scratches all over her body stung under the hot shower. She winced as she soaped up knowing it could have been a lot worse. She had messed around and made out with boys before but no one had ever been rough like that. She made a mental note to avoid Sully and never go near that house or even that street again.

Twenty-three

A FEW DAYS LATER, a girl whispered to Riley as they passed each other in the school hallway. "Stephanie Briggs wants to kick your ass."

Riley turned to Bones behind her. "Who the hell is Stephanie Briggs and why does she want to kick my ass?"

"Oh my gawd," said Bones. "That's not good. Stephanie Briggs? She's put people in the hospital. You don't want her after you. I'll try and find out what's going on. Go out the back door and once you get home from school, stay there."

The list of people to avoid was growing. Riley was already avoiding Sully and his boys and now this Stephanie Briggs. It seemed like every street corner, convenience store, housing project, and park was claimed by a gang of kids who had known each other forever. Riley had a hard time making friends. Most people didn't even know her real name. They just called her Quincy Girl.

Bones was a misfit too. People knew her, but she didn't really belong to any group, and while no one seemed to have anything against her, they just dismissed her.

If there hadn't been a stupid rule about riding bikes to school, Riley knew she could easily escape, but on foot she felt a sense of doom. By the end of the school day the stories about what Stephanie Briggs had done to her victims were flying and everyone Riley passed in the hallways told her she was dead meat. She took Bones's advice and went out the back door by the dumpster.

When she got home, she locked the door behind her, went immediately to the drawer with the phonebook, took it out, and looked up karate studios in Quincy. Not knowing anything about karate, she finally decided on one that advertised Taekwondo. She disguised herself with a ball cap and sunglasses then took the red line to the Wollaston stop.

Riley peered through the studio window at boys of various ages wearing karate uniforms. They were fighting each other on mats, working out on punching bags and kicking the air. She slid through the front door and looked around to see who was in charge. Besides a few moms flipping through fashion magazines waiting for their sons, there wasn't a single female in the gym.

Sideways glances and outright stares from the boys made her feel awkward. She was relieved that she didn't recognize anyone. The boys she had hung out with in Quincy were more likely to be down some alley smoking cigarettes, or if they were lucky, pot. Finally, a tall, powerful looking man with short, dark blond hair came over to her.

"Are you looking for someone?" he asked.

Riley noticed his black belt and swallowed before speaking. "Umm, I want to sign up for a class."

"Oh," he said taken aback. "Sorry. I don't run any classes for girls."

"Well," Riley summoned her courage, "could I take a class with the boys then?"

The man did a quick scan of her and responded. "No, I don't think that would be a good idea. Wouldn't want you to get hurt, honey. If I had enough interest, I'd run a class for girls but there's not enough interest."

THE NEXT DAY at school, Bones told Riley that Stephanie Briggs was going to beat her up because Susie Madden thought Riley was trying to steal her boyfriend. Stephanie Briggs was just muscle for hire. When the final bell rang, Riley hurried out the back door by the dumpster again. Stephanie Briggs was already there, waiting with about ten other kids. Riley walked past them. They followed her. The pack of teens grew. Riley quickened her pace. They taunted her. "Kill the slut! Kick her ass! Quincy girl's gonna get a beating!" She looked back over her shoulder and realized she was being followed by a crowd of almost thirty.

Like a wolf pack, they seemed to have a collective mind. As soon as they passed the red and white Budweiser sign of Al's Variety, they corralled her into a small vacant gravel lot strewn with trash. Stephanie stood before Riley like a truck. She had thick legs and giant arms and was eager to fight. Riley tried not to cower under Stephanie's glare but the hate and malice coming from her eyes was frightening. They'd never met before. Why the hate?

Maybe it was Stephanie's unfortunate face, which looked like it was permanently pressed against a piece of glass that made her so eager to rearrange the faces of others. Riley sighed, pulled an elastic band from her pocket and tied back her long, thick hair. The crowd that gathered was larger than normal because everyone in Southie wanted to see the strange new girl from Quincy get her ass kicked. Everyone jostled for a better view of the slaughter. Riley looked around. Sully stood at the edge of the crowd smirking. There was no way out. She tried to quiet the thumping in her chest and size up her opponent.

The crowd started chanting, "Cat fight, cat fight..." Riley was pushed hard from behind. She careened right into Stephanie Briggs who immediately put her into a headlock and punched her in the stomach and face. Riley managed to twist back Stephanie's thumb and break the headlock. When she was free, she stepped back, caught her breath, and then went in with a right hook to Stephanie's left eye then a left uppercut to her stomach.

The kids went wild. They had expected a quick kill. Stephanie lunged for Riley, pinned her to the ground then stood up and started kicking her. Through her pain, Riley managed to grab one of Stephanie's legs and topple her. They were both on the ground. Stephanie got hold of Riley's hair and held her head back while she punched her in the face.

"Cops!" someone yelled. The crowd began dispersing. Stephanie let go of Riley's hair and ran. The kid's voices receded. Riley hung her head and watched blood drip from her mouth onto the gravel. She tried to get up and run but her body wasn't ready so she kept her head down and waited. The cop came over to her. Even though she feared he'd drag her down to the station or back to the school, she was grateful because she couldn't have taken much more.

He asked her if she was all right and if she wanted to go to the hospital or file a complaint. She stayed focused on the ground and shook her head no. They both knew that would make it worse. Telling, in this neighborhood, always made it worse. The cop, more than anyone, would understand that.

RILEY crept painfully up the stairs to her apartment, slid the key into the lock and turned it slowly. After peering around and determining that her father wasn't home, she went into her room and lay on her bed. She wanted to look in the mirror but was scared that she looked how she felt.

When she finally got up and looked at herself in the mirror over the bathroom sink, her pain increased. It was worse than she thought. She pulled some scissors from a drawer. If she looked like a boy maybe people would leave her alone, maybe she could get into that Taekwondo class and learn to fight. They'd come after her, try and pick on her because she was small, and then she'd pull some crazy Bruce Lee shit that left them on the ground crying for mercy. After that no one would mess with her anymore.

Riley remembered the time when she was five, and her mother had lost her patience while trying to remove gum from her hair. She'd cut Riley's hair so short that she made her look like a boy. As a little girl, she'd hated looking like a boy, but as a teenager, being a girl had brought nothing but trouble, and she wished she'd been born a boy—the son her father had wanted.

She began cutting. The raven locks fell to the bathroom floor in a thick pile. When she was done, she gathered them up and threw them into the trash. She was relieved that she finally looked as ugly as she felt.

Twenty-four

ALL EVENING RILEY waited for her father and worried. Her head had swollen to the size of a pumpkin and her left eye looked like a fleshy bruised clam. The lower right side of her lip drooped and periodically wept blood. What could she tell him had happened to her? The truth, as usual, was out of the question.

At seven she cooked a TV dinner. She peeled the lid back and cheese-scented steam wafted up to her face. The prospect of warm food momentarily comforted her. She managed to maneuver a few forkfuls into the left side of her mouth without disturbing her cut lip. Her movements were so slow and pained that the small saucy rectangular entrée cooled and hardened before she could eat it. Most of the cheese had stuck to the sides leaving a hard inedible layer, which looked like melted plastic.

Still hungry, she did her homework and watched TV. Bones called and asked if she was all right. At midnight, she lay in bed reading a story about four children who were tortured and held captive by their own mother and grandmother. The story reminded her that life could be much worse. Her father still wasn't home. She turned off the light and went to sleep.

The next morning Riley woke to the smells of alcohol, sweat, cigarette smoke and cheap perfume. From the doorway, she peered into her father's room. She saw flesh, woman's flesh, tangled with her father's and a nest of dark-rooted frosted blond hair. Riley turned, went into her room and gagged both from the odors and the disgusting vision, which she feared had already etched itself into her memory. "Ugh, ugh, ugh," she said aloud and paced her small room. She had to get out of the apartment. She picked up some jeans and an oversized sweatshirt from the floor. She pulled them on and covered her butchered hair with a Red Sox cap.

The taste of blood still lingered in her mouth. She stepped into the hallway and collided with the woman as she was coming out of the bathroom. All Riley wanted to do was pee, brush the metallic taste of blood from her mouth and get the hell out of there, but the woman had stopped and blocked the bathroom door.

She pulled a package of cigarettes from her acid-washed denim jacket. A gold cross dangled over her crêpey cleavage, which sprouted from her tight, black tank top. She lit the cigarette and exhaled in achievement as if she had just accomplished some monumental feat. Her small hard eyes peered out from thick black-lined lids. She narrowed them on Riley and studied her in detached defiance. Riley watched the smoke waft into her teased hair. She wore giant gold loop earrings, which could have been perches for parakeets except all that smoke would probably have killed them. Gaudy, her mom would have said—gaudy, tacky and cheap. Had her dad really—? Ugh!

Her father appeared in the doorway wrapped in a bathrobe. He had dark raccoon circles under his eyes. Gray facial hair covered his face up to his cheeks and Riley realized he didn't look much better than the woman who had come out of the bathroom.

"Riley. You're up early. This is…" He scratched the back of his head and looked at the floor. "Help me out here." Riley heard him mumble to the woman.

"Linda! Jesus Mikey, you didn't tell me you had a son?"

Riley's eyes widened, and she looked at the woman with all the hate and fury she usually kept bottled up. She narrowed her eyes and looked at her father as if he were some demon.

He looked back at her and finally noticed her hair and face. His jaw dropped and he whispered, "Oh my God. Honey, what happened to you?"

"Fuck you. Fuck you both," yelled Riley. She turned, stormed down the hallway and slammed the front door. She barreled past apartment three and then two. The gold-plated number two hung sideways, and for some reason, Riley never failed to notice it— that sideways hanging two which marked her comings and goings. She had to grab the wooden railing so she didn't fall down the narrow stairs. On the ground level next to the front door sat a pile of morning papers. Outside, she let out the breath she'd been holding and inhaled deeply. The thick salt air settled into her upper lungs and she wished that it was thinner so that it wouldn't suffocate her.

After she had screamed at them, the woman had whistled like, "Get a load of this one." Riley kept hearing that whistle as she charged down the street. She felt lowly and out of control. No. That trashy woman her father had slept with—who spoke so easily in whistles; she was the lowly one.

Instead of going to school, she went to sit and think on the retaining wall at Carson beach. The Red Sox cap was big enough to hide her bruised face and shade her swollen eyes from the sun. She squinted out at Dorchester Bay. Her mother had been dead less than two months and her father was already sleeping with another woman. She wondered if he had been doing it even before her mother had died. No. He hadn't been like that. It was drinking that made him like this, turned him into someone else. Made him do things he'd never do if he were sober.

With the way she looked now, she doubted anyone would recognize her. She didn't care about skipping school. Even if her father found out, what could he say? What right did he have to say anything about what she did? A force from behind hit her between the shoulder blades and launched her off the wall into the sand.

"What the hell?" she screamed standing up and brushing herself off.

"Hey Quincy girl!" Sully jumped over the wall and grabbed the hat off her head. "Oh my God, your hair and face look like shit." He pushed himself into her and felt her up. "But your tits still feel good."

"Get away from me," scowled Riley as she struggled to push him away.

He backed up and mocked a few punches in the air. "You got in a couple of good shots. But then she got you by the hair. Is that why you cut it? What? Are you planning on fighting her again? You don't have a fuckin chance. But you know, I can keep her off you." He put his face close to hers and whispered, "cause she likes me. She's hot for me." He looked out at the bay and screwed up his face. "Yeah, too bad. I don't want anything to do with that butch bitch." He looked back at Riley. "If I tell her to, she'll stay off ya."

Riley had never heard Sully talk this much. He was excited, amped up almost, and she wondered if he was on drugs.

He put his face close to hers again. "All you have to do is give me a blow job and she'll never touch you again. Just like that. She'll be off your ass forever."

Her lack of response fired him up. "Oh my God," he said in a low whisper. "You don't know what a blow job is, do you? Do you?"

"Of course I do."

"Then tell me."

"I'm not going to say it."

He projected his voice like there was someone out in the bay listening. "Oh my God, I can't believe it! She doesn't know what a blow job is." He turned back to her. "Where you been? Playing with dolls in Quincy?"

Riley thought about the dolls she'd had in Quincy and remembered Skipper, that boring flat chested, goody-two-shoes. Her mother had banned Barbie because her big tits were too risqué. Riley thought of how desperately she had once wanted a real Barbie doll because all the other girls had one. By the time her mother had decided she was old enough, it was too late. She'd already graduated from playing with Barbie to torturing her. She and her friends had cut off her hair, put a noose around her neck and dangled her out of a second story window. Now it seemed like forever ago and it was hard to believe that the acquisition of a Barbie had once been her biggest problem.

She looked out at the water. "Yeah Sully, that's exactly what I was doing—playing with dolls in Quincy. And I didn't even have a real Barbie, just a fucking Skipper."

He reached inside his faded denim jacket, took a cigarette from a Marlboro Red box, and tilted his head as he squinted, lit it and exhaled. "Who the hell is Skipper?"

She didn't answer. He scooted closer to her on the wall and put his hand on her thigh. "Most guys aren't going to be into you, now that your face and hair look so ugly. But me, I don't really care about stuff like that. You see, I'm more interested in the neck down anyway."

Riley yelled, "Jesus Sully! Look at me. Look at my face. For this one day, can't you just leave me alone?"

"Oh, poor baby." He grabbed her face and squeezed it till she winced. "I'll leave you alone till your face gets better. Then you can give me a blow-job. But you better find out what one is first."

Riley grabbed her backpack and hopped off the wall. She looked at Sully with tired disgust, shook her head and walked away.

THE BLACK BELT who had told her the classes were only for boys leaned over the counter with his square jaw resting in his thick hand. Today he wore jeans and a black t-shirt. He hadn't seen her come in. She watched him for a moment and noted the meaty veined forearm that held the weight of his head as he concentrated in a bored perturbed manner on some papers. He looked up and jumped when he saw her.

"Yeah? Can I help you?" He looked back down at the papers shaking his head.

She looked like a boy with her short hair, hat, and loose boyish clothes, so she might as well try and get something out of it.

She responded in a low voice trying to sound like a boy but not so ridiculous that he would be onto her.

"I want to sign up for classes," she mumbled.

"Okay," he said looking up again briefly and then back down. He turned without looking at her and pulled some papers out of a file cabinet. When he turned back to her, he did a double take on her face, looked closer and asked, "Did someone beat you up kid?"

"Um, yeah."

"Take off your hat."

Riley slowly took off her hat and hung her head avoiding eye contact. When she finally looked him in the eye, he cringed. He grabbed her chin and slowly turned her head from side to side studying her bruises as if he were a doctor. "You're the girl who was in here yesterday. Look honey, I told you we only have classes for boys." He let go of her chin and sighed, "Maybe in the future if there's enough interest we'll start something for girls. But I can't put girls in with the boys. It causes too many problems."

Normally Riley didn't beg but her whole future depended on this. "Please," she implored. "I'll keep my hair short and I'll wear baggy clothes. None of the boys even have to know I'm a girl. I have to learn to defend myself, or I'm going to die." She broke down. Her face crumpled and her shoulders shook.

The black belt stood before her like a rock with his arms folded. Trembling and crying she pulled the coffee can from her backpack and dumped all the money she'd saved on the counter. "Please. I can pay in cash."

He took another look at her face, winced and wavered. "Okay listen. Stop crying—you have to stop crying. Everyone is going to know you're a girl if you come in here crying. Dress and act like a boy all right? You're small so I'll put you in with the younger boys. They're clueless. It's okay kid. I'll teach you how to defend yourself."

He said it with such certainty Riley believed him, nodded, and composed herself. She was afraid to say anything else in case she sounded too much like a hysterical girl and he changed his mind.

Since her hair was so ugly, none of the girls at school were jealous of her anymore. Without the long mane she didn't attract attention. A few of the boys at the Taekwondo gym called her a fag and said she looked like a girl, but she didn't mind.

She learned a series of kicks that were the foundation of the practice. Thanks to the flexibility and balance she had developed in gymnastics the kicks came naturally. At first she felt silly yelling,

Hiya. It was so overdone on TV by Bruce Lee and Miss Piggy. But after yelling it for a while, she found a voice of power and unfiltered energy inside her that she had never known existed.

Tuesdays and Thursdays she took classes at the gym but every morning she practiced alone at the beach after running two miles. After a couple of months, if she went to competitions she might have won, but she wanted to stay under the radar so she only went to practices. The glory could go to some hungry boy driven to win. She only wanted to learn how to defend herself. But what she found in those months of solitary practice was something much deeper.

Part III

Falling
For
Johnny

Twenty-five

ON HER MORNING RUNS and training sessions, when the first pink rays of sunlight broke through the clouds, Riley felt free. There was something different about training outside, even when the smell of low tide filled her nostrils and the seagulls scavenged for rancid food from trash cans along the waterfront. When she saw the first light of day and felt the morning air mingling gently with the vestiges of night, her practice was transformed. She always wished that small window between night and day would last longer.

The practice of Taekwondo was like finding an old friend. As her body became more powerful, she overcame her insecurity. Kicking, striking, stretching, breathing, and sparring made her muscles strong and flexible. While sparring with an opponent, she sometimes saw his moves before he executed them, and so the timing of her blocks was uncanny.

The gym amplified egos and competitiveness but during morning training, natural elements—sun, wind, rain, even flakes of snow—infused her practice with power that was free of petty entrapments. At first she studied Taekwondo for self-defense, but she soon discovered that through her practice, especially the morning practice, some of her trauma was healed. As her physical body grew more powerful, she felt less the victim of accidents, of violence, of other people's lust.

Most people out walking at sunrise were old, and after a while, some of their faces became familiar. She would nod, smile or say hello to a few of the regulars as she ran to get the blood flowing. She could feel the muscles in her legs, buttocks and stomach expanding and contracting. Her breath was deep and focused except when some foul odor forced her to curl her upper lip into her nose.

After running, she did a series of exercises on the retaining wall between the sidewalk and the beach. The wall was a perfect place to practice balance. In these moments, her concentration intensified and even the rankest odor couldn't break her trance. Upside down with her weight on her hands, there was a place between trying too hard and letting go. In that place, she could hold her handstand without effort. The simple magic of it was inspiring. The possibility of falling kept her focused and fed her brain adrenaline, which gradually eroded her sadness.

DURING one of these training sessions, she noticed an older man watching her. She knew her strange routine might draw attention so she didn't really mind. Although he was in her field of awareness he did not distract her. The ability to focus and tune out distractions was an important part of the training.

When she finished, she smiled at the man who had watched her from the bench with his small, obedient dog beside him. She'd seen him almost every morning walking his dog. Tufts of white hair poked out from under his Red Sox cap, so he was probably old. Yet his skin had a healthy glow, his features were still angular, his eyes filled with some secret amusement.

"That was impressive," he said.

"Thanks. I've still got a long way to go though."

"Oh yeah, what are you training for?"

"I don't know really, but I want to be ready when it comes."

He laughed. "Well, it's nice to see young people taking care of themselves instead of poisoning their bodies with drugs and alcohol like most of the punks around here."

"Thanks," said Riley. She wasn't really so pure. She'd smoked cigarettes, drunk beer, and even tried pot a few times. "From the looks of it, you're looking after yourself too. I see you walking your dog all the time. You look like you're in great shape for an, uh—" Riley faltered and bent down to pet the small terrier. She was about to say "old guy". He was probably about fifty but people his age didn't like to be called old. She couldn't think of anything else to say.

"For an old guy? Don't worry, I know I'm old. But I'm still in pretty good shape." He flexed his arm. "Come on, feel that," he said. Riley reached over and squeezed his bicep.

"Rock solid." She squeezed again to confirm. "Yeah, rock solid. I'm impressed." The dog licked sweat from her ankles. She reached down to pat him again. "Hey you—that tickles. What's your dog's name?"

"Caesar."

"Oh yeah, a little general. I can see that. I have a cat named Chairman Meow."

"Chairman Meow? That's different. "

"He's a pretty good cat, except lately he's been leaving dead mice in my bedroom."

"You can't hold that against him. It's just his nature. That's his way of taking care of you. He's trying to show you he's capable."

"Yeah, I guess you're right. I never thought about it that way. Still grosses me out though."

After a few moments of easy silence taking in the morning light, Riley looked at her watch. "Well, I better get off to school now. It was nice talking to you."

"You, too. See you again tomorrow morning."

"Yeah, see you tomorrow." She started to jog away. "By the way, what's your name?" She called back.

"You can call me Johnny. What's your name, dear?"

"Riley."

It became a ritual—morning running, training on the retaining wall, and then sitting on the bench with Johnny after he'd finished his walk. Sometimes they talked and other times they just sat and watched the sun rise.

Twenty-six

AFTER HIS BRISK WALK Johnny sat down on a bench, its paint long since peeled from exposure to the salty air. Benches dotted the walkway all the way to Columbia Point, but he always chose the same one. He looked out at Dorchester Bay and planned for the next stage of his life.

He'd read many books about management and business. Although he had tried to incorporate the general principles into his syndicate, he was damned glad he wasn't in the legitimate business world where he'd have to abide by bullshit regulations. If he had trouble with someone, he knew he could always employ the final solution.

For the past fifteen years he had engaged in the same morning ritual, and nothing much had broken his routine. Even late night jobs didn't interfere with his morning walks. He didn't need much sleep anyway. Sleep was about the only thing that terrified him.

During the day he had almost complete control over everyone and everything around him. Meticulous planning and his keen instinct kept him one step ahead of the game. Yet sleep meant going into a world of nightmares and hallucinations. The nightmares were the bane of his existence and disturbed him more than any of the problems in his waking life.

He slept from 10am till 3pm—the hours of legitimate business. Not much had ever changed this. He walked the same way then sat on the same bench in an uneventful pattern. In the late afternoons, he conducted meetings, often walking with his associates along the causeway so they could make plans where there was no chance of being bugged or overheard. Early mornings had always been his time to think alone.

At least until recently when he had met the girl. He'd seen her running and couldn't help but smile at her freckled face, self-absorbed and yet open to the world and people around her. In another era, a girl that young could have been married off to an older man like him. He convinced himself that his feelings toward Riley weren't like that. She reminded him of Katie. Her dark hair fell in a way that sparked painful memories. She was about the age his daughter would have been, if she had lived.

She chose a spot on the wall near his bench to do exercises, which were eerily reminiscent of those he had done in his cell at Alcatraz. The acrobatic way she moved reminded him of Eva and how she moved on the trapeze. He watched her openly despite the ache it caused.

He had the knack of attracting people and yet when he didn't like someone, or they compromised his business, he could make them go away, for good if he wanted. He had drawn her in with a compliment and had kept her a little longer each day with his steady, quiet charm.

Soon she was sitting with him each morning. Through all her physical strength he sensed a weakness, a vulnerability that aroused him with a strange mixture of predatory and protective feelings.

Twenty-seven

THAT WINTER everyone in Boston complained about the ice, the gray, the cold, the wind chill factor, and the frozen sludge which was too thick to go down sewers. Winter was their common enemy. If they could rid themselves of it, they believed their problems would melt away. They wanted to escape to Florida. It was their elixir, the ultimate fixer to all that was wrong with the world. Yet without the demon winter to draw them together in collective angst, without that source of misery to rally against, they'd soon become lonely. At least for part of the year, they needed something tangible, something outside of themselves, to be fed up with.

One morning Riley woke to the high eerie whistle of a cold December wind. The pipes in her apartment clanged and banged as they fought to maintain warmth in the building. She looked out the window. Snow swirled from rooftops. A chill penetrated the pane. As goose bumps broke out on her bare arms, the warmth of her bed beckoned to her. She fought the urge to succumb—this was her time, the time that kept her sane, and if she returned to bed, later in the day she would feel depressed.

Before she could talk herself out of it, she pulled on Lycra tights, a sweatshirt and sneakers. The wooden stairs in the hallway creaked as she descended. Outside, the wind cut through her tights and chilled her legs as she ran across the empty streets toward the beach. Brittle leaves danced by in groups, trailing a tinkling chorus. When she reached the walkway, she looked out on the choppy wind-swept bay. She expelled her breath in steady, cloudy bursts. As she ran faster, her internal heat rose as it fought to break through her frozen skin. She could not stop now. If she stopped running, her sweat would turn to a thousand icy fingers.

She was alone on the walkway. Near her building she had passed huddled bodies shuffling with heads bent against the wind toward town, people on their way to work. Not many chose to be out on a morning like this. The temperature, humidity and wind, made it a bone-chilling cold. The wind whipped tears from her eyes. She wiped them and squinted into the distance. A man walked toward her with his dog. It had to be Johnny.

The wind blew from behind him, ballooning his black Members Only coat into the shape of bat wings. He approached and smiled a tight, sideways grin. "I thought that must be you. You're the only one crazy enough to be out here on a morning like this."

"Yeah, look who's talking." Riley said. She ran in place.

"Okay, you and me, kid. Come on, enough of this. Let's go get some hot coffee and breakfast, my treat."

She followed him to his car. He opened the passenger door of his black Lincoln Town Car and she slid in, relieved to be sheltered. His car smelled new and faintly of cinnamon Dentyne. Many times, she'd sat with him outside on the bench, but she didn't know his smell. Riley didn't feel like she really knew people until she could recognize their scent. It didn't matter if it was just the type of laundry detergent they used and not their deep down personal stink. She just needed some smell to associate with people. Maybe cinnamon Dentyne was Johnny's scent. He ground a piece between his teeth so subtly that she would never have noticed if she hadn't smelled it.

Except for an ice scraper and a dog blanket on the backseat, the car was empty. Riley's father always had to spend about five minutes moving things off the front seat before she could even get in his car. With the junk in his trunk you could probably survive on a remote island for a year. He even kept his hockey equipment in there just in case ice became available. In her father's car, she could always smell sweat, motor oil, the brine of an old buoy and metal from a pile of change he kept to feed the meters. She could barely squeeze in amongst all that stuff. Yet in his clutter she had somehow felt secure.

The cleanliness and order of Johnny's car made Riley aware of her disheveled state. He wasn't wearing fancy clothes, but he still looked tidy and sported expensive leather gloves. Even dressed up, Riley felt sloppy. Maybe it was her unruly hair, or maybe it was because she had tried to live up to her mother's impeccable grooming. No matter how hard she tried, Riley always felt she was coming apart at the seams. She tucked her nose down the front of her sweatshirt and took a whiff to see if she stank. Most likely his nose was not as sensitive as hers, but she was relieved that she had not worked up a strong dose of body odor on her morning run. For some reason, she wanted Johnny to like her.

"Your car smells new," she said.

"It is fairly new."

"Automatic windows, huh?" She pressed the button and the window lowered a little. Johnny turned a steely gaze toward her. She put it back up. "Fancy," she said.

"Have you got time for breakfast before school? I don't want you to be late."

"Yeah, I got a little over an hour. The other day I went to take a shower before school and my dad's trashy girlfriend had used up all the hot water. A cold shower really sucks."

"Well, I can't think of anything worse than a cold shower right now, besides maybe a bullet to the head," Johnny replied.

"That would be worse. I'd choose the cold shower over that." Riley nodded in agreement and looked out the window.

Johnny drove to Linda Mae's on Neponset Boulevard.

"Ever been here?" he asked.

"Oh sure. We used to eat here all the time with my grandpa before he died."

"Great breakfast." On the way in, he took a newspaper from a dispenser.

THE DOOR to Linda Mae's resisted his pull then flew open with the force of its surrender. They were greeted by a blast of warm air smelling of bacon, eggs, coffee, and a hint of hangover gas. The girl wore black running tights and a gray sweatshirt that said UMASS. As they followed the hostess to their table, Johnny noticed a man slouched over his coffee, his eyes fixed on her ass. He glared at the man. Jesus, how many more men would he have had to kill if his own daughter had lived?

They squeezed into a booth and opened menus. They closed the menus and sat in easy silence looking through the newspaper. The waitress came by and poured them coffee. Johnny watched smiling to himself as Riley put three sugars in hers, exactly what he had done when he was her age. Then the years had gone by and he'd learned to take it black. His taste for sweetness was gone now, except sometimes when he really needed sleep.

He didn't struggle with cravings for food or drink the way some people did. He appreciated good food and a drink but neither had power over him. Sex on the other hand popped into his head when it had no business being there and those urges lingered. His girlfriend Jean, fifteen years his junior and glamorous, should be enough to satisfy a man of his age. When she wasn't, he wondered what or who could. The waitress came back and took their orders.

117

"Wow. I can't remember the last time I ate a hot breakfast." Riley smiled and rubbed her hands together.

"Oh yeah? Doesn't your mother make you breakfast, kid?"

"My mother's dead."

"Oh, sorry."

"It's okay. It's not your fault." She smiled tightly and looked away.

"What do you normally eat?" he asked.

"Cold cereal. I usually skip lunch then I have fast food or a Budget Delite for dinner."

"Budget Delite? Yuck. I wouldn't feed that stuff to my dog— way too much sodium. You got to eat better. If your dad doesn't cook, then you should learn."

The waitress came back and topped up their coffee. Johnny took a sip and looked around the restaurant. Good, no familiar faces. So many people had grudges against him—he never knew when or where they might try something. He could handle it, but he didn't want to scare the girl.

"Oh, by the way, you won't be seeing me around for a while. I'm taking a little trip and I won't be back till after New Year's."

"Really? Where you going?"

"To Europe for a couple of weeks."

"Really! Where in Europe?"

"I'll land in Paris and then who knows—Italy, Spain. We'll see."

"Business or pleasure?"

"Oh, a little of both."

She whispered. "Alone? Or with a companion?"

"What is this, the third degree?" He took another sip of coffee and put it down. "With someone else, okay."

"A woman?"

"Yes, a woman."

"Your girlfriend?"

He sighed, looked around the restaurant and back at her. "Yes, my girlfriend."

"Ohhh, what's her name?"

"Enough questions, kid. What, are you writing an article for the 'National Enquirer'?" He shook his head and started to read the paper again.

"What is it you do for work anyway? I figured you were retired."

"I'm in business."

"Really, what kind?"

118

"I'm in the business of making money. All kinds of things really—I try and diversify." That sounded better than extortion, racketeering, and money laundering.

"I've never been that interested in business. It seems boring."

"It could be boring, but I have my own special approach, which keeps it interesting. So what about you? What do you want to do with your life? When do you graduate from high school?"

"One and a half years, but hey, who's counting. I'd like to do something really different and exciting like join the circus or be a fireman." She took a sip of her coffee and grinned. "If I can make it to college, I might study psychology or something."

"You know, I travelled with the circus, when I was about your age, actually."

"You're kidding. What did you do?"

"Believe it or not, I hopped a circus train. Then I became a roustabout— that's just a fancy term for someone who sets up the tents and does all the general labor. But I learned a few tricks from the performers."

"Yeah? Awesome. Wow, I can't believe you did that. You can't really do stuff like that nowadays. Why did you quit?"

"Well the pay was peanuts, and I wanted to make some real money."

"Very funny." She grinned and nodded. "So you went from the circus to business. Do you ever miss it?"

"What, the circus? No. Some good memories though." He remembered Eva—God what a body—what luck, to have a woman like that as his first. Among all the women who had followed, there'd been none like her. He wondered what had become of her and the circus people when they had aged. They'd probably ended up rotting away in a trailer park. "Those circus people work so hard, but you know, even the performers, they don't get paid that much. Not enough to retire on. Then they get old and what happens to them? No, I don't miss the circus. Business has been good for me. I like to make money and save it for a rainy day. You never know what's going to happen in life. Without some money saved you've got nothing to fall back on."

She nodded and stared into her mug, "Yeah, my dad said my mom's death was an accident, but I have a feeling it had something to do with money."

Johnny raised his eyebrows and nodded. "My mother used to say 'Money is the root of all evil.' I think it's the lack of money that's at the root of evil. How did your mom die?"

"A fire—an explosion really—at our house."

119

"Sounds like a really bad accident. What makes you think it had something to do with money?"

"About a week before it happened, my mom and dad had an argument about some money of his that she found and spent. I'll never forget the way my Dad looked. He was terrified and said the money wasn't his."

Johnny put his arm up on the back of the booth and looked around the restaurant. He tried to keep his expression neutral, but Jesus Christ, she could be the girl whose mother they'd accidently barbequed, of all the strange coincidences. Chills crept up the back of his neck and his skin started to feel like tiny bugs were marching on it. Was she Mikey-fucking-Donavan's girl? Unbelievable— and he had liked her so much too, really liked her. My God, what a shame! This was how Donavan was looking after his daughter. She had to eat cold cereal for breakfast and Budget Delite for dinner.

"I'm so sorry to hear that, dear. Does your father have problems with gambling or drugs? Sometimes when people get messed up in that stuff, they end up owing a lot of money and it leads to violence."

"I don't know. That's what I don't get. My dad gambled and drank, but he gave all that up years ago. Until my mom died, he was active in A.A. and G.A. It was like his religion. It's just hard to believe he'd talk it up so much when he was doing something else. But he's fallen off the wagon now, that's for sure. He's taken up with this awful woman—a total barfly—and my mom hasn't even been dead for three months. That's what really pisses me off."

"That's too bad. You know people jump to all kinds of crazy conclusions when something like this happens. I think that's because most people watch way too much TV. I bet it was just an unfortunate accident. It'll take time and you'll both miss her, but you'll survive."

"Well if it wasn't an accident, and someone did this to us on purpose, my Dad will be hell-bent on revenge. He's that type of guy—normally calm, but when something gets him going, then forget it. For a smart guy, he has no common sense."

It wasn't over with Donavan and Johnny hadn't even gotten his money. The waitress came over and set down their steaming plates. The heat from their food eased his anxiety. It was cozy for a minute, eating hot breakfasts together. But every time someone opened the door, the whole place chilled. "You know, we're sitting here having breakfast, and I don't even know your last name."

"Donavan. What's your last name?"

"Gavin. Donavan, huh? That's a good Irish name."

120

It gave him pleasure to see the girl eat. He had watched her exercise and run each morning as if her life depended on it. She seemed strong, but also neglected and run down. Sometimes there were purple circles under her eyes, like maybe she lacked sleep or iron. She put her fork down and pushed away her plate.

"Finish your eggs. With all the exercise you do, you need the protein."

She seemed about to protest but she picked up her fork and finished them. Good girl.

"Okay, I'm really full now." She groaned and put her hand on her stomach. "Thanks for breakfast. That was really good."

The waitress dropped their check.

"You're lucky you'll be in Europe for Christmas. I'm really not looking forward to Christmas this year." She stared into her coffee cup as though she could see her miserable Christmas day at the bottom. "Thanksgiving sure sucked. At least we found a Chinese place that was open, but I'm not sure I can stomach Chinese food at Christmas."

Johnny looked around the restaurant again. All that brown vinyl, damn it was depressing. At least the food was good. "Hey, one day I'll take you to Paris for Christmas, huh? That would cheer you up. But you know, come to think of it, I got a little something I want to give you before I leave. So let's make sure we see each other before then, huh?"

"You got a Christmas present for me?"

"It's just a little something I picked up last week."

"What is it?"

"I'm not going to tell you. You have to wait. How about Thursday?"

"Okay, Thursday," she said. "What can I get for you?"

"I got everything I need. All right? Don't be getting anything for me."

"Yeah, okay. Maybe."

He held up a finger and pointed it at her until she relented.

"Okay, I don't have any money anyway."

Twenty-eight

PARIS. Even if he didn't mean it, the thought of being somewhere else, the possibility that she could ever go somewhere like that, lifted her spirits. Day and night, planes flew low across Southie on their way to Logan airport. They seemed close enough to touch. Yet it felt like no one from where she lived would ever go anywhere. She felt like she'd be stuck there forever.

The very air she breathed oppressed her. Even when the weather was nice, she felt an invisible cloud hovering. All she wanted was to get as far away as possible. If she didn't see her father much, what would that matter? It would save her the pain of seeing him self-destruct.

In the old days, when Johnny was young, you could just run away and hop a train. Life was different now. There were things like AIDS, cocaine, crack-heads, gangsters, rapists and serial killers to worry about. Sickos like Ted Bundy picked up girls and killed them just for fun. A guy they called the South Shore Slasher was on the loose. He had sliced up several women who were out jogging, and now Riley was nervous on her morning runs.

The world was a lot uglier these days, and she knew from TV shows what could happen to runaways. Her only hope was going to college. She would go as far away as possible—thousands of miles—maybe even to the University of Alaska.

ON THURSDAY it was cold again, so after running and walking, she and Johnny hopped in his car and headed back to Linda Mae's. In the car, he handed her a box. She opened it and smiled as she held up a purple and pink Nike running jacket and pants.

"Wow. This is nice, stylish too."

"It's supposed to be the best fabric for exercising in cold weather."

"Thanks."

"Hope it fits. I got the smallest size they had."

She rubbed the material on her cheek. "I like the fabric—it feels soft. This is great. I'm a little low on clothes. We lost everything in that fire." She pulled her sweatshirt away from her body. "I'm all sweaty. I think I'll put it on when we go inside."

"Wait a minute though—I got you this." She yanked a small, wrapped rectangle from the pocket of her hooded sweatshirt.

"Hey I said no gift, remember?"

"Just open it."

"All right." He tore off the wrapping paper and read the title of the small book. "French-English Phrasebook for the Traveler."

"For your trip to Paris. Don't tell me you're already fluent in French?"

"No, but—"

"Okay, secret is out. Look." She took the book out of his hands, opened the cover and showed him an inscription. "I didn't buy it. I already had it and I'm passing it on to you. It's called re-gifting. Kind of tacky, huh? "

He read the inscription. "'Ma Chér, Bonne chance. Je t'aime, Mom.' This was a gift from your mother. Are you sure you want to give it to me?"

"To be honest, I find French a bit pretentious. My mom made me take it even though I wanted to take Spanish. We had a big fight about it. She had some snobbish notion that everything French was better. Now, I'm taking Spanish and every time I look at that French book I feel guilty. I can still feel her disapproval, almost coming out of that book." She frowned at the book. "So when you said you were going to France, I thought it would be the perfect gift for you."

"Guilt is a useless emotion, dear." He shook his head and looked at the book. "Are you sure you don't want to keep it for sentimental value?"

"I'm not very sentimental. Hey, when you ain't got nothing, there's nothing to lose."

He looked at her. She was right. She didn't really have much of anything. But she had a fighter's spirit. "You've lost a lot kid, but you got a lot to offer. You'll bounce back."

He looked down at the book again. "Okay then. Thank you. I'll study up on my French so I can communicate with the snobby Frogs."

In the bathroom at Linda Mae's, Riley changed into the Nike jacket and pants.

She returned to the table and smiled. "Fits perfect. Thank you."

"Yeah, that looks great, and it should keep you warm and dry unless this whole fabric thing is a crock of shit. You test it out and tell me."

Twenty-nine

JOHNNY usually went around to Jean's place for dinner. Most of his nights were spent working, seeing people in the bar, dealing with problems and roughing up people who didn't cooperate. He needed a vacation as much as anyone else. Since neither of them had kids, they decided to spend Christmas in Europe. He could kill two birds with one stone and stash some money while he was there.

Nightmares made him a restless sleeper. He tossed, turned, mumbled and even screamed in his dreams. Jean was a deep sleeper. When they slept together, she never woke up no matter how much he tossed, turned and yelled. Sometimes he woke up from a nightmare and couldn't get back to sleep. His dog had gotten used to going for walks in the middle of the night.

The honking of European cars penetrated their closed hotel window. He got out of bed and looked down on the Parisian street. He was a tourist now. He could return to his country if he wanted. But the future already occupied a place in his mind, and he moved through the present with a kind of premature reminiscence. Soon he'd be a fugitive.

He climbed into bed next to Jean. Her back was to him, rising and falling in the rhythmic breath of sleep. He thumbed through Riley's book searching for useful phrases. When his eyelids felt heavy, he placed it on a bedside table on top of a book about Napoleon. He started to fall asleep, but the descent into dreams was too sudden and violent. He found himself awake again, terrified.

Sleep finally came. He was alone in his boat steering it toward some spot in the middle of the ocean. He squinted against the sun's blinding reflection. When he arrived at what seemed the right place, he cut the motor, rummaged with his fishing gear and cast a line. The boat gently rocked. Relaxed, he closed his eyes and turned his face toward the sun.

When he opened them, he nearly jumped out of his seat. A woman stood at the bow of the boat with her back to him. The breeze lifted her red hair around her head like a static halo. The fine white hair on her arms and legs caught the sunlight and created a shimmering glow around her whole body. His eyes followed her slim coppery legs up to a crisp white tennis skirt.

"It's nice out here," she said loudly over her shoulder. He could just hear her voice over the screeching gulls and the waves slapping the boat. When she turned and walked toward him, he was stunned by her emerald eyes and her perfect nose. He longed to touch her and undress her. She reached out and grabbed his wrist turning his palm face up. Her thumb pressed hard on his pulse.

"You," she commanded, "take care of my baby." Her eyes stirred some deep phantom longing within him. She turned her head and looked out at the water. Her hair covered her face. Her touch burned. He pulled his hand from her. She looked at him. Suddenly, flames consumed her face, the flesh melted, dripped till her bones showed. He smelled the horrific smell of burnt hair and flesh. She screamed in agony. Unable to look anymore, he turned his head. When he looked back, she was diving into the water. Small white pieces of fabric, burnt around the edges floated in the air—pieces of her tennis skirt. Scorched flesh and bone disappeared over the edge of the boat. There was neither sound nor splash. When he looked over the side of the boat, all he saw were fish darting away.

He sat up in bed, sweating and panting, the dream still vivid. "Take care of my baby?" he asked himself. What was that supposed to mean? He looked at Jean. Her back was still to him, rising and falling. He tried to go back to sleep, but the dream and the woman's image haunted him. Some urgency in her voice had spilled into him. He didn't believe in ghosts, so it must be his guilty conscience feeling responsible for Riley and what happened to her mother.

In Paris they took the elevator to the top of the Eiffel Tower, strolled down the Champs Elysée and visited the Louvre. He was interested in Roman history when France was Gaul and ruled by the ancient Celts until one by one they were conquered by Caesar. Although he descended from the Celts, he admired Caesar. He had named his dog after him. His dog had none of the traits of a great general, but he could be a tyrant if he didn't get his walk every day. He hoped Mrs. O'Leary, the dog sitter, had the energy to keep up with him.

Thirty

RILEY CRAVED nature the way an addict craves drugs. The peeling paint on their apartment walls, turned yellow with decay, sometimes closed in on her. She longed for a different life, to be free from the past and start over. Out there beyond Dorchester Bay, where she sat with Johnny in the morning, was the ocean, holding infinite possibilities but also danger. She felt simultaneously seduced and intimidated by it.

One Saturday in March, Riley rode her bike out to the Blue Hills Reservation to climb the 600-foot hill. It was the highest point within ten miles of the coastline till you got to Maine. She wore light gloves and a hat to keep off the chill. If she covered her head while riding her bike people usually left her alone, but if her hair flowed out behind her, and it had now grown back to her shoulders, she was often harassed.

She rode fast and made it there in about half an hour. She locked her bike to a fence. In shady spots, patches of snow from the last storm still dotted the ground. Before she climbed the hill to the lookout tower she fed the one lonely deer they kept in the enclosure. She felt bad for the deer because he had been alone all winter. In Quincy, she had spent all her time hanging out with friends, but now, just like the deer, she spent most of it alone. Sometimes she hung out with Bones and once in a while she went to parties, but mostly she was by herself. If it weren't for her time with Johnny in the mornings, she would have been really lonely. It felt weird and disrespectful to call him Johnny, but he had told her to. He mostly called her kid or dear and that made her feel kind of special.

Riley crouched in front of the wire fence of the deer enclosure and pushed a handful of granola through a hole. As the deer ate, his wet, rough tongue tickled her palm. It tilted its head to get the last crumbs. While staring into the deer's dark, moist eyes, she pulled her hand back through the hole and reached for the box of granola. When she looked up, Johnny was there. She'd never seen him other than in the morning, and he looked somehow different in the afternoon.

"It's you," he said. "I thought I saw you ride by on your bike. You know it's kind of dangerous riding on these curvy, narrow roads." He looked around. "I don't think it's very safe for a young girl to be alone out here either."

Riley shrugged. "It feels a lot safer than my neighborhood."

"Really? Why is that? Is someone bothering you?"

"Yeah, but he'd never find me out here. That's for sure."

"What's his name? Maybe I can help?"

His voice was filled with urgent concern and she wished she hadn't said anything. What could Johnny possibly do to help her? "Don't worry. He's a scum ball. But I can avoid him if I watch my step."

Johnny looked around at the empty cages and chewed on his bottom lip. "Do you come here often?" he asked. "You know I used to visit these poor animals but I haven't been here in years."

"Not a lot. Once in a while I come and feed this deer. He really likes me."

"Well yeah. What's this you're feeding him?" Johnny picked up the box. "Quaker Granola. Got to be like prime rib for this guy. Most of the time, he gets fed that stuff." He pointed to some pellets in a metal dispenser that cost a quarter.

"Oh." Riley laughed. "And I thought it was just me he liked."

An awkward silence filled the March afternoon. They had often sat watching the sun rise out over Dorchester Bay, but it felt strange to meet here. "I wish you'd tell me who's bothering you. I grew up around there. I might be able to help."

Riley petted the dear through the fence. "Hey, do you want to hike to the top?"

Johnny sniffed and looked up the hill. "Sure, why not? Now that I'm here, some fresh air and exercise can't hurt."

They started up the steep trail. Granite stepping stones scattered the hillside and created a path in the thawing earth, which led through the forest to the top of the hill. They stepped from stone to stone avoiding the soft suction of mud pulling at their shoes.

"You're in good shape," Riley said.

"I try to take care of myself," he answered.

"Johnny, I'm glad to run into you. You're probably the only normal person I know."

Thirty-one

JOHNNY SMILED. She seemed perceptive and yet she misread him. He was not a kind man, and definitely not a normal man. He was feared and known for ruthless brutality. The waters running down the hill on which they walked flowed out to the tidal marshes of Neponset Bay and washed over the decaying bodies of people he had killed with his own hands.

Yet the truth was he didn't feel like a killer in her presence. There was a freedom in shedding his ruthlessness, in being with someone who knew nothing about his work. He could be a nice guy. He looked after families in South Boston, people who had once been good to his family.

There were two towers at the top of the Blue Hills Reservation. One was a weather station and the other was an observation tower, which stood forty feet tall and was made of blue granite interspersed with ocher and pale yellow stones. They climbed the winding stone steps of the graffiti-marred, urine scented stairwell until it opened to a viewing area. From there, they could see for miles in every direction.

They looked out from a thirty-foot-high wall. Riley hoisted herself onto it. Her legs dangled over the edge.

"What the fu—what are you doing?" he asked as if she were crazy. She stood on the wall and scrambled up the slanted wooden roof.

"There's an even better view from up here," she said nonchalantly as if this were something she did all the time. "Johnny, you got to come up!" She leaned down toward him and pointed at the roof. "You just stand up on the wall, and then hold on right here and there. Use the wall for your feet. It makes it a lot easier."

He looked at where she pointed. The structure could be climbed without much difficulty. But something at the bottom of his stomach prevented him from joining her.

"Sorry, is this freaking you out?"

"No." He was determined not to be outdone by a fifteen-year-old girl. Without thinking, he hoisted himself up.

"So, what's the point?" He sat next to her on the roof.

"There's no point," she said smiling. "It's just fun. Look at the view."

"Yeah?" he said looking out, then down thirty feet to the ground. "Yeah, okay I can see the thrill in it. Most people just do drugs."

"This is a lot better for you and cheaper, don't you think?"

"Well yeah, unless you fall that is."

"You're not afraid of getting arrested are you?" she asked looking around.

"Getting arrested?" he repeated with a surprised laugh.

"Yeah. We could get arrested for this. So we probably shouldn't stay here too long. I don't want to be responsible for a nice guy like you getting arrested. It could ruin your business career."

"That's true."

They sat looking out at the Blue Hills Reservation—a canopy of conifers and deciduous trees that were finally sprouting tiny, green buds on their skeletal branches. They faced the Boston skyline to the north. The blue of the Hancock tower stood alone a couple of shades darker than the light blue sky. The old, gray Prudential building a short distance to the south made the Hancock building look like a whimsical child. To the east was Quincy Bay and beyond that the endless blue of the ocean.

For a moment, they were separate from the buzz and hum of the world that usually contained them—the world of streets and houses, of people, of striving and failing, pettiness, greed, unnoticed heroic acts, and violence. In that world, the living, the dead, and the living dead, swirled and vibrated, tangled in a chaotic mass of energy that most people did not consciously notice.

But at the top of Blue Hill, the breeze, unhindered by buildings, danced with the tree limbs, diffused human tension, and brought pure elemental awareness into something that just maybe resembled the soul. It wasn't the Catholic soul they had been taught about, which atoned for sin and lived in an afterlife of heaven, hell and purgatory. The breeze carried spring's wordless secrets of life returning to earth, of light born of darkness, of life followed by death in an endless cycle.

They did not try to name it, hold it, or even to understand it. They just felt it, absorbed it, let it pass through their bodies and felt grateful for the moment.

"Ever imagine jumping?" asked Riley.

"Jumping? Off what?"

"You know—ever get up someplace high and imagine jumping? Not because you want to kill yourself or anything, but doesn't the edge kind of draw you toward it?"

129

"To tell you the truth, I usually avoid heights, and the way you're talking, so should you." Johnny slid off the roof. "Come on. Better not stay too long—wouldn't want to get arrested for stealing such a priceless view."

"Yeah." She slid down after him. "That would ruin my chances of going to college."

"Good for you dear. Plan for the future. Why don't you study business so you can make a lot of money?"

"I don't really care that much about money. I don't think it's what makes people happy."

"Sure makes me happy."

When they got back to the parking lot, Riley bent over and started unlocking her bike from the fence.

"How long did it take you to ride your bike all the way out here?"

"Oh, not long. It's not a bad ride. It's just the drivers that are bad."

"Why don't you let me give you a lift home then, huh?"

"No. It's okay. I don't want you to go out of your way."

"I'm going that way anyway, dear. I'll just throw your bike into my trunk." He sized up her bike. Several bodies he'd had to dispose of had been at least that big. "It'll fit."

"Okay then. If you're sure it's no trouble. Thanks. It is a bit nerve-racking riding on the roads in the evening." He maneuvered her bike into the trunk then opened the passenger door for her.

"So, where do you live anyway?" she asked as they were pulling out of the parking lot.

"I live in Quincy, but I do most of my work in town."

"Oh really? I grew up in Quincy. What part do you live in?"

"I live in North Quincy, at Lewisburg Square."

"Wow. Those are nice condos. My dad looked at moving in there after my mom died but they were too expensive. Then he just gave up and moved us into a dump near the T in Southie. I thought there must be something in between those condos and where we live now. But I don't think my dad could be bothered looking. He's depressed."

Johnny took the back way from Blue Hills, avoiding the expressway. He knew all the back roads. Donavan should snap out of his depression and look after his daughter. "Lewisburg Square is nice. I like it there. It's fairly quiet backing onto the bay and I'll tell ya, the view of the Boston skyline at night is spectacular. I have a telescope and sometimes I can see the planets. The city lights are

130

usually too bright but sometimes I can see Venus, once in a while Mars. You know I'm really sorry you lost your mother, kid."

"You don't have to be sorry. It's not your fault. Everyone says sorry when someone dies, but it's not like they killed them. You know, I thought if we moved into a fancy place our lives would be perfect, even without my mother. I thought if we lived in the right place and I wore the right clothes I could forget her. But I don't know. I doubt it would be any different."

"It sounds like you're dealing with it better than your father."

"Things were pretty bad at first. I was at a real low point not long ago. I kind of wished I was dead. Then I started Taekwondo and I met you." She looked at him and smiled.

"Did you and your mother look alike?" He kept his eyes on the road.

"Oh, no. My mother was beautiful. She had red hair and green eyes, and everything about her was absolutely perfect."

That description made his brain tingle and his skin turn cold. She could be the woman from his dream. "You're beautiful too."

"I was never good enough for my mother."

"Well, I think you're pretty good."

"Thanks." She looked out the window.

As they drove, he thought about how much he'd liked his condo, until he realized it was bugged. He felt paranoid now, couldn't relax, even after he'd bought a top-of-the-line detector and tore out the bugs. He always had a gun next to the bed and lately he even slept with a knife strapped to his calf.

Soon he would disappear and change his identity. He had to avoid going back to prison at all costs. He'd done hard time in his twenties and he would not go back. His nest egg was larger than he ever imagined, and yet he obsessively stashed money, passports, all kinds of things in safe deposit boxes scattered all over the country and the world. It wasn't easy, and most of his time and mental energy was consumed with covering his tracks.

Everything was becoming computerized these days and since he didn't know much about computers he'd hired a consultant, a friend's kid at MIT, to advise him on that aspect. He paid the kid well and wasn't too worried about him ever talking since most of the details were vague. He learned everything he could from the kid so he'd never have to trust anyone else to take care of something important for him.

There would come a time when all fingers pointed to him and they would have enough evidence to convict him of something— maybe not everything, but they'd get him for something all right. For years, Agent Mulligan had thrown in a monkey wrench every time they set up a sting, and Johnny had rewarded him dearly for it. He could only continue so long before someone put the pieces together and by all indications it was happening now. Mulligan was a flashy goofball and even though Johnny had told him to keep it down, he still paraded around in new cars and fancy suits. It was almost time to go on the lam, but until then he would continue the cocaine distribution up and down the eastern seaboard, which was pulling in millions each week.

Thirty-two

THE BULLETIN BOARD at the L Street Community Center was a colorful, messy, collage of notices: lost cats and dogs, babysitting and handyman services, guitar lessons, chess clubs, support groups, legal services, help wanted, course offerings—even a few people looking for love. Riley scanned the ads and lifted a couple to see if anything interesting was hiding underneath them.

She had overheard her dad on the phone arguing with the insurance company, and she knew he was stressed about money. She needed a part-time job, but she had no skills and no employment history. She'd discovered this when she went to fill out an application for a job at CVS and had to leave both those sections blank. She'd almost written martial arts in the special skills section, but doubted that was a desired skill for employment at a drug store.

She often stopped and read notice boards, always with some vague hope that she might see something—something destined for her to see, which might change her life for the better. She was about to walk away when she saw a pastel blue ad hanging on the bottom left corner of the massive, cork board. She'd been looking up and had almost missed it. People were always looking up and failing to notice what was below.

The sign read, "Earn Money: Become a Certified Life Guard." She was a strong swimmer. She could become a lifeguard. There were tons of hotels around the city that needed lifeguards. She'd seen their ads in the paper. But the course was fifty dollars. She'd have to scrimp and quit going to Taekwondo. The thought of that didn't bother her much. Everyone at the gym knew she was a girl now that her hair had grown back. Now the boys all stared at her and sneered or grimaced. Even though she wanted to progress in Taekwondo, she felt awkward at the gym and had started to dread going there. She'd continue her practice, get books out of the library, try and learn as much as she could on her own and then when she had some money, she'd look for a co-ed gym. She took the ad from the bulletin board, folded it, and put it in her backpack. If not enough people signed up for the class, maybe they'd lower the price.

Thirty-three

MICHAEL DONAVAN stood on the corner with a steaming coffee cup in his gloved hand. He wore heavy work clothes and construction boots. The clothes allowed him to mingle unnoticed with all the other construction workers who were grabbing morning coffee and doughnuts before a hard day's labor. There were rumors of a huge construction project to dig a tunnel, channel traffic from the Central Artery and create another route to Logan Airport. The construction industry was buzzing with excitement, and all the men felt certain they would have jobs in the years to come.

His suit and briefcase were in his car two blocks away. Although he would be late for work, he would still take a long lunch so he could come back to this spot again and keep an eye on the Camel's headquarters. A body shop fronted for the gang headquarters in the back. All day a mix of customers and criminals visited on various orders of business. It took him a few weeks of observation to distinguish the Camel's gang from the real mechanics. He recognized one of the guys who had tried to come after him in the alley. He was a large guy with arms the size of most guys' legs. Michael followed him and learned that almost every evening he stopped by O'Malley's Tavern on his way home.

ONE EVENING, Michael left work early, slipped into the construction clothes and arrived at O'Malley's before the guy. He settled onto a barstool a couple of seats down from where the guy usually sat and ordered a beer. His long salt-and-pepper hair, his mangy beard, and the construction clothes made him look and feel like a totally different person. People he'd known for years and ran into on the street didn't even recognize him.

After he took a hearty swallow of his beer, he focused on the tiny bubbles marching in an infinite and perfect line toward the top of his glass. They were illuminated by a slanted ray of sunlight that had penetrated the dusty, west-facing window behind him. Toward the end of his first drink, he felt the dull knife-edge of tension melt from his shoulders. The second drink relaxed his facial muscles and slackened his jaw. As soon as he set the second glass down, the third drink called to him like the irresistible allure of a glamorous woman despite the probability that she was a whore. Just as his

134

third beer began to put a twinkle in his eye and spark a fire in his belly capable of great mischief or overindulgence in greasy food, the door opened and the Camel's man entered.

"Hey, Markie, how ya doin?" called the bartender. "We missed you last night."

"Yeah, busy week."

"That right? What you got going on? Gonna blow up the Governor's mansion? Wish someone would take that wing nut out. I'm tellin' ya."

"Yeah, yeah, very funny." He glanced around the room and gestured with his hand to keep it down. "Just get me a beer would you."

Michael kept his eyes fixed on a TV above the bar. He tried to keep his face vacant. His beard made him inconsequential. He was a man without status and without a razor. No one could be bothered with a man who couldn't be bothered to shave. In fact, it was often hard to get service, and he wished the bartender would offer him another drink.

Blow up the Governor's mansion? Yeah, obviously a joke, but why joke with a man about blowing something up? Every joke had some truth in it. This could be his man. After months of searching, the man who bombed his house and killed his wife could be sitting two bar stools down from him. What was he to do now? He hadn't really planned this far.

It took everything he had to mask what was going on in his mind and slow the blood that pumped faster in his body and compelled him to act. The whole mess had started that way, with adrenaline from being surprised, and then his gut reaction of attacking the men who had approached him. He could have negotiated and taken a little beating. They probably weren't going to kill him that night. So what? He'd suffer a beating and a bruised ego. Eventually, he would have come up with the money to pay the Camel. He had to get to them before they came for him again. He had to come up with a plan. He couldn't fly by the seat of his pants like he so often did in court, getting by on his eloquence and fading good looks.

Thirty-four

BONES' BIRTHDAY fell on a Friday evening in late April. The last warmth from the day mixed with the cool evening air. A relaxed excitement hovered. You could almost reach out and touch it. They snuck a bottle of whiskey from Bones' house. Hidden by the shadow of the Carson Beach retaining wall, Bones and Riley sat on the sand and drank the whiskey mixed with orange juice. When they ran out of juice, they drank it straight.

Two and a half months and school would be over. Riley was nearly done with all the certifications she needed to get a lifeguard job. Her grades were good, and she hadn't had a run in with Sully for while. They passed the bottle back and forth giggling about the stupid but funny things that had happened at school that year. There were parties to go to, but it was nice to just hang out for a while and not worry about a party scene. When Riley stood up, she stumbled and fell back into the sand. Suddenly realizing that whiskey was more potent than beer, she looked at Bones who strained to hold her own head up, as if it weighed as much as a bowling ball. Riley tried to look at her upside down and they laughed in hysterics.

"Strong stuff," she said and pointed to the bottle, which was more than half gone.

STROLLING DOWN THE CARSON BEACH walkway with his friend, Looney, Sully noticed the shadows of some obviously drunk girls down on the sand. He couldn't believe his luck when he saw it was Riley. He gave a sideways smile to Looney, who caught his eye and smirked. There was no reason to be rough with girls who were this drunk so he turned on the charm instead.

He straddled the wall facing the bay. "Evening ladies. Nice night for some whiskey." He nodded toward the bottle. "Got any left or did you polish that off?" '

The girls froze as if the Grim Reaper had just appeared. Finally, Bones handed him the bottle.

"Sure Sul, have as much as you want."

"Why, thank you." He toasted her subtly, tipped back the bottle and handed it to Looney. They hung around nonchalantly, seeping into the atmosphere until the girls relaxed in their presence. Sully smiled at the drunken sway that had taken over Riley's body.

"Hey, why don't we go to my place, before the cops come and bust us?" He slid the bottle under his jacket and waved his arm for them to follow him.

"Good idea." Looney grabbed Bones' wrist and pulled her toward them.

"Okay." Bones looked like a hooked fish getting reeled in.

"I think I should go home," mumbled Riley. She turned and stumbled a few feet away from them.

Sully grabbed her arm. He pulled her toward him and smiled. "Come on. Let's put everything behind us and be friends, all right?"

"Riley, you can't go home like that," slurred Bones. "You are soooo drunk."

They started walking toward Sully's place. Riley reluctantly stumbled along behind them. Every now and then Sully looked back over his shoulder to make sure she was still there.

They walked up the stairs and went into his house, through the kitchen then past his sleeping brother curled up on the living room couch. Sully put his finger to his lips and shuffled them into his bedroom. He scooped laundry from a mattress on the floor and threw it toward the corner of the room. It landed on some crushed beer cans which skittered on the hardwood floor. He squatted down and switched on the radio—WBCN, the rock of Boston. The red Rolling Stones tongue hung on the wall next to the Zeppelin. Sully turned off the main light and turned on a lava lamp which cast florescent pink and green rays over the room causing the colors on the black felt posters to glow.

"Sully, aren't you going to get in trouble with us here?" asked Bones.

"I just live with my uncle. He doesn't give a shit. He's never here. My brother, on the other hand, will beat the hell out of me if we wake him up. So be quiet."

Riley was pale and looked like she was going to throw up. "Riley, are you going to puke?" He took her by the arm and guided her into the bathroom. He stayed with her while she threw up glad that he had got her there on time. He grabbed a towel from the bathroom floor, ran it under the sink for a minute and wiped her mouth. She pulled her pants down and turned to go to the bathroom. He grimaced, oh God, this was going to be so easy.

From the toilet, she suddenly came to life and looked up at him. "I can't believe I'm going to the bathroom in front of you," she slurred.

"I have to admit, I'm surprised too," he said still grimacing.

When they opened the door to his room, Looney and Bones were on the bed kissing. Looney was on top of Bones who squirmed underneath him.

Sully kicked Looney gently in the ass. "Hey, go hump that skeleton somewhere else."

"What?" Looney looked over his shoulder annoyed.

"Go in my uncle's room."

"What if he comes home?"

"He won't," assured Sully. Looney got up slowly, rearranging himself and his clothes. He grabbed Bones' arm and pulled her to her feet misjudging her weight, nearly sending her flying forward onto her face. They stumbled out of the room. Sully followed them and made sure they got to his uncle's room without waking his brother. When he came back, Riley was slumped against the wall. Her head lolled as he maneuvered her over to the bed.

"Les be friends then, kay?" she slurred.

He looked down at her body splayed out on his bed like a piece of cake he was about to devour. "Oh yeah, we'll be good friends."

"Sul!" called his uncle's strong, loud voice from the kitchen.

"Shit!" Sully cursed his luck. His uncle never came home at this time. He slipped out of his bedroom and shut the door behind him, before his uncle had a chance to come in.

"What are you renting my room out by the hour or something?"

He looked toward his uncle's room, "No, I, uh—"

"I got rid of them," his uncle said in that cool, unreadable way of his. Sully just never knew from his voice, his face, or his actions if he was pissed off or not. He might just cuff him and he'd never see it coming. His uncle looked at him hard and blank. There was obviously something else on his mind, more important than the teenagers he had found humping in his bedroom.

"You want any coke, Sul?"

"Oh you know it. That's all I've been thinking about man— that and pussy."

"There a girl in your room?"

"Yeah."

"She passed out?"

"Yeah."

"Didn't think you could get a girl in your bed unless she was unconscious."

"So, where's the blow?"

"Well, that's the thing. You got to do something first."

138

"Oh no, not that shit again man. I can't do that." Sully started pacing the room.

"It's the only way. We don't have any money. Listen, you do this, we get an eight ball, do some ourselves, then split it up, sell it for a profit, buy some more with the money we earned and never look back."

"Why don't you do it?" whined Sully. "I ain't a fag!"

"This guy ain't a fag either. He's just got this, you know…fetish—likes to get blow jobs from young guys sometimes. It's not that weird." He lowered his voice in a conspiratorial whisper. "Some people like to get whipped, some people like to get strangled, or pissed on even. That's all it is. Don't think of it like you're turning gay. Think about how much time you're spending and what you're gonna get in return. Huh? Otherwise we're dry."

Sully thought how badly he'd been craving some blow. Every day he obsessed about it, tried to sniff it out at every party, from anyone he knew. But word had got around and he'd done as many free lines as he was going to get.

"Look. He's waiting. You go on out to his car. Do what you need to, come back, we'll do a few lines, and then you can go enjoy that girl in there."

Sully tried to sound tough and to maintain his masculinity, which he was about to trade for an eight ball. "This is the last time."

HE CAME BACK PISSED OFF and disgusted with himself, eager to numb his feelings and feel good again. His uncle cut some lines on a mirror, rolled up a bill, and handed it to him first. "We be smart with this Sul, and we're golden."

Sully's brother had already woken up and gone out, and he knew his uncle wouldn't hang around for long either. He got a cold beer from the fridge and went into his bedroom. He looked at Riley passed out on the mattress.

Doing her now might be too much like doing a corpse. With curious disgust, he remembered all that fetish shit his uncle had talked about. The image of what he had just done popped into his head and he threw the Budweiser can at the wall. He didn't feel any better as he watched the foamy liquid run down the wall. He just wondered remorsefully how much beer was left in the fridge.

"Damn it," he said looking at Riley wishing he could summon some of the desire he'd felt before his uncle had called his name.

As soon as the cocaine entered his blood stream, he felt good again. He looked admiringly at the bag of coke his uncle had left him and convinced himself it was worth it. He undressed Riley, who stirred but was too out of it to comprehend what was going on. She was very different now from the hellcat who fought him off most of the time. He smiled at her naked body, rubbed her breasts and shoved his fingers as deep into her as they would go.

He could wake her up and give her a line of blow just to get some life into her. No it didn't matter. Her pussy was still tight and alive. Fucking a corpse was probably way different than fucking someone who had passed out. No, this was going to be too easy. She would never even know what happened. No one would ever know if he could manage to keep his mouth shut about it. He finally felt excited enough to stick it in, but when he tried it wouldn't go very far and seemed to hit something like there was a wall inside her. He pushed and pushed and all the pushing made him soft.

Then he lost it, and in a rage started beating her as if she were just a lifeless punching bag. She curled up, tried to scream and cover her face with her hands. Yet he couldn't stop. He raged at his junkie mother who had left him, at his unknown father, at his brother for all the unfair beatings, at his conniving uncle, and at himself for what he had just done.

Thirty-five

EVEN THROUGH HER DRUNKEN STUPOR, Riley felt intense pain. It felt like someone was trying to kill her. She wondered who, and why, and if she would die. She tried to scream for help but her tongue was too thick from the whiskey.

The next morning, struggling to open her eyes, she squinted against the daylight. When she finally managed to open one eye, she realized with horror that she was lying in the packed mud and dewy grass next to Sully's house. Her other eye was swollen shut. She raised herself and felt the cold ground beneath her hands. She wiped some mud from her cheek with the back of her sleeve and looked around.

When she tried to stand up, needles of pain stabbed her head, the ground underneath her spun, and she vomited. She fought the urge to lie back down as foggy details from the night before trickled forth. "Shit, shit, shit," she said as tears stung her eyes and she looked around in panic. The beating came back, the pounding blows, the terror and helplessness. In her drunken state all she could do was curl up and pray for it to stop. She wondered if he had also had sex with her. But if he did, why did he have to beat her so badly? There was no memory. A vague uncertainty of what happened gnawed at her and this lack of certainty about something so personal made her feel not just violated but hollow. She felt totally incomplete and disgusted with herself for misplacing her virginity.

JOHNNY HADN'T SEEN RILEY for a week and he felt strangely unsettled. It bothered him that he cared about her that much. He sat on the bench and looked down the walkway hoping to see her. It was a gray Saturday morning, which made Friday's beautiful weather feel like a dream. Riley's bright eyes would cheer him and break the monotony of the misty somberness that had blurred the line between sky and ocean.

He saw a small figure shuffling down the walkway. The hair looked similar, but it couldn't be her. The movement was tentative, if not pained, and the girl always had a bounce in her step. She approached slowly and sat shyly at the end of the bench.

"Morning," she muttered.

His blood pounded in his temples and his heart beat faster as he took in her battered face and the painful way she moved. His muscles fired and twitched as he fought the sudden desire to lash out and kill whoever was responsible. All of his murders had been planned and motivated by a strategic need to eliminate a foe. Now he knew what Joe "the animal" must feel when he lashed out with his bare hands in a fit of rage. Johnny needed action. He would go kill whoever had done this to her right now. It could not wait till the cover of night.

He got up, knelt in front of her and grabbed her shoulders. "Tell me who did this."

She looked at him through one eye. Her face was almost unrecognizable. She was not the girl who just a week ago had smiled and laughed with him.

"I'm sorry," she cried. "I should have never come here and let you see me like this."

"Jesus. No. Don't apologize to me. No. I'm glad you came. I've been wondering what happened to you." He struggled to compose himself, and allow his emotionless calculating mind to take over. His angry outburst had only scared her and he would have to calm down if he wanted to find out anything.

"Who did this to you, dear?" The most gentle and concerned voice he could muster masked his rage.

She looked at him, then quickly down at the ground and out at the bay. "I wish guys today were more like you. My grandfather, he was a hat tipping gentleman. Now his whole generation is almost gone. Guys these days are assholes. Do you think there are any hat tippers left?"

He stood up, took off his baseball cap and ran his hand through his hair. The memory of strangling Kathleen Dunn with a piano wire popped into his mind. His hands had squeezed the wire, which he had wrapped around her neck. Her heavily made-up face had been frozen in horror like a cheap china doll as she gasped for her last breath. The wire left angry marks but her expression was finally peaceful, and he was glad that at the last moment she had resigned to her fate. He was far from a gentleman. But this girl seemed to think he was the best thing since sliced bread. He faltered, momentarily forgetting who he was. He sat back down on the bench and looked at her.

"Hey, I'm not that old you know, and I only tip my hat to shade my eyes, see." He tipped the brim of his Red Sox cap to cover his eyes from the sun that was just beginning to break through the clouds. "You didn't answer my question dear. Who did this to you?" He couldn't believe the twists and turns their conversations took.

She looked at him dismissively. "It doesn't matter. There's nothing you can do."

He tried not to persist, noting the intensity of her shame and the hopelessness she felt.

They were silent for a while. "What did your father do when he saw you like this?"

"I haven't seen him yet."

"When did this happen?"

"Last night."

"How come you haven't seen your father since last night?"

"I don't know. I guess we just missed each other. You know," she said softly, "it was my fault."

"What could you have done to deserve something like this?"

"Whiskey. It's a lot stronger than beer. I drank too much and passed out. I'm lucky someone didn't kill me, I suppose."

"Yeah, well I can smell it. You should stay away from hard liquor. A girl could get in big trouble passed out in the city. But I don't think this was done by a stranger. I think it was someone you know. I think it was the same guy you mentioned was harassing you before. Why don't you tell me his name?"

"And then what? What would you do? Tell the police?"

On the tip of his tongue hung everything—who he was, his power, what he could do to protect her and punish whoever did this. It all hung there for a second, the words about to spill out. Then he swallowed them. Always think before you speak. Think of your words, who you're talking to, what they reveal. In his business, he calculated every word, weighed it for effect and made sure he never revealed more than he wanted or needed to. Of course he was guarded. A hundred people would like to put a bullet in his head and about a hundred more wanted him in prison.

He didn't need to give himself away. He liked what he had with the girl and there was no reason to shatter her illusion that he was a kind gentleman. He could be that for her for a brief time in the morning. He would find out who had done this to her and they would feel his wrath. If he couldn't find out from her, there were other ways.

"Don't worry. There's nothing you can do about it. It's enough that you even care," she said.

Why do I care about this karate ragamuffin who seems to have no people of her own? He thought of the daughter he'd lost and the emptiness he'd felt for years.

"All this training I've been doing for self defense and I go and incapreciate myself," Riley said changing the subject again. "How stupid. I've only ever drunk beer and wine coolers before. Whiskey's dangerous."

"Incapacitate."

"What?"

"The word is incapacitate."

"Incapacitate." She repeated and looked at the ground.

"Many people have lost their lives because of too much whiskey. I don't touch the stuff myself. Few beers, glass of wine now and again, that'll do me. I suggest the same for you."

"Doesn't matter now. What's done is done. I'm never getting drunk again and if anyone tries to mess with me when I'm sober, I'll kick his ass."

He regarded her small figure out of the corner of his eye. "Don't ever try your karate on someone with a gun, all right?"

"Taekwondo."

"Whatever it is. Just remember it won't work if they have a gun or a knife." He sniffed, feeling the dagger against his calf and the other one tucked at an angle behind him. His posture had benefitted from the blade at his back. He never slouched, always stood straight with his hands on his hips ready to grab it at a second's notice. He could open the jugular of a two-hundred-pound man with one clean slice. One clean experienced slice. He imagined what he'd do to the guy who had done this to her.

He looked at her closer, studied her cuts and bruises. "Come here then. Let me take a look at you. You don't need stitches do you?"

"I don't know." She curled up and hugged herself.

"Stand up—lift up your shirt. You might have broken a rib." She stood in front of him and raised her shirt to the top of her rib cage. He winced. He had seen plenty of gruesome bodies, murdered by his own hand, without the slightest bit of sympathy, but this disturbed him.

He shook his head, "No one should do this to a girl and get away with it." He tried to block the flooding memories of strangling Kathleen Dunn. She had been a grown woman, a trashy whore, and a serious liability to his organization with all that she knew and her big mouth. It had to be done.

"I think you need a few stitches right here." He pointed to a place where her cheek had split. "Otherwise you might end up with a scar."

"I'm not going to the hospital."

"I can do it for you."

"Really? Where'd you learn that?"

"Oh, old guys pick up a few tricks over the years."

"That's so cool. Do you really think I need them though?"

"Yeah, just a few. It'll heal quicker."

With the sun, the Saturday walkers came out in force, and for the first time he was embarrassed to be seen with her. People might assume he had done this.

Thirty-six

IN SILENCE, they drove to his condo. Riley sat at his kitchen table while he went upstairs to get a first aid kit. His place was dark and sparsely furnished. The windows were covered with heavy shades. There was no mail lying around, no sticky notes or magnets on the fridge with photos of smiling children. A neatly folded newspaper sat on the countertop next to his wallet and keys, which he had placed in a decorative bowl as they came in. The bowl must have been a gift. It didn't seem like something he would buy. Riley rose from the table and had a quick peek into the living room. She listened for him, so she wouldn't be caught snooping. Nobody liked a snoop.

In the living room was a couch with a few throw pillows. A collection of statues sat on the mantel over the gas fireplace. They were soldiers, generals, chiefs—war stuff. One was a copper Indian on a horse slumped over a spear. The stairs creaked. She rushed back to her seat at the table.

He set down a huge first aid kit and began rummaging through it. "Wow. I've never seen a first aid kit like that." There wasn't any part of her Life Saving or First Aid course that taught how to stitch up a cut. "Johnny, how do you know how to do this? Were you ever a doctor?"

"No. I just like to be able to take care of myself and my friends. I don't like going to hospitals. Now this needle and thread," he said holding up a needle to the light and threading it, "are totally sterile. This stuff isn't from a sewing kit. It's the same kind of needle and thread they use at the hospital if you get stitches there."

"Good." His confidence and all the fancy supplies eased her anxiety.

"I can give you a painkiller, but it won't kick in for about twenty or thirty minutes. You're already in so much pain anyway, that this won't feel like anything." He walked to the couch in the living room and grabbed a small pillow. He placed it on the table in front of her. "Here, put your head on this. Close your eyes and try to relax. It'll only take two minutes."

She did as he told her but couldn't help opening her eye a little. She felt a pinch as the needle pierced her skin. He was right. Compared to the pain she'd been through and still felt, the pinch of the needle was nothing. Yet she winced as it pierced her skin again.

"Try to relax your facial muscles," he said. Riley tried to relax. Yet, she couldn't help opening her eye. Johnny looked so silly with his tongue stuck out between his teeth. People who stuck out their tongues when they concentrated had always cracked her up. Her body started shaking as she failed to hold in her laughter.

"Does this hurt? Or are you laughing? Hold still!" His tongue went back into his mouth and his face went from ridiculous to stern.

Riley tried to explain. "You just looked so funny biting your tongue like that." Warm, salty tears rolled down her cheeks.

He waited for her to stop laughing then dabbed the tears away with cotton. "Don't look at me, if it makes you laugh. Close your eyes and don't move so I can get this done properly. I've never had anyone laugh when I was giving them stitches." He shook his head. "Hold still. You don't want a big scar on your cheek."

Riley took a deep breath through her nose and shut her eyes. "Okay, sorry." She recomposed herself. When he finished, she let out a deep sigh.

"Remind me and I'll take them out in about a week." He put the supplies away and closed up the first aid kit. "You know, I'd take you out for breakfast, but I got to be honest, I don't want to be seen with you." He crossed the kitchen, opened the refrigerator door and looked in. "It's not about looking gruesome, and I won't lie, your face looks pretty gruesome. It's because every time a man goes out with a woman or girl who's all beat up, everyone assumes he did it. So how about we have some eggs and toast here?"

"Sure. I understand. To tell you the truth, I don't really want to be seen with myself. Now I know what the Elephant Man felt like."

He glanced at her and took out eggs, a pan, and a loaf of bread. "At least it's not permanent. One more week and you'll look a lot better. Hopefully there won't be any scarring. If you ever get stitches again though, try not to laugh so much."

"Sorry about that." Riley watched as Johnny took an egg with one hand, cracked it on the side of a frying pan and tossed the shell into the trash. "Too bad I'm not a guy. A scar would actually be pretty cool."

He repeated the flawless action with the next egg, leaving no shell pieces or trails of egg white goo. "Wow! You're an expert egg cracker. I make a mess even when I use two hands."

Johnny split the scrambled eggs onto two plates and pulled some toast out of the toaster. He slid Riley a plate and some utensils and sat across the kitchen table from her. "I'm good with my hands."

"I'll say," she said and picked up her fork. She scooped some eggs into her mouth. The motion hurt. "You're a good cook too. These eggs are perfect."

JOHNNY shook his head, chewed his bottom lip, looked down and tapped his fork against the side of his plate without taking a bite.

"I'm sorry. Is my ugly face putting you off your breakfast?"

He looked up at her and then back down at his plate. He took a bite of eggs and shook his head. "No it's not that. I've seen worse beaten-up mugs than yours. I just want to know who did this to you."

"Well, I'm pretty certain I know who it was. The only thing I really remember is feeling someone beating me. I must have totally passed out because I woke up lying on the ground. So I can't be one-hundred- percent sure."

"I don't need certainty. Who do you think it was?" He looked her straight in her one good eye and waited for her to reveal the son of a bitch's name.

She hesitated and looked around at his place. "Believe me, it's no one you would associate with," she said.

He looked around at his upscale condo and saw the kind of impression she had of him, as a successful business man uninvolved with the seedy side of life. Normally, when he needed information from someone who didn't want to give it up, they nabbed the guy and took him to a warehouse where no one could hear him scream. Then they tied him to a chair and tortured him. Maybe they'd pull his teeth out or maybe something else. Whatever they ended up doing to the guy, it sure was a hell of a lot easier than this. The guy always talked. Most of the time, they'd kill him anyway so he wouldn't keep talking. This situation, trying to get information out of a fifteen-year-old girl who he did not want to hurt, was much harder and damn frustrating. He'd relied too long on violent methods of dealing with people. He couldn't torture the name out of her. That would defeat the purpose. He sighed loudly and got up to clear the plates.

"Well kid, I got some business to take care of in town. So I'll drop you off on my way. You should take it easy. Just lie in bed and read a good book for a couple of days, all right? It would mean a lot to me if I knew who did this to you. But if you want to keep it

148

a secret, there's nothing I can do. I can't tie you to a chair and beat it out of you, now can I?" He smiled wistfully.

Thirty-seven

THEY OFTEN sat in silence watching morning break over the bay. Sometimes it happened as if the sun could barely summon the strength to rise and sometimes the sun was determined against all odds to bring warmth and light to the world. One morning Johnny was studying the holes in Riley's sneakers while she watched a pigeon pursuing another in aimless circles.

"Looks like you need some new sneakers, kid."

She looked down and crossed one foot over the other, hiding the one with the most holes.

"Well, guess what Johnny?"

"What?"

"I have a job interview today for a lifeguard position at the Park Plaza Hotel." She emphasized the Ps.

He whistled, "A lifeguard position at the Park Plaza Hotel? Sounds great. Are you qualified?"

"Yeah, I've been taking a life saving class at UMASS. I just finished my First Aid class. It pays nine dollars an hour. If I get the job, I'll buy two pairs of sneakers and save money for college."

"How do you have time for that? Are you still going to Taekwondo?"

"I had to give up the classes for a little while, but I'm still learning new moves from a book I got. I've been pretty busy. It's good though. It keeps my mind off things. But look at my face. No one's going to hire me looking like this. "

He turned to her, leaned closer and inspected her face. "Hey, it looks a hell of a lot better than it did last week. Come on, it's about time you told me who did that."

"Johnny, I just want to forget about it. But damn, it's bad timing, looking like this for a job interview."

WHEN RILEY walked into the Park Plaza Hotel, she felt like a street urchin. The chandeliers, soft classical music, elaborate woodwork and subdued shine of the brass railings made her want to hide her bruised face. She wore her only skirt, which was slightly wrinkled and too short. She had over styled her hair into a nest and her nail polish had already chipped. Her cheap, vinyl soled shoes echoed on the floor as she crossed the lobby to the reception desk.

"Yes. May I help you?" The concierge looked at Riley's face and barely concealed her horror. Riley wished she could crawl under the Persian carpet and hide.

"I'm here for an interview."

"Go through that door." The woman pointed to a door that said, "Employees Only." "Go down the hall, take a left and have a seat in the hallway. If you come again you need to use the employee entrance off the alley."

Riley went through the door and down the hallway. She took a sharp left and sucked in her breath. Three teenage boys occupied the chairs outside the office. She leaned against the wall and slumped down wishing she'd just worn pants and a t-shirt. Her attempt to dress up probably just made her look like a cheap slut. She wanted to sit on the floor and make herself smaller but that could be awkward in a skirt. The boys looked at her then glanced at each other and chuckled. They were all big, well built, and seemed like members of some prep school shark wrestling team.

"Jesus, what happened to your face? Were you born that ugly or did you get in a cat fight?"

Her insides burned. She imagined punching the kid in the nose. She didn't respond because she couldn't think of a comeback. She should have known not to get her hopes up about the job, but she had been fantasizing about it ever since she got a call for an interview.

"What are you interviewing for?" another boy asked her. "A position in the laundry room?" They all laughed.

She tried to keep her eyes on his smug face and sound confident. "No. I'm interviewing for a lifeguard position."

"Oh really? You don't look like you could save anyone. If I were drowning, I'd sure hope you weren't the lifeguard. Of course, I wouldn't be drowning. Have you ever guarded before?"

"No. I just got my certification." She strained to steady her voice and will the water from welling in her eyes.

"Well, you don't have a chance then. We were all beach lifeguards last summer and they're only hiring two. You're wasting your time. Why don't you try and get a job at HoJo's? Get it HO-Jo's?" He turned to the others. They laughed.

She waited while they were interviewed. Each boy came out of the office and flashed a triumphant smile. The interviewer popped his head out of the office door.

"So you must be Riley. Last one. Come on in and have a seat."

She followed him into the office and sat in front of a big desk. He sat behind the desk, did a double take on her face, shook his head, looked down at his folded hands and did a quick thumb roll. "So Riley, do you have all your certifications?"

"Yes."

"Do you have them with you?"

Riley nodded, retrieved them from her bag and put them on the desk. He inspected them and nodded.

"Looks good. You got the job," he said.

"I got the job?"

"Yeah, you got the job." His voice had an edge and he was looking at her in a strange way as if he almost begrudged it. She looked at him and squinted into his eyes, searching for that thing hovering in the office that wasn't being said.

"Great. I'm excited."

"Okay then, let me make some copies of these certificates and we'll put you on the schedule. Working around school hours till summer, I assume?"

"Yes."

Thirty-eight

JOHNNY HAD ENTERED the lobby of the Park Plaza Hotel two hours before Riley. Like anyone from a working-class background, he had felt cowed by its opulence, but the twenty million he had spread around the world in safe-deposit boxes made him stand straight. He swaggered in his leather jacket to the reception counter.

"I need to talk to the manager or whoever's responsible for hiring lifeguards."

The concierge knitted his brow and took his time as he mulled over Johnny's request.

"That would be Matt. Sorry, I think he's in a meeting right now. Would you like to leave your number?"

The concierge's eyes fell to the thick gold rope that hung around Johnny's neck. That's right fucker, this necklace costs more than you make in a couple of months. "No. It's urgent. Get him out of the meeting now." Johnny stared at the man with his menacing, commanding eyes until he picked up the phone. He locked his stare on the man's face while he spoke.

"Matt. There's a gentleman here who needs to see you right away. I don't know. He says it's urgent." With the phone in his neck, the man glanced up at Johnny and nodded.

Johnny walked into the office without knocking and found young Matt straightening his hotel issued sport jacket.

"You the guy responsible for hiring the lifeguards?"

"Yes," he said, "but I don't think you—"

"A girl's coming in for an interview today. Her name's Riley. You need to hire her." As Matt raised his hand in protest, Johnny pulled a fat envelope from inside his jacket and slid it across the desk. Matt hesitated before he picked it up.

"Wooah, that's a lot of money to get someone a lifeguard job. What's this all about?"

"It's about a girl who's going to get a job here today." Johnny shook his head and smiled at the man as if he were crazy. "No questions."

"But sir…" Matt glanced at the contents of the envelope again. "This is probably more than she'll make. Why not just give her the money?"

"Why do you think?"

"Yeah." Matt nodded. "Okay."

Johnny looked into Matt's squirrelly eyes. "If you're thinking about taking the money and not hiring her, you better wipe that thought right out of your tiny mind." Johnny smiled. A bead of perspiration ran down Matt's temple.

"I...I wouldn't do that, sir. What makes you think I'd do something like that?"

Johnny smiled. He looked down at the black name tag with the gold lettering—MATT. "You tell me." He grabbed some mail from a tray on Matt's desk and began to flip through the envelopes. "Matt Goodson, 29 Old Country Road, Braintree. Oh Braintree, that's a nice town!"

"Would you put that down, please? You don't need my address. I said I'll give her the job."

Johnny turned to leave. "Thanks for your cooperation." He turned back. "Oh, one other thing—she is not to know about this."

"I'll make sure she never finds out."

"Good. Have a nice day."

Thirty-nine

JOHNNY PROPPED his foot up on a bench at Castle Island and felt a nice stretch in his quadriceps as he leaned forward. He was giving orders to Markie and Kilpatrick. They clustered around him nodding their heads. Johnny stopped talking and looked at them. He had lost their attention. They were focused on something behind him. He spun around to see Riley walking toward them smiling. He turned from the men and walked toward her.

"How did it go?"

"You won't believe it."

"What?"

"I got the job."

"I had a feeling you would." She wrapped her arms around him and squeezed. Keith and Markie exchanged glances.

"That's fantastic. This could be the beginning of great things for you."

"Yeah." Riley smiled. "I sure hope so."

"I got some business to take care of with my associates over there, so I'll, uh, see you tomorrow then."

"Okay. See ya." Riley glanced over at the men before she turned to go.

Johnny turned and walked back to Markie and Kilpatrick. As Markie watched Riley walk away, Johnny said, "You see that girl Markie? I'm going to give you her address. I want you to follow her to and from school everyday till you can tell me who did that to her face. Got it?"

"Who is that?" asked Markie. "She looks kind of familiar."

Kilpatrick stared after her diminishing figure. "Would be an attractive girl, cept it looks like someone put her face through a meat grinder."

Johnny turned a soul-crushing look at them. His voice turned sharp. "Never mind who she fucking is. Just do what I told you. Now can we get back to business? It's like I'm talking to five year olds with attention problems."

They discussed business on the pathway by the waterfront because the garage, Hangman's, and their cars had been bugged by the state police. Johnny had suspected that they were watching him long before Mulligan could confirm it. He had seen them sneaking around the garage dressed as construction workers and following him in unmarked cars. Their covert surveillance was blindingly obvious.

The end was in sight, but they wouldn't shoot him dead on the street like they had John Dillinger or put him in jail for tax evasion like they'd done to Al Capone. He had a plan. No one but Kilpatrick knew of his preparations for a new life and he didn't know much. They would question him after Johnny disappeared so Johnny had fed him lots of bullshit, just in case he talked. He wouldn't live a life on the run as most people imagined it, running from place to place, with the cops at his heels, letting them hunt him down like prey. He hadn't spent the past twenty years building a criminal empire and amassing millions of dollars to live out the rest of his years like that. He had sacrificed too much and killed too many people to let it all end that way. He had planned this next phase of his life with painstaking attention to detail.

Jean was supposed to come with him but he could feel her reluctance, and as much as he wanted her company, in the end it would be a liability. She would miss her family, the neighborhood, and her roots. Some people just couldn't be uprooted. He would also miss his family—the people and places he'd known for so long. There was a price to pay for his notoriety and the illicit fortune he'd saved.

Forty

MICHAEL DONAVAN had thought long and hard about how to approach the man called Markie. There was no way to bargain. Yet he'd played poker with no hand and had won bluffing. He'd have to do that now. There was no other option. He was a skilled liar if not a gifted orator.

He couldn't decide whether to approach Markie as the construction worker who had been hanging out at O'Malley's nearly every night, or as himself, the downtrodden lawyer, seeking to avenge his wife's murder. He had spent so much time wearing the construction clothes, hanging around the newsstand in the morning, and drinking beer in the evening that the line between his disguise and reality was starting to blur. A few times he'd even stumbled home and passed out in the construction clothes.

Approaching Markie would be dangerous enough. Approaching him with a fraudulent ultimatum was probably suicidal. But what was the alternative? For months he had done nothing but stew, and now he had a lead. It was a baseless lead that would get him laughed out of the police headquarters. It was just a passing comment overheard in a bar, a joke even. Yet something told him that Markie was his man. How many guys could the Camel have that went around blowing places up for him?

MARKIE SAT on a barstool at O'Malley's sipping a beer. He half watched a Red Sox game on the overhead TV while thinking about his ex-wife and daughters. If he hadn't been such a louse, instead of spending evenings at O'Malley's he'd have a nice home to go to. His apartment was very nice. It was so nice that it made him feel guilty, even though his ex-wife and daughters had a nice enough place of their own too. That's what working for McPherson got you—enough money to pay for two households when most working stiffs could hardly afford one. Yet their place wasn't with him and that left him at his place feeling lonely. So almost every night he ended up drinking beer and eating dinner at O'Malley's. The food wasn't bad, but his pants were getting tight.

He couldn't blame Michelle for leaving him. He'd cheated on her, many times. She also didn't like his work, although she had no problems spending the money. Markie was lost in thought when a

157

man with an overgrown beard, wearing dusty construction clothes sidled up to him and bought him a beer.

Markie looked down at the beer and inspected the man beside him who looked one step away from a street bum. Around Markie's wrist was a thick gold watch and on his finger was a twenty-five-carat gold Claddagh ring with a real emerald in it. That hand alone was worth over two grand. So why was this dirtbag buying him a beer?

"Looks to me like I'm the one who should be buying you a drink. What the hell do you want?" he asked.

The man scratched the back of his head. "Just a word. A few minutes, that's all."

Markie let out a heavy sigh and got off the bar stool. They walked to the corner of the tavern and slid into a booth. Markie searched the man's face. There was something familiar but he couldn't place it.

The guy stared at him with a strange intensity. "I know who you are," the guy finally said.

"Oh, yeah? That's good. Who am I then? And who the hell are you?"

"I'm Michael Donavan. Remember me? I lost my wife and house in a suspicious explosion. And I know you did it."

Markie looked at the guy again—saw behind the beard and clothes. Yeah, it was the guy who'd struck him hard in the throat that night. Then he'd watched him leaving his house every morning wearing a suit and carrying a briefcase. This guy, his wife and daughter had all come and gone for what seemed like eternity till finally he was sure he had a nice window of time when no one would be home. Then that fine redhead, in her little white tennis skirt, had to run back into the damned house and get herself killed. That had caused him a lot of aggravation with the Camel.

"Sorry pal, I think you've got me confused with someone else." Markie put his arm on the top of his side of the booth and looked back at the Red Sox game.

Donavan leaned closer across the table. "Yeah, well all the evidence seems to point in your direction."

"What evidence?"

"You'll find out at your trial. Unless you decide to cooperate."

"I already told you. You got the wrong guy."

Donavan slapped his hand down on the table. "I don't want you. I know you're just a low guy on the totem pole—a pawn. I want your boss." Donavan tapped his finger on the table in cadence with his words then leaned back and put his arm on the back of the booth. "If you want to rot away in prison to protect him, that's your choice." He shook his head.

"You know what happens to rats?" Markie placed his arms on the table, leaned in and glared at Donavan.

"Yeah, but I got connections." Donavan leaned in and spoke low. "How would you like to have a nice warm life with no more Boston winters? How does Puerto Rico sound? Or the Dominican Republic? I can get you in the W.P.P. You like Latin ladies, I can tell."

Fed up with the bullshitting weasel, Markie reached across the table, grabbed him by the front of his jacket and pulled so their faces were inches apart. He grumbled low and guttural. "Do you have a death wish?"

Donavan shook his head. Markie looked into his bloodshot eyes and smelled hard booze on his breath. "What are you drunk or something? You smell like whiskey for Christ's sake. Listen, if I ever see your face again, you are a dead man. Got that?"

Donavan nodded. Markie released his jacket and Donavan sank back into the booth like a deflated balloon.

Markie finally placed the girl at Castle Island. "By the way, how's your daughter?"

Donavan fired up again. "My daughter? Leave her out of this."

"Then get up, smile, go out that door and don't ever let me see your face again."

Donavan stood up and stared at Markie. With his eyes locked on Markie's, he backed toward the door, turned and left.

Markie sat back in the booth wondering what the Camel was up to. Why the hell did he want him to follow Donavan's daughter? What was he doing with her anyway? They looked awful close. His own daughters were about the same age. Damn it. What had he gotten himself into? Who had he become? It better not come down to hurting Donavan's daughter. He didn't think he had it in him to do something to a young girl, especially his own daughter's age. When would it end? Was he just a pawn? Was that all he was? He thought of himself as powerful with the money, the drugs, the women, and the flexible schedule. But was he really? Did he really have a choice in anything he did? Could he ever get out, even if he wanted to?

Forty-one

MICHAEL DONAVAN ROLLED from his thin mattress and put his feet on the floor. He tried to steady his spinning head in his cupped hands. He rose slowly and rubbed his lower back. All night the mattress springs had dug into him. Every morning he reminded himself to do something about it, but by night he always forgot. The side of Linda's face pressed against the mattress and her mouth hung open. He knew Riley hated when Linda came home with him. But somehow he always ended up with her. He couldn't even remember how he'd run into her last night. Had he sought her out?

He hadn't really expected Markie to cooperate. Yet there had been something in his eyes that had said he wasn't entirely unsympathetic. He looked at the clock. There was still time to stake out the garage for an hour or two before work. He'd follow Markie again and see if he could get any more info. He couldn't give up now. He felt close to something big. He dressed for work. Since he'd approached Markie in the construction clothes, he'd have to find another disguise. Linda stirred. He shook her elbow. "Hey, Linda, don't hang around the apartment okay? It upsets my daughter. He pulled a small roll of bills from his pocket and peeled off a twenty. "Here, I'll try and meet you at The Egg and I for breakfast in a couple of hours."

She rolled in the bed and the sheets twisted around her body. "Okay, Mikey."

He parked half a block from the garage and sat in his car drinking coffee while pretending to read the newspaper. He waited for Markie to pull up in his maroon Chevy. A parking spot right in front of the garage seemed to be reserved for short-term business. The guys in the gang who parked there always ran in and out pretty fast. When someone else unwittingly parked there some thug or mechanic came out of the garage and shooed them away. After about twenty minutes, Markie's car pulled up. The thick man waddled into the garage on muscle-bound legs. His arms hung at his sides like oversized bratwurst.

When Markie got back into his car and pulled away from the curb, Michael did too. He had to cut someone off and the guy leaned on his horn. "Jesus, will you shut up already," he muttered and prayed that Markie wouldn't check his rearview mirror to see what all the fuss was about. He let a few cars pass and kept his distance. They were driving out of town, back toward Southie. Markie pulled over and parked a few doors down from Michael's apartment.

A few cars back, Michael pulled over and sank down in his seat. Every few minutes, he craned his neck so he didn't miss anything. He figured Markie was waiting for him to come out of the building. Panic stirred his stomach acid and last night's alcohol into a cauldron of bile that nauseated him. He fought the urge to vomit.

Riley bounced down the steps with a backpack slung over her shoulder. She seemed to be on automatic pilot as she made her way down Columbia Street toward South Boston High, oblivious of anything or anyone around her.

Michael felt his heart beat like a drummer on speed as Markie slipped from the curb and began tailing his daughter. He never should have approached Markie. After his karate moves, it was probably the second stupidest thing he'd ever done. He was exploding inside. Part of him wanted to grab his gun and blow his own brains out—just to end it all.

He followed Markie, who tailed Riley at a slow pace, pulling over every so often to let traffic pass. Markie followed her all the way to South Boston High. Then he parked in front of the school until she went inside. After the bell rang and all the teenagers filed into the building, Markie drove to Castle Island. Michael followed and watched as he picked up a newspaper and coffee from Sullivan's. He strolled over to a bench, sat down, sipped coffee, and began reading the paper.

Michael steamed in his car and whispered, "I hope that coffee tastes good." He removed the gun from inside his jacket and checked the chamber. "It's the last cup you're going to have." His hand shook. It wasn't just a tremor—it was a violent shaking. He grabbed the wrist of his shaking hand. Unable to steady his hand, he threw the gun on the passenger seat and squeezed his head.

"Shit," he moaned and rolled his head back and forth on the steering wheel. He took a deep breath and looked at the glove compartment. "God, grant me the serenity to accept the things I cannot change, courage to change the things I can, and the wisdom to know the difference."

He reached over, opened the glove compartment and grabbed a pint of vodka. "Just one sip to steady the nerves." He took a quick swig and exhaled. "Liquid courage."

He got out of his car and crouched behind some other parked cars until he was about twenty feet behind the bench where Markie was reading the newspaper. Even though no one was around, he'd have to make this quick. He crouched between two cars and took the gun from inside his jacket. His hand shook again but it was broad daylight and he couldn't risk taking aim for too long. He found the back of Markie's head in the sites and took a quick shot before he lost his nerve.

WHEN HE heard the loud crack, Markie jumped off the bench and ducked under it. He looked behind him and saw Donavan running like a spooked cat toward his car.

Donavan's tires screeched as he backed out and sped away. Markie grimaced, shook his head and sighed. There was a small hole on a sign about ten feet from the bench. "Man, that guy's a terrible shot." Markie chuckled. He almost felt bad for him. Yet he tried not to feel too bad because soon he'd have to kill him.

Forty-two

SOMETHING SEEMED FUNNY about Paul Marks. He'd been nervous and kissing ass ever since he'd botched the job on the Donavan house and barbecued Riley's poor mother. Johnny felt bad about that. All she did was marry a tight-ass, prick of a husband who refused to pay up. Johnny had really stuck it to Markie for that. But he also took pity. He saw in the kid's eyes not only remorse but a deep need for his approval.

With that bomb, they'd sent a message all right, just a little stronger and clearer than he had intended. To most people it would look like an accident, but to those in the know he would appear ruthless, which had advantages. He had given Markie a "talk" and another chance to prove himself. Now something was different about him—not post-fuck up nervousness, but something else.

Markie was hiding something. Johnny's feeling wasn't based on anything in particular. It was just a feeling, which started in those fine tiny hairs at the back of his neck. Then he couldn't relax. He couldn't relax for days because in the fiber of his being he knew something was amiss. Johnny had built a criminal empire on his instincts, and he wasn't about to ignore them now, however loyal Markie seemed.

Johnny decided they'd take Markie for a little drive. He wanted to see if he could gain any insight before putting the squeeze on him. The enclosed space of an automobile provided a perfect venue for initial interrogations. Even if the guy was a Broadway actor, Johnny could still smell his sweat, and how it changed as he sweated fear. All the information he needed, the unsaid molecular information would vibrate in the small space of a car, telling him more than words ever could.

Markie sat alone in the backseat. Johnny drove and Kilpatrick sat next to him in the passenger seat. Kilpatrick was Johnny's right-hand man. Kilpatrick and Markie had a little rivalry going. Johnny had seen Kilpatrick bristle at Markie's initial successes and his quick rise. He had also noticed Kilpatrick's pleasure when Markie had screwed up. It was amusing. They sometimes seemed like children to him, children in men's bodies.

"So, what did you fellas want to talk about?" Markie let out a nervous chuckle. "No offense, but some people have been known to go for rides with you guys and disappear for good." Johnny did not respond. He glanced in the rearview mirror and saw Markie swatting at a hornet. He locked the windows.

Markie tried to put his window down. "Hey, Johnny, put the window down, will ya? There's a hornet in the car."

Johnny didn't put the window down. He pulled off Morrissey Boulevard and drove to the back of the Stop and Shop. With the motor cut and the decreased road noise, the hornet's angry buzzing intensified. Markie ducked each time the hornet came near him. Beads of sweat sprouted on his hairy brow.

"You seem a little nervous about this insect in my car, Markie. Is there a problem?"

"Yeah, there is. I'm allergic to these little suckers. Man, this one hornet could kill me. Put the window down, will ya?"

"Really? A tiny little insect could kill a big man like you?" Johnny held his finger out at a horizontal angle. It took about thirty seconds for the hornet to land on his finger and stop buzzing. He brought his finger close to his face, looked into the hornet's beady eyes, smiled, put the window down and set the hornet free.

Kilpatrick looked quizzical and laughed uneasily. "Hey Boss, I didn't know you were a bee charmer."

"It looks like we've found your Achilles' heel, Markie." Markie's attitude changed. He was thinking, watching his step and hiding something.

"Yeah if I didn't get to the hospital on time that hornet might kill me." Markie tried to recover his breath.

"Get out of my car, Markie. You got work to do. Come see me Tuesday morning."

Markie got out of the car and leaned into the driver's window.

"See you guys around then, okay? Are we good? Is everything good?" Kilpatrick and Johnny remained silent. Markie backed away from the car. He turned around and quickened his pace. He looked back over his shoulder a couple of times.

"By the way he's walking," said Kilpatrick, "I think he half expects a bullet in the back." "Yup, I told you he was hiding something. Time for the squeeze."

Kilpatrick looked at Johnny. "How did you do that thing with the hornet?" He held up his finger as Johnny had.

"When I was a kid, I used to steal honey, straight from a beehive. Boy, I had a sweet tooth. " Johnny chuckled. "I have an idea about how to get Markie talking." A sinister smile swept across his face as he imagined what he'd do.

Forty-three

AS HE MADE HIS WAY across the parking lot of the Stop and Shop on Morrissey Boulevard, Markie wondered what the hell was going on. He had been nervous ever since crazy Donavan had taken a shot at him. That guy really didn't know when to give up. What did he think he was going to do, take down the Camel? There were already so many Bureaus and special agencies investigating the Camel, Markie couldn't keep them straight. There was the FBI, the DEA, the Boston Police, the Staties, and probably even the CIA for running guns to the IRA. There was no way in hell some lawyer with a small time bookmaking business was going to touch him.

He should have told the Camel about Donavan but he didn't really want to kill him or his daughter. The whole situation just made him feel kind of sick. A week had gone by since Donavan had shot at him and he hadn't tried it again. Markie wasn't scared of the guy. How could he be scared of a guy like that? He shot like a girl.

The image of the Donavan girl popped into his head. He wondered what the Camel was doing with her. Markie shook his head. He hoped the Camel wasn't screwing her. That would be pretty twisted. She was not much older than his daughters. He had to stop thinking about it because it was driving him nuts.

God, what about that hornet? How did they know he was scared to death of hornets? He had a good reason. He had almost died when he was stung as a kid. Markie wondered if it was just a coincidence or if they had planted it in the car. Sweet Jesus, what did they want to talk about? They never did say. Now he wished he'd just told as soon as it happened because the Camel obviously knew something was up. You couldn't hide anything from that guy so it was best not to even try.

As he went around to the bars and other businesses to collect the weekly patronage, he replayed the situation over and over in his head, wondering what to do. He really didn't want to kill Donavan. The guy had balls. He was only trying to avenge his wife's death and protect his daughter, which was exactly what Markie would have done. Even though his wife, Michelle, had left him, he'd still try to avenge her murder. Hell, he still loved her.

ON TUESDAY, when Markie showed up at the garage, the Camel told him they needed extra muscle on a couple of errands. They drove in a brand new Chevy. That wasn't unusual. The Camel often switched cars ever since he'd found a bug in one. Markie sat in the backseat. The music blared from the back speakers and he couldn't hear anything the Camel and Kilpatrick said up front.

The Camel turned down the music. "You've been awful quiet these days, Markie. You don't seem yourself. What's going on?"

"Aww, nothing much really, had some things come up with Michelle and the girls. That's all."

"You sure there's nothing I need to know about?"

"Ahh, can't think of anything." He looked out the window and didn't recognize the route. Shit. "Where we going?" he asked.

They pulled down a dirt road covered with overgrown trees. The Camel stopped the car, turned around and pointed a Python revolver at his head. Kilpatrick jumped out of the passenger side, opened the rear door, dragged him out of the backseat, cuffed his hands behind his back and pushed him toward the trunk.

Like a surgeon, the Camel slid on some black leather gloves while Kilpatrick stuffed him into the trunk. Markie had to curl into a fetal position to fit his body inside the trunk. Before the trunk shut all the way, the Camel reached in. He held a huge glass jar between his gloved hands. From the light which streamed in, Markie could see hornets crawling and buzzing inside the jar. The hand methodically unscrewed the lid of the jar and the trunk slammed shut.

"I'm going to ask you that question again, Markie, because I got the feeling you were lying to me," said the Camel over the buzzing hornets. "Is there something you need to tell me? You're going to have to speak up so I can hear you."

"Yeah, there's something. Please let me out and I'll tell you."

"Why didn't you tell me before, when I asked you nicely?"

"I didn't want to bother you with it because I didn't think it was important. Please let me out of here before I die."

"If you stay calm they won't sting you."

Kilpatrick piped in. "I went through a lot of trouble to get those bees, Markie. I think you should stay in there a little longer to make it worth my time. Personally, I thought it would be easier if we just tortured you. But Johnny said this would be poetic."

Markie felt the tickle of hornets crawling on his skin and cursed himself for wearing short sleeves. He always wore short sleeves as soon as it got warm so he could show off his muscles. Now he regretted it. He closed his eyes and felt the damn things crawling on his head and his face. He tried to calm down and keep still. Would he die from a hornet sting? Would they kill him even if he survived the hornets? Would he ever see Michelle or his daughters again?

The Camel said, "I'm waiting—" and was silent.

Markie's could only hear his own labored breath and the buzzing hornets. The itching was unbearable. He broke. "That guy, Donavan, remember the bookie, who didn't pay up, the one whose house I blew up with his wife in it?"

"How could I forget?"

"Well that guy tracked me down and wanted me to testify against you, said he could get me into the W.P.P."

"Donavan asks you to testify against me and you don't think you should tell me?"

"He's talking out of his ass. He's got nothing. He didn't even come with a cop. The guy's a wind bag, used to be a lawyer. You know the type. I thought I got rid of him. Then he saw me following his daughter and he sort of took a shot at me."

"Sort of took a shot at you. What the hell does that mean?"

"He hit a sign like ten feet from me. The guy's got a screw loose. He's such a terrible shot. It was almost comical."

"Almost comical? I think you got a screw loose. Did you kill him?"

"Aww, well I took a shot back and that scared him off. I would never kill him without orders. "

"When and where did all this happen?"

"The other morning right after I followed his daughter to school. I picked up a paper and some coffee. I was just sitting on a bench over there near Sullivan's. It was a real nice day."

"You two loonies exchanged fire in broad daylight?"

"Uhh, it was early. I don't think anyone noticed. Or if they did, they didn't say nothing."

"Why didn't you tell me about this?"

"I, I, he's such a loser. I just don't see him as a threat to you." A hornet that had been crawling on Markie's lip made its way into his mouth as he spoke. "Ahh!" he screamed. "Come on! Let me out. I just got stung on the wip. "

The Camel opened the trunk and the bees flew out. Kilpatrick took a few steps back but The Camel didn't flinch. "He took a shot at you and tried to get you to rat me out and you don't think he's a threat?"

"I threatened his kid. He won't be back."

"What? I told you to find out who beat her up. You didn't even notice that her fucking father was following you when you were following her? Did you do something to her?"

"No, I didn't touch her. I didn't even talk to her. I just made him think that I would so he'd back off."

"And you think that is as good as killing him?"

"I thought I should talk to you before I killed him."

"But you didn't talk to me. You didn't say a word till I locked you in the trunk with a jar full of bees. Why?"

"I didn't think it was worth your time."

"Not worth my time? Well look how much time this has cost me now, huh, and Kilpatrick's time. Do you have any idea how much time it took him to get those bees? Find Donavan and kill him." Johnny put his hands on his hips. "Make sure the body never turns up. We're not trying to send a message now. We just want him to disappear. He might be a windbag blowing hot air. But I don't need the aggravation. Anyone who even hints that someone should testify against me is gone. That's it, the final solution, not negotiable. Now this is the last time you get to screw up and take another fucking breath, got that?"

"Yeah, I got it."

"Get out," Johnny commanded.

With difficulty, Markie got out of the trunk. He stood with his hand pressed to his lip.

"How's your lip?"

"It hurts," said Markie through his swollen lip.

"Yeah, well you got stung by several more bees." The Camel pointed out some pink swollen patches on Markie's arm. "You know, those were honey bees not hornets. What are you allergic to?"

Markie wasn't really sure what had stung him as a kid. It could have been a hornet, but on the other hand it could have been a bee. The Camel stared at him, waiting for an answer.

"Don't you even know the goddamn difference, you idiot? The devil is in the details. How many times do I have to tell you that, for Christ's Sake! Know your enemies. Are they hornets? Or are they honeybees? Because there's a big fucking difference!"

Markie wondered if the devil wasn't actually standing in front of him. The Camel's face got this look sometimes and he became a different person, like Lucifer just stepped into his body. Then he went away and the guy was as nice as pie again.

As they drove into town, Markie sat in the back seat with his head against the window. He wasn't as smart as either of the men who had just nearly killed him. Kilpatrick could do sums in his head, remember them, and tell you exactly how much anyone owed on any given day without looking at ledgers. The Camel, he just knew everything. Markie wished his punishment was over and he could get away from the fatherly disappointment that filled the car. If he lived through this, he would have to find a way to get out of working for The Camel. Sooner or later he was bound to screw up again and get himself killed. He was still alive but his throat could close at any minute. Would it be out of line, to ask them to swing by Saint Margaret's and drop him off at the E.R.?

Forty-four

HE'D BEEN LUCKY that day with the hornets. The doctor had said if he'd gotten to the hospital any later he probably would have died from the allergic reaction. Now Markie had to kill Donavan. The task lay in front of him like a pile of mushy string beans on the table when he was six, not going away, and getting more unappetizing by the minute. Markie knew Donavan was a drinker so he asked around and found out where he drank.

On Thursday night he spotted Donavan walking into Lucky's. He parked his car a few doors down and waited. He hated what he had to do. Yet it would be impossible to leave the gang and live for long. He'd be too much of a liability. Even if he managed to quit his criminal career, how would he provide for his girls? What could he possibly do to make the kind of money he took in working for The Camel?

He pulled out his new Cobra, placed it on his thigh, and immediately felt his prick stiffen a little. He tilted his head, picked up the revolver, opened and spun the loaded cylinder. Hot off the market, .44 caliber stainless steel. Jesus, what a piece. It had cost him over four hundred and he was somewhat reluctant to use it on a hit. He didn't think he could bring himself to part with it, if it came to that. He put the gun back in its case and slid it under the seat sticking his tongue out and breathing heavily from the effort of contorting his body. He kept his eye on the front door of the tavern and hoped Donavan would come out soon.

Two hours later, Donavan stumbled out the front door and began walking east away from Markie's car.

He drove alongside him as he walked down the street. "Hey!" he called.

Donavan stopped, peered into his car, and seeing him, backed up to the sidewalk and quickened his pace.

"Come here. I want to talk to you about your offer."

Donavan stopped in his tracks and spun around.

"Yeah right. You're just going to take me somewhere and whack me."

"Just get in."

Donavan hesitated, opened the door, and slid onto the front seat next to Markie. As soon as Donavan got into the car, Markie knew it was going to be an easy hit. He slid his hand inside Donavan's coat and took his gun. Donavan didn't even protest. He must have knocked back quite a few while in the tavern. His facial muscles were so slack it looked like his whole face might just drip off onto his lap.

"We need to go somewhere we can talk," said Markie.

"Why not talk right here?"

"You can never be too careful. There might be bugs."

Donavan swatted the air in front of him. "I don't see any."

"Not those kinds of bugs, you idiot. You know, listening devices."

"Who's bugging you?"

Markie put his finger to his lips and shook his head. He got onto the southeast expressway. A few exits later, he got off in Quincy, drove west up a hill and parked the car.

"Don't say anything. Just get out," said Markie.

Donavan got out of the car and looked around. "Quincy Quarries. Now I know you're going to kill me. Look, the whole thing, forget about it, okay? Just forget I ever approached you at O'Malley's. I'm sorry I took a shot at you. That was a mistake." Donavan opened his arms wide in front of him like he expected a hug or something.

Markie grabbed him by the shoulder, turned him around, and shoved Donavan's own gun into his back. He patted him down again then led him toward the quarries at gunpoint. Rectangular slabs of granite covered with graffiti scribbles were stacked like the blocks of a careless child. Those blocks were piled high around a quarried granite cliff that grew from a pond of murky water. It was dark but the bright moonlight reflected off the graffiti-covered granite rocks where teenagers had attempted to immortalize themselves. "I just want to talk somewhere quiet where we won't be seen or heard." Markie reassured Donavan. There was no sense making it unpleasant.

They walked past the Swingles Quarry, which had been partially drained in the summer of '85 in order to search for the body of a fifteen-year-old boy who had never resurfaced after his jump. Probably cut up by one of the hundred cars at the bottom. His body was never found.

Donavan looked around. "I haven't been here in years," he said.

Markie held the gun to the back of Donavan's neck. "Me neither." Markie had wasted many hot summer days, sweating in the heavy, humid air that always smelled like warm doughnuts. He had jumped from the high cliffs into the cool, green water, felt pressure in his ears, and then relief when he finally resurfaced and gulped his first breath.

"You ever jump off that one?" asked Donavan. He pointed across from where they stood at one of the highest jumps, called Rooftops.

Markie decided to allow Donavan a trip down memory lane before he died. He put the gun to his side and looked around. It was the least he could do. There were junked cars in the water and probably decomposing bodies as well, but it was a place where boys could be boys and some of the best memories of Markie's own youth had been at the Quincy quarries. "Yeah, with my ass puckered so I wouldn't shit myself or get split up the anus with a car antenna. You?"

Donavan scratched his head. "I heard the antenna went into the eyeball not the ass. You know—" Donavan stepped toward the edge of the cliff and peered over. "I doubt anyone would have noticed if you shit yourself in that water. Hey look. There are those damn telephone poles. What a pain it was trying to jump around those. Do you think that antenna story was true?"

"Watch your step, Donavan. You're a little close to the edge there." Jesus, it would be a headache if Donavan fell into the water before he was dead. "Don't know. They never seem to find the bodies of people who drown in there."

"My father was a stonecutter in this quarry." Donavan nodded his head and looked around as if he could still see the men working.

"Is that right?" Markie kicked some scrap metal on the ground and put his foot under an old tire wondering if it would be heavy enough to drag Donavan's body to the bottom.

"That's what my mother told me. She also said he was dead. Then he showed up one day and took me to a Bruins game. Never saw him again."

Damn it. The guy kept talking. The more he talked, the harder it was going to be to put a bullet in his head. Markie thought of his own father, the day he had promised to take him to a Red Sox game and never showed up. Markie had waited, listening to the game on the radio—it seemed like forever and he had kept hoping. The game had ended—his father had never shown up, and he had never seen him after that day either. Donavan was lucky—he got to go to the game. Markie didn't want to talk anymore, get sentimental and reminisce about the past. He had a job to do and all this talk was interfering with his professionalism. "Have you ever thought

172

about your role in this whole thing?" He tried to get mad. It helped to be mad when you had to kill someone.

"My role?" asked Donavan.

"Yeah, you could have just paid. Everyone pays The Camel. That's the way it is. That's the way it's been as long as I remember, and that's the way it'll be till the guy finally croaks, which won't happen anytime soon because he's strong as an ox. What the hell am I talking to you for? I'm sorry pal, but I got to kill ya."

They stood on top of a thirty-foot cliff, one of the smaller jumps. Markie pushed Donavan down to his knees and held the gun to his head. Donavan was about to die, so Markie figured he was about the only guy on earth he could be honest with. If you valued your life, you just didn't say a word against The Camel to anyone. Markie had already walked that line, had already been in Donavan's shoes, and he never wanted to be there again. He didn't want his daughters growing up without a father. Maybe he wasn't the best role model. But he kept them housed and fed, bought them nice clothes and other things they wanted. His girls wouldn't be ridiculed like he had been, for wearing the Bargain Center specials and pants that never quite reached his shoes.

"Before you kill me," said Donavan with amazing calm for a guy who was about to get his head blown off, "can you promise me one thing?"

"What? No! I don't make promises to the guys I take out. That's not the way it works. We shouldn't even be talking."

"Just don't hurt my daughter. Make sure nothing happens to her. C'mon. Don't you have any kids?" Donavan turned his head and looked up at Markie.

"No. I don't have any kids," Markie lied. "What about me looks Dadish?" He wondered if he had an image problem. Even though he was a dad, he tried not to look like one. He worked out and went to the tanning salon and wore fashionable clothes.

"I'm sorry. I just thought you might know what a father would feel. Look—" Donavan's repose crumbled and tears ran down his face. "My daughter—" He choked. "I screwed up. I screwed up her whole life. I haven't even talked to her or taken her out for an ice cream cone. Hell, I don't even know if she still eats ice cream cones now that she's—she's—oh hell, she turns sixteen tomorrow. Promise me nothing will happen to her. That it ends here with me."

Markie looked at the blubbering mess the man had turned into and felt a mixture of revulsion and pity. On the verge of tears, Markie yelled. "That's enough! Enough!" He couldn't stop thinking about his own girls, and after seeing Donavan's daughter with The Camel, he certainly couldn't make any deathbed promises to keep her safe.

"Damn it. I won't hurt your daughter, all right? But I can't promise someone else won't. Sorry." Markie held the gun up to Donavan's head and took a deep breath.

Donavan pleaded. "One more thing, do you know the name of the cliff we're on? I want to know where I'm dying, and I can't remember the name. It's on the tip of my tongue."

Markie sighed, looked over at Rooftops and Heavens then down at the smaller jump they stood on. The name of the jump that was spray-painted below came back to him. He dropped the gun to his side and screamed out all the tension he'd been carrying since who knew how long—forever it seemed. He let out one big, "FUUCCK!" It carried through the night, toward the moon like a wolf's lonely howl. He shook his head and looked at Donavan. "I should never have let you talk. Fucking lawyers—always talking their way out of everything!"

The jump was called "Dads."

Forty-five

MICHAEL DONAVAN BREATHED. A mosquito bit him on the neck. He heard the buzz of others. It didn't matter. He was alive. He had shut his eyes tightly and prayed—prayed to a God he wasn't sure he believed in. He had cried out silently in the snowy darkness of his scrunched and terrified eyes, turned in with a sudden acute awareness of how badly he had failed his daughter. It wasn't the lawyer in him who had been talking—it was the failed father, not the absent father—the one who had never even tried, the father so many of them had never known. Was the emptiness left by their absences worse than the twisted memories of those who'd stayed and screwed up? He opened his eyes and dropped his head back in relief. Above him faint stars glowed in the semi darkness edged by a cloud of light sprawling from the city.

"You have to disappear," said Markie.

The voice came from another world. "What?" he asked.

"If I don't kill you, they're going to kill me. So you got to disappear tonight. Don't show your face to anyone, not your daughter, not anyone. Get as far away from the Atlantic as you can. Go to Iowa or Kansas or somewhere. Just don't ever let anyone around here see or hear from you—ever. Or I promise I will kill your daughter."

"But my daughter, who will—"

"Your daughter will be better off without you, pal. What have you done for her lately? Should I kill you instead?"

Leaving Riley without saying goodbye or telling her why he had to go would be awful. She would think he was a deadbeat like so many others. A final betrayal. He would never do that. Yet, he was being forced to. He wondered if a bullet in the head would have been easier.

"Come on, let's get out of here." Markie took his finger off the trigger and ran his other hand through his hair. "Listen, I'll drive you to your car but you're going to have to ride in the trunk. When we get to your car, just get into it and get the hell out of town. Don't go home first and drive all night. Now, where's your car?"

"How come I need to ride in the trunk?"

"You know, you ask a lot of fucking questions for a guy that's lucky to be alive. I don't want to be seen with you, and I don't want you blabbing your big mouth off in my car. You've talked enough tonight." Markie jabbed his finger into Donavan's chest. "You've talked me out of killing you, and I'm not too happy about it. What I'm doing right now could get me killed."

Michael nodded. "I really appreciate it. If there's ever anything I can do—"

"Just get in the trunk already and do what I told you."

AFTER DONAVAN was securely snuggled into the trunk, Markie slammed it shut. He drummed his fingers on top, and looked up at the moon for an answer. Out from under the car seat, he pulled the new gun case. He opened the case and started to feel better as he gazed down at his brand new .44 caliber six-cylinder, double-action, Cobra revolver. He walked back to the trunk and fired six bullets right through the metal into Donavan's body. He'd been dying to use that gun. He shook his head at the gun in his hand, reprimanding it, as if it had a life of its own. Though, it was the Camel who had given the order. Markie was, after all, only the hand.

He drove up the road to the faint jeep trail that led to the top of Swingles Quarry. He drove the car to the edge of the cliff, grabbed his gun case and a few other things from the glove compartment, put the car in neutral, hopped out and went around to the bumper, where he gave it a good push. It hardly took any effort to get that thing over the edge. He looked down and watched it bounce, heard glass shattering and saw the splash when it hit the water. He'd always wanted to do that. The car was a piece of shit anyway. He'd file a stolen car report and maybe the insurance would spring for a new one. He shook his head and watched the bumper disappear. Poor Donavan.

Forty-six

ON JUNE TWENTY-FIRST, the morning of her sixteenth birthday, Riley woke and went straight into the kitchen. Her gaze landed on the empty table. She had been expecting a present and a card. Later in the evening, after school, she figured her father would take her out to dinner. That had always been their birthday tradition. For a few days she had been thinking about where they would go. It had been so long since the two of them had gone to a restaurant or even had eaten together in the apartment.

Her father was not in his room. He could have stayed the night at Linda's. Ever since she'd confronted him about having Linda around, she barely saw him anymore. But he'd never forgotten her birthday before, and even though their lives were a mess, she was certain he would not forget it this year.

After school, she returned to their apartment and searched her closet for something special to wear. Her dad would be home soon and then they would go out and celebrate. She changed her outfit several times and messed around with her hair, trying out different styles she'd seen on girls at school.

After six, she wondered why he hadn't called to let her know he was going to be late. She turned on the TV to pass the time and hoped he would walk in the door any minute. A few times she heard noise from the street and went to the window to see if he was there. After several TV shows began and ended, Riley's heart sank, and she wondered what she would do if he never showed. When darkness fell and she realized it was past eight o'clock, she gave up hope. Some sweet sixteen.

She wondered what she could have done to deserve all the shit that had happened to her in the past year. Maybe she was cursed. It felt like a curse. She could not see the television through the blur of her tears. Her stomach muscles and throat tightened as grief overtook her. She went into the small kitchen and hoisted herself up onto the counter so she could reach the bottle of whiskey her father kept in a high cabinet. This was what people did to feel better. She took a swig but the taste only brought back that terrible night with Sully.

She put the bottle back, shut off the TV and curled up into a tight little ball on her bed. Chairman Meow jumped up and stared at her. His large cat pupils rolled back and forth. Riley tried to focus and reach out to pet him but her sadness was too much. She pulled her hand back and hugged herself to steady her shaking body. The Chairman walked in circles a couple of times before settling next to her and purring like a soft motor.

At two-thirty a.m. she heard a knock on the door. She switched on the light and looked in her father's room. He still wasn't there. Maybe it was him at the door. Maybe he'd forgotten his key. She put her hand against the door and stood on her tiptoes to look through the peephole but she was too short. "Who is it?" she asked.

"S'mee. Linda. Is Mikey there?"

Riley cracked the door but she did not unchain the lock. She looked at Linda with disgust. "My father's not here. I figured he was with you."

Linda looked around confused, checking that he wasn't in fact with her after all. "No, I haven't seen him for a few nights." Her face looked apologetic, but she was just drunk.

"Go away," Riley hissed and shut the door.

In the morning, she felt empty, almost lighter, like everything inside her had spilled out with her tears. Her anger and disappointment turned to panic as it dawned on her that she hadn't heard him come home the night before her birthday either. It wasn't like him to disappear for this long. He hadn't been with Linda. Unless he had and she'd forgotten.

Riley looked into the mirror. A red, blotchy face with puffy eyes looked back. She wanted to go back to bed and avoid the humiliation of going to school like this. But school was almost over for the year and final grades would go in soon. Every Friday, the Spanish teacher gave a test. She took off five points if you were mysteriously absent. Riley decided to get dressed and go to school. Her only hope for happiness now was in thoughts of leaving for college and starting a new life somewhere else.

At school she felt better. She aced the Spanish test even though she had not studied. After school, she lingered outside and sat on a wall. She stared at the red brick, which radiated the sunlight it had absorbed all day. For a long time, she was transfixed by light particles moving about. She felt like she was on the cusp of some monumental change but she didn't know what it was. After thirty minutes, she realized there was no answer on the wall. Her eyes, red and tired, burned from staring at it for so long. She walked back to the apartment hoping her father would be there.

She wasn't angry at him for missing her birthday anymore. She just wanted to see him.

There was no sign of him and no sign he had been home. She sat on the couch staring at the grimy walls, the remnants of a fly that had been swatted but not cleared away. A breeze wafted into the window carrying scents of clean laundry and grilled meat. Riley couldn't bear to spend a beautiful June Friday evening in this decaying apartment feeling nothing but self pity. She called her old friend, Michelle, in Quincy to see what was going on. Michelle convinced her to go out to Squaw Rock for a big keg party.

After a few hours of changing outfits, Riley finally decided on some black leggings with a green striped t-shirt and a zip up sweatshirt. It was practical; she could ride her bike in it and the sweatshirt had an inside zip pocket for her keys and money. The outfit seemed stylish but not dressy. She didn't want to appear too dolled up, like she had put a lot of thought into her appearance.

She rode her bike down Columbia Ave past Carson Beach. She picked up her pace as she passed the Columbia Street housing project, recovered her breath by the JFK library, and then rode fast again past the Boston Globe building into Neponset Circle, over the Neponset River Bridge and down onto Quincy Shore Drive. She rode on the sidewalk in front of the parking lot of Johnny's townhouse. She could stop in to say hi but that would be awkward if he was with his girlfriend or something. Johnny was stable. If he was her Dad, he wouldn't disappear, or forget her birthday.

She turned left at Dunkin Donuts and took the causeway out to Squantum, where she had lived briefly as a kid. Someone chucked a bottle at her from a car window. The glass shattered on the sidewalk in front of her, and she wondered if she should have stayed home after all.

Forty-seven

Push about the can~ With strong waters flowing~ Let the song go round ~We shall soon be going; Let us, while we stay~ Spite of wind and weather, If we do get high, All get drunk together. ~Lobsters, tom-cods, clam, We no longer want'em Brandy, Gin and Rum~ Flow full fast at Squantum.
Party Song from Squantum Rocks, 1812

FOR GENERATIONS, revelers had come to Squaw Rock to feast, yet most of the modern partiers were unaware of the reserve's history as a gathering place. Thousands of years ago, Native Americans had spent summers feasting on mollusks in the tidal waters and salt marshes of Squaw Rock Reserve. After the Anglo settlers came and wrested the land from the natives, they too were drawn to the area. One legend claimed that the actual "squaw rock" at the eastern edge of the reserve was named for a heartbroken Indian woman, who, after being used and slighted by a male colonist, had thrown herself to her death, her spirit and likeness forming in the rock.

In the early 1900s, a sewer line was constructed from Boston to Moon Island. Raw sewage was pumped into Dorchester Bay. The abundant sea life that had once nourished ancient people became poison. By the 1980s even swimming was banned. Hoards of underage drinkers habitually partied on an abandoned concrete platform strewn with broken glass, cigarette wrappers, used condoms, cans and other trash. The police made vain attempts to chase them away.

ON THE EVENING OF JUNE 22, 1986, RILEY DONAVAN locked her bike to an abandoned fence and walked a wooded path up to the concrete platform where teens were starting to congregate. Within half an hour, darkness fell. Across the bay, the Boston skyline shimmered like a Christmas display and the reality of a trash strewn wasteland was forgotten and replaced by the excitement of a sparkling summer night. Riley walked to the edge of the platform and sat down next to her friend Michelle. The scent of urine wafted from the bushes below. Light cast from the city obscured most of the stars, but failed to eclipse the full moon. Riley stared at the moon's reflection in the water. The keg hadn't arrived yet. Anticipation hung in the air. Teenagers milled about thirsty for beer and eager for the party to begin.

Michelle was complaining about her boyfriend, and trying to decide if she should break up with him. Even though she didn't like him anymore, there was only one week till the Junior Prom, and she doubted if she could get another date that fast. Riley knew she wasn't going to her own Junior Prom. She wondered what her life might have been like if her mother hadn't died in the explosion and they hadn't moved. Listening to Michelle made her wish that her biggest problem was finding a date. Sometimes she felt so old.

She figured her parents might eventually have gotten divorced if her mother had lived. But just about everyone's parents were divorced now anyway. Her mother wouldn't have approved of her obsession with martial arts, and she would have hated the fact that Riley rode her bike everywhere and never wore skirts or dresses. She would have hated anything Riley did that wasn't ladylike, and so she was probably turning in her grave.

A familiar voice rose above the others and filled her with panic. She turned and saw Sully standing with a group of guys. It looked like money was being exchanged. She crouched down so he wouldn't see her.

"Shit," she said, interrupting Michelle's saga.

"What?" Michelle stopped talking and looked around.

"See that kid?" Riley ducked lower.

"Who?"

"That kid, right there, with the Celtics shirt and the giant gold shamrock necklace."

"Oh, yeah. Who the hell is he? Why are you hiding?" Michelle half smiled.

"He's from Southie and he likes torturing me."

"So do you like him?"

"No! Of course not."

"Why?" Michelle looked over at him. "He looks kind of cute. Actually, he's a fox. Does he have a car?"

"He's a first class scumbag. He beat me up one night."

"Oh." Michelle pursued her lips and nodded.

Sully sauntered over to them with two red plastic Solo cups. "Hey, Quincy girl. I thought I might find you here. Sneaking back to Quincy? What, Southie not good enough for you? I'm just shittin' ya. The keg just got here. I brought you two ladies some beer." He handed them the cups. "Aren't you going to thank me and introduce me to your friend?"

They looked at each other, shrugged and sipped the beer. Riley was quiet.

After a silence, Michelle said, "I hear you like beating up girls."

Sully looked at Riley. Her stomach fluttered and her pulse quickened. She took another sip of beer and looked away.

"What?" Sully stepped closer to Michelle and looked down at her. "Who told you that?"

Michelle didn't break his gaze. "My boyfriend might have a problem with you standing that close to me, so I'd back up if I were you."

He bristled. The moment had the kind of tension that could escalate into a brawl. Riley had seen it before. She wished he'd take Michelle's bait and become involved in a melee so she could sneak away unnoticed.

"Riley!" Sully dropped his aggression toward Michelle and turned to her. "Don't make up lies about me just because I won't go out with you. That's what I get for buying you beer?" He shook his head. "Nice to meet you, Michelle." He smiled and walked away.

"What did he beat you up for?" asked Michelle.

"I have no idea. But it was bad. See that?" Riley pointed to the scar on her cheek.

Michelle looked at Riley's cheek. Her eyes widened for a minute and then narrowed as her mouth set in disapproval. "Okay, no joke. He's a scumbag all right. What's he doing here anyway?"

"Probably selling coke."

"Oh, he really is scum then. Someone's been giving that shit to my little sister and now she's a fiend. My mom caught her stealing two-hundred dollars out of her purse—says if she does it again she's going to send her away to one of them homes."

RILEY was on the periphery of the party, staring at the lights across the bay when things started to look strange. An anxious feeling washed over her, like she was trapped inside her own body clawing to get out. Every molecule of air seemed to pixelate as if she were watching things on a very snowy TV screen. Things that were not moving began to vibrate and swirl into fractals. She thought she was losing her mind until she remembered Sully handing her and Michelle cups of beer. He'd probably dosed her with acid. She'd heard people talking about crazy hallucinations from acid. Their stories had frightened her so much she never wanted to try it.

The anxious clawing feeling intensified and she looked for somewhere to hide. As she stared into the night, which was buzzing and moving in a thousand different directions, she tried to decide what to do. Back at the center of the platform, a circle of people were drinking, laughing, and jostling each other. Flames leapt from a fire and cast strange shadows on their faces.

Riley saw the teenage bodies orbiting in a slow circle around the fire like planets to the sun. They had lit a fire not only to take the chill off the night, but also for something to gather around. The flames mesmerized her and without knowing why, she found herself walking toward them. Ordinary things now appeared extraordinary. Everything came to life, every detail of the June evening from the fire's smoke and heat rising in a rhythmic dance to the cells of skin marching on her hand, which she held up in front of her and studied as if seeing it for the first time.

"Is something on your hand?" A voice pierced the bubble of her fascinated examination. Riley looked up and saw an animated face with green eyes that swirled like paisleys. It was Eric Silvers, but he seemed like a lost character from a failed cartoon. His white blond hair looked like the end of a Q-tip that had just been pulled from a waxy ear.

"Riley? Oh man, what happened to you? What are you on?" he asked.

Riley knew in every hyper-activated cell of her body that she should get away from people. No one would understand her current state. She had to go hide somewhere and ride it out alone. From across the crowd she could feel Sully's radar stare tracking her movements. She could feel a line of energy like a tether between them, and she had to break it.

All around her, hands clutched red Solo cups like drowning people clutch buoys. That red cup had been her undoing. Riley threw it to the ground and ran before it exploded. She imagined that if the partiers let go of their cups they would float away and sink in the poisoned waters of Dorchester Bay under centuries of sludge and sewage. She knew there was a hidden place somewhere out there in the reserve, and if she could just get to it she would be safe.

She stopped at the edge of the platform where human life ended and was replaced by tall reeds, trees and bushes. She had to escape from Sully. She had to break the chain of his gaze and slip away without him noticing. If he saw her leave, he would follow her and trap her alone. That would be much worse than any form of embarrassment. She wondered if she could get to her bike without him noticing. If she could do that, she would ride as fast as she could through the back streets of Squantum to a secret place she knew where he would never find her.

There was a clear path from the concrete platform where the keg party was raging to the abandoned fence where she had locked her bike. The fence, a remnant from the past, just stopped, protecting nothing. But that path leading to her bike was like a runway, open and exposed. He would see her if she went that way.

Riley wandered a maze of faint paths through the reserve. Sometimes the stench of feces was so strong she stopped and gagged. She moved slowly because it was all alive and dangerous. The sound of something human stopped her in her tracks. She looked around, listened carefully and tried to locate its origin.

"Help me. Help me," called a faint, desperate voice.

Blended into the weeds, sat a small pile of moving clothes. Matted ends of disheveled hair hung from a heaving head and brushed the earth. Riley knelt next to a sick, miserable girl and placed her hand in the center of her upper back, rubbing in a gentle clockwise circle, as her mother always had when Riley was sick to her stomach. The girl turned to her. It was MaryAnn, from fourth grade. Every day she had meticulously sharpened her pencils and crayons to perfect points that had always been on the verge of breaking. MaryAnn looked at Riley's face.

"Riley? Help me. Are you real?"

MaryAnn seemed to have no more substance than a tattered, discarded rag doll. Riley wondered what was real. Maybe she wasn't real. The smell of vomit activated her gag reflex and brought her back to the present. She stood quickly so she could escape the horrid odor rising from a small chunky pile next to Mary Ann.

In the distance, the whiteness of someone's t-shirt reflected the moonlight and moved through the tall grass. Riley knelt back down and whispered, "MaryAnn, what should I do?"

"Do you have a car?" she asked.

"No car, just a bike."

"See if Donna McGovern's still here. She has a car. Tell her where I am." MaryAnn barely squeezed the words out before she threw up again.

184

The shirt was moving toward them. Riley ran through the tall grass deeper into the reserve. The shirt, alerted by her sudden movement, began to move faster, then suddenly stopped.

Forty-eight

SULLY NEARLY TRIPPED OVER A PUKING GIRL. Chicks really couldn't hold their booze. Vomiting just from beer was pathetic. It would take a lot more than beer to make him throw up. He stepped over her. He didn't want to lose Riley, but he wouldn't humiliate himself by running after her. It was fun to see her scurrying around like a small frightened animal. He went over to the fence where she'd locked up her bike, took a knife out of his pocket and picked the cheap lock. He was surprised the bike hadn't already been stolen. He hid her bike in the bushes and went back to the party, keeping an eye on the fence. She would eventually return for her bike.

As the night wore on, he lingered and talked to the last boring drunks who had no place else to go. He knew of at least two other parties, but this was a standoff and he would win. He put Riley's bike back against the fence and hid in the bushes waiting for her to return.

He had to prove something to himself. Since that night with Riley in his room, he hadn't gotten laid, hadn't really even tried because of what happened. He had to prove something and then he could move on and be done with her forever. He wanted to get her out of his system—never think about her again. You didn't pine for the cake you'd eaten. You didn't even remember it. You moved on to the next piece, and he wanted to move on. Acid was probably not the best thing to slip someone you wanted to take advantage of, but he had a surplus now that everyone had moved on to coke, and it was funny to watch her tripping.

FROM HER HIDING PLACE IN THE BUSHES, Riley could see the spot where she had locked her bike. Yet the fence stood purposeless and abandoned without anything attached to it. She felt trapped without her bike and retreated back into the reserve looking for somewhere to hide. Layers of rocks separated the edges of the reserve from the tidal marshes. Riley scrambled over Squaw Rock. She slipped and tried to hold on to slimy seaweed and bladder wrack. Barnacles and periwinkles scraped her arms and feet as she tried to break her fall.

She landed in the deep, stinky mud of low tide. She tried to lift one of her feet from the muck. It swallowed her shoe and her foot emerged bare, dripping with mud. Tired of fighting, she plunged her foot back into the muck and leaned against the giant rock she had just slid down. The moon shimmered on the water and city lights sparkled in the distance. Festive voices from boats passing in the channel mingled with the sound of lapping water.

As the moonlight danced and sparkled on the bay, she began to relax. She was not alone after all. There were people all around. Some with canoes nearby waded out in the channel, the muscles in their strong backs flexed as they pulled nets. Women with long, flowing ankle-length dresses stumbled, giggling with half-cocked parasols. They dissolved. Riley shuddered.

She decided to be still, as if she were something that had grown out of the mud. Her feet took root deep below the surface. After a while, she decided she would never move again. She'd turn to rock and for thousands of years the moon would wax and wane, the earth would continue to turn, and she would watch hermit crabs scoot sideways in and out of mud holes at low tide. No one would ever suspect that she was alive—the tiny pores of her stone surface actually breathing. She stood in the mud for a long time. The moon continued moving west, the stars swirled, the crabs clicked sideways, the noise of the party faded.

Cool saltwater licked her legs and finally startled her out of her stillness. Time had passed, hours perhaps. She must have out-waited Sully. It wasn't in his nature to have this much patience. He was gone, had to be gone, to the next raging party, chasing drunken tail, in search of more blow. Whatever it was that motivated him, he would have followed it by now. She clambered shoeless over the slippery rocks back to solid ground.

Although a few cars were abandoned in the parking lot, she heard no voices as she crept quietly out of the reeds toward the platform where the party had been raging. She felt rocks and glass beneath her feet but ignored the sensation because she had to get away.

If Sully had a car, she did not know what it looked like. She'd seen him driving cars before but always different ones. Her bike was leaning against the fence where she had put it. Had she missed it earlier? She could not trust her mind. The intensity of hallucinations was slowing but they still crept up from time to time. Barefoot, with mud caked up to her calves, she walked slowly toward her bike. She smelled of low tide. She wanted to wash it off, wash the whole night off, and wash her mind free.

When she leaned over to unlock her bike, her head was wrenched backward. Her muddy feet scrambled across the gravel lot to ease the pain on her scalp. Sully had grabbed her by the hair and was pulling her toward the parking lot. She tried to sweep her foot around his leg but he was too far in front of her moving toward a rusty white sedan. She cursed her hair. She had let it grow out because she wanted to feel it blow in the wind. She had felt naked and exposed without long hair. Now Sully had it wrapped it in his hand like a rope.

Riley tried to remember something from Taekwondo. Dread and panic rose like the tide, and her mind went blank. This was not like sparring practice. Sully had not bowed to her before he attacked her. He was a foot taller and seventy pounds heavier.

He shifted his body to open the back door of the Sedan. With all her force, she spun and kneed him in the groin. He doubled over and clutched himself releasing her hair. She began running back into the reserve but stopped when something sharp pierced her right heel. She lifted her foot. Bright fresh blood mixed with the mud.

"Bitch!" Sully yelled in a loud but weakened voice.

She crouched behind a small boulder and looked at her foot again. The caked mud helped to slow the bleeding, but it still seeped from a deep slice on her heel. There was no time to go back and hide. He was coming down the path and she had to stop him. The acid in her brain infused him with demon powers, but she felt a power too. It was something deep within her, yet somehow not of her.

He came down the path looking from side to side. She sprang out from the rock sweeping at his ankles. She knocked him off balance. He landed on his back and tried to push himself up. His hands were behind him and his chest was exposed. Malice shone in his eyes. He was about to lunge at her from his low position.

In a fury, she aimed the side of her left foot to the right of the gold shamrock dangling by his sternum and kicked him hard in the chest. The impact stopped him. He clutched his heart, gasped for air and fell to the ground.

Riley limped toward the parking lot hoping he wouldn't rise and come after her again. She looked back over her shoulder. His body was dead still. After he did not move for two minutes, she turned, limped back and stood over him. He lay flat on his back, clutched his heart and looked up at the sky. Riley titled her head back and followed his gaze. The moon had moved west and dropped out of sight, but the stars shone above. The sonar hum of night insects filled the silence. She crouched on the ground and hovered over him.

He looked into her eyes and his face softened. "No one's ever looked at me like that before." He groaned.

"Like what?" Riley asked.

"Like they cared that much," he said with effort. "Kiss me." He rolled sideways and winced.

"What?"

"Kiss me," he groaned. He lay flat on his back again and looked at her with sad, pleading eyes. "I won't hurt you. I'm dying."

Her body tingled as if an electrical current ran through it. Was he really dying? If so, would he use his final moment of life to wrap his fingers around her throat and squeeze the last breath out of her? Her fear dissipated into pity because she could see his fading spirit and how his whole life had been a series of unfortunate events and misdirected desire.

She knelt over him. Their eyes locked and she lowered her lips to his. Her hair fell over him like a dark veil. When their lips first touched she felt warmth—a subtle movement. Then it was gone and his lips went slack. She raised her head from his corpse, knowing without even checking his pulse, that he was gone. He was gone and she could still feel on her lips, would forever feel on her lips—that tiny window between life and death. Knowledge reserved for those who dared to kiss the dying.

She looked down at the foot she'd used to kill him. It seemed separate from her body. She looked at his chest where she'd struck. There was dirt but no blood. She must be mistaken. No blood anywhere—he couldn't be dead. She crouched by him and felt for his pulse, switching between the brachial and arterial pulses as she'd been taught. After several minutes she gave up. She couldn't leave him lying there looking passed out when he was dead so she picked some sumac and cat o' nine tails and laid them across his chest as if they might help him in the next world like the guns and swords buried in the tombs of kings and generals.

In a stunned trance, she stood and walked toward her bike. She swung her muddy leg over it and barefooted, began to pedal away. The wind lifted and blew her hair. She looked over her shoulder then back at the road ahead, feeling free for the first time in a long while. Pedaling down the deserted road, an early morning chill crept into her bones as salty tears warmed her cheeks.

Forty-nine

JOHNNY WAITED for Dennis Mulligan at Anthony's in Swampscott. From his table, he could see the parking lot and a slice of the Harbor. Anthony's was a safe distance from where either of them lived or worked, so they were unlikely to run into anyone they knew. They'd been meeting here several times a year for the past decade. Johnny liked the food— clean and fresh without heavy sauces. He'd order fish, grilled or broiled, lightly sautéed vegetables paired with a pinot noir. He was in great health, except for some minor heart trouble, which he kept under control with exercise and a good diet.

He looked at his watch and felt irritation settle into his jaw. Mulligan was ten minutes late, and he was the one who had called the meeting. It wasn't the time so much as what it meant—a lack of respect.

A dark green Jaguar zipped into the parking lot and occupied a handicapped spot. Mulligan popped out of the car wearing dark glasses, coiffed hair and a flashy suit—swaggering as if he owned the world and it didn't quite meet his standards. Jesus. Johnny shook his head and tried to control his rising anger.

Mulligan breezed in, inquired with the hostess, caught sight of Johnny and headed for the table. He stood in front of Johnny and looked around the restaurant.

"I'll get us a better table," he said.

"Just sit the fuck down. What are you going to do—propose or something?"

Mulligan sat down and reeled himself in. He cleared his throat. "Sorry, I'm a little late. This big dig is killing me—every direction, every time of day—traffic. Ahh, what da ya gonna do, huh? Let's get a nice bottle of veno." He opened the wine menu and pursed his lips.

After the waiter brought wine, filled their glasses and walked away, Mulligan said, "I got some bad news, Johnny."

Showing no emotion, Johnny kept his eyes locked on Mulligan's. He waited for him to continue. Mulligan coughed into his fist and watched a good looking waitress carrying a heavy tray above her head across the room. "It's time. They'll be coming for you soon." He lowered his voice and looked around the restaurant again. "This should be our last meeting. Somehow I've come under

190

suspicion for colluding with you. I'm getting a lot of heat at the Bureau."

Johnny looked out the window. His eyes were fixed on Mulligan's Jaguar. "Hmmm, I wonder why anyone would think you're on the take. It couldn't be….that car….or the watch you're wearing, or your fancy suits, or the way you strut around like a peacock with his head up his ass. Jesus, Mulley, I warned you about all that. I told you to keep a low profile!"

Mulligan nodded and looked repentant."Yeah, Johnny. I know it. I just couldn't help myself. A kid from the projects with all this money—how could I not spend it?"

Johnny softened his tone. "I got a plan. But what about you? Have you done anything to protect yourself?"

Mulligan smiled and shook his head. "Oh, they've got nothing on me. It's just the rumor mill, you know. But a man's reputation is everything. So that could hurt me."

Johnny took a sip of wine. "I'm not worried about your reputation. I'm worried about your ass landing in the big house. Somehow I don't think you've got what it takes to do hard time." He stared at Mulligan's hair, which was fluffed up like a girl's.

Mulligan scoffed, "Ha! You know where I come from. Under the fancy threads, I'm the same tough nut I always was. Even if I've gone soft, it doesn't matter, because I'm not going to prison. And you're not either. That's why I'm telling you this now. Go as soon as you can."

Before they parted ways, they gave each other an awkward, half-hug manly squeeze on the shoulder, knowing that their decades long relationship was about to end—forever.

Fifty

THE VEIL between the real world and the spirit world is said to be thinnest sometime between three and four o'clock in the morning. Those awake at that time will tell you it is true. Strange things happen, even to those who don't believe. At three-twenty a.m., on June 23, 1986, Johnny McPherson woke from a restless sleep. Later that morning he would begin his life on the lam. He'd gone over the particulars with painstaking care. He'd covered all the bases and then covered them again because he could not afford any mistakes.

To someone watching, it would have never seemed that he was about to disappear and take on a new identity. After his meeting with Mulligan, when he had casually dropped by to see his brother, sisters and mother, it had been to say good-bye forever. Yet he could not say goodbye, could not let them know what he was doing. If his family knew he was leaving forever, it was not because he told them. They said what they needed to say while saying something else.

He was already nostalgic for everything he was about to leave behind, but he was also anxious to begin his exile. His unlikely bonding with Riley, and the fate that had befallen her parents, weighed on him. It was unfortunate yet necessary. Her mom was an accident, but her dad was a loose cannon who had to be taken out. Of all the people Johnny had known for generations, why did he think about Riley the most? She was probably better off without her crazy father. But who would look after her now?

He leashed Caesar only out of habit. There would be no one out at this time of the morning. He walked east on Victory Road heading toward the marina where condos multiplied like jackrabbits. The humidity of a pending thundershower hung in the air. After Caesar did his business, Johnny turned around and headed back before it began to pour. He stopped and wiped his feet at the door even though he'd be leaving the place for good in four or five hours. As soon as he entered the kitchen, rain began to pelt the windows and drum on the roof. Weariness replaced his anxiety, and he put the kettle on for a cup of tea.

THE FIRST DROPS of rain felt like tiny needles. Initially, it was refreshing. Then the drops came down harder, lashing Riley's flesh like cold whips. She bent her head against the long wet fingers sweeping in from the bay. Beneath her bike, the street flowed like a small, brown river. Mud splattered from her tires into her face. The spiked pedals hurt her feet. Blood dripped from them and dissolved in the flowing gutter. Her body shook and her hands became so stiff and achy she barely had the strength to grasp her handlebars.

She wanted to make it to her apartment, stand under a hot shower and wash the muck and chill from her body. Yet it seemed impossibly far. The road in front of her blurred, and she fought to keep the bike upright. Each second seemed to drag on as if time had slowed. Every unpleasant sensation was amplified. Agony pulsed through her body like bad music. Was this what torture felt like?

When she died, she hoped it would be quick. More than anything she feared a slow, painful death like those of the martyrs and saints she'd read about as a child. She wondered what her mother had felt, burning to death. Imagining her mother's pain brought forth a wave of tears and anguish. This pain did not come from the cold that numbed her, but rather a hot place deep within. At least the heat of this grief thawed her stiffened hands.

Set back on her right, nestled close to the bay, were the quaint, stacked townhouses of Lewisburg Square, old-fashioned-style brick row houses—solid yet inviting. She rode into the parking lot. A faint light shone from Johnny's upstairs window. She didn't want to be a bother. What would he think of her, showing up like this in the middle of the night? But she had to stop the uncontrollable shivering that racked her body, and she really needed a friend now. What if she went home and her father still wasn't there? What if he never came home? What would come of Sully's death? Would she be accused of murder?

She got off her bike and stood at Johnny's door. After she reached out and rang the bell, she crossed her arms over her chest and tried to quiet her chattering teeth. The door flew open and the barrel of a gun was thrust into her face. She screamed.

The man holding the gun did not look like the Johnny she knew. The man holding the gun had eyes that were shallow and dull like the steel of a cafeteria spoon. His weird smile was a sideways snarl accentuating a pointy canine that she had never noticed before. She looked from his mouth back to his eyes and saw his expression change as recognition washed over him. He dropped the gun to his side and the angry mask dissolved—but she was still screaming.

193

HE WRAPPED an arm around her head, covered her mouth and dragged her into the apartment. He placed the gun on the kitchen table and put his finger to his lips. "Shhh, shhhh! It's okay. I thought you were a burglar."

His hand stayed clamped on her mouth until she finally relaxed.

"Good God." He sniffed. "You smell like low tide. What's going on? It's the middle of the night." He took a step back and looked her over. "Where the hell are your shoes?"

"Jesus, Johnny! You scared the crap out of me with that gun. You know, burglars don't usually ring the door bell." She wrinkled her nose at the gun on the table like it was a dead squirrel. "Johnny, you've got to help me. That guy, he came after me again and I… I accidently killed him."

She did not look like the girl he'd spent so many mornings with, watching the sunrise, her face filled with wonder and naïve hope. She looked broken and wild, like a wounded animal. He was torn between the impulse to mend her, or put her out of her misery.

"What are you talking about? Sit down." He guided her into a chair at the kitchen table. "What happened?"

She began by telling him how her father had been missing since her birthday. The tea kettle screamed. He removed it from the burner and turned off the stove. She was under the table with her hands over her ears. He grabbed her by the shoulder, placed her back in the chair and searched her eyes. "Are you on drugs?"

She told him how Sully had put acid in her beer and trapped her out in the reserve. He was the same kid who had beaten her up before.

"I tripped him, and then I kicked him as hard as I could. Right there…" She reached out and held her small finger over Johnny's heart. "He clutched his chest, said he was dying and asked me to kiss him. I felt so sorry that I did." She ran her fingers over her mouth and stared down at the floor. "My lips burned then turned ice cold."

Johnny shuddered, swallowed and tried to make sense of what was happening. He had killed people who had tried to tell him bullshit stories. Her story was unbelievable. Yet when people lied they tended to tell believable stories. Had she really killed a guy by kicking him in the chest? If so, that was fairly impressive. He tried to imagine it. Then his head hurt because of the timing of this mess with everything else he had to think about.

He put his hands to his head, brushed back his hair and paced the kitchen. "You never should have been out at a place like that drinking and carrying on. You open yourself up to all kinds of trouble."

"I killed him," she whispered, "Killed him. He's lying out there dead. And I'm a murderer." Her hands went to her face, her shoulders caved and she convulsed.

Johnny looked around his place like there might be an answer written on the wall somewhere. "Hey, don't feel bad about that. I would have liked to kill him myself. He had it coming." He looked back at the broken girl crying at his table and sighed. "Yeah, that's too much for you isn't it." He put a hand on her shoulder. He moved in front of her, took her hands from her face and looked into her eyes. "Listen, you're not a murderer. That's called self-defense, kid. Good for you. You're strong and brave. You kept him from raping you, maybe worse. Now tell me again, how exactly did you do it?"

"It was an accident. I didn't mean to kill him—I just wanted to hurt him enough so I could get away."

She described the kick again, and how she had executed it after she tripped him.

"That Taekwondo stuff has paid off."

"I thought you'd be mad."

"No, I'm disappointed that you were drinking at a place like that. You said you were never going to touch alcohol again, remember? But if you really killed that dirt bag yourself, I'm proud. You did good." He shook his head and raised his eyebrows. "Unbelievable, though."

"Well somehow I don't think the police are going to see it that way, so I'm running away."

Johnny regarded her wild hair and muddy clothes again. He glanced down at her bare feet and legs caked with mud. "Like that?"

Her voice shook. "I'm scared. I have this awful feeling something terrible has happened to my dad. Sometimes I don't see him for a couple of days, but he always writes me notes and leaves money on the table. I just can't believe he'd miss my birthday and disappear for four days if something isn't seriously wrong. His slutty girlfriend came by and she hasn't seen him either. I don't know what to do."

195

Johnny put his hands on his hips and started pacing the kitchen. "Maybe he's just on a bender."

She shook her head and stayed focused on the floor. "No. He's not the bender type. That's why he gets away with drinking so much. He's high functioning, even when he's totally hammered. My mom said he took the bar exam drunk."

Johnny put his hands on her shoulders again and locked eyes with her. "Listen, you shouldn't run away. You didn't do anything wrong. Where would you go? It's not safe for a young girl. You don't know the kind of things that could happen." He took his hands from her and ran them through his thinning hair again.

Shit, what was going to happen to this crazy girl? He couldn't cut her loose in the world with no one to protect her. What a mess. He knelt in front of her. "Okay, look at me. Are you sure you killed this kid? Did anyone see it? Where exactly did it happen?"

She looked at him briefly, then back to the floor. "We were alone. I don't know if anyone has found him yet. It happened less than an hour ago, I think. He's probably still lying in the grass. There was no blood. That was the weird thing—no blood. But I'm sure he's dead. I tried to take his pulse for a long time."

"Tell me exactly where the body is."

She looked at him. "What are you going to do? Are you going to call the cops? Please—"

"Listen, I'm not going to call the cops. I'm going to call someone I know who takes care of situations like this. He can get rid of the body so no one will ever find out what happened."

"You know someone who—takes care of dead bodies? Murdered bodies?" Her eyes narrowed on him and then she glanced at the gun on the table again.

"In this case, dear, it's not a murdered body. It's a scumbag who deserves to be dead. So tell me where the body is, and I'll make this phone call because we don't have any time to lose." He leaned against the counter. "Do you want something to drink?"

"Yes, please. I'm very thirsty."

"You know, I'm glad I got to see you tonight so I could say goodbye. I have to get out of town for a while because of a little legal trouble. I'm leaving later this morning." He opened the fridge. "Orange juice?"

"Sure. Johnny, what do you mean? What kind of legal trouble are you in? Too bad my dad's missing. He's a lawyer. He could help you."

"I don't think he could help me now. It's too late." He slid a glass of juice across the table.

"Why? What's going on?"

"Taxes I didn't pay." He waved his hand in the air as if he could flick it away.

"That doesn't sound too serious. I'm sure they'll give you a break for something like that."

Johnny cocked his head to the side and pointed at her. "Don't be too sure. You know, Al Capone was sent to Alcatraz for tax evasion. Almost died there too." He nodded knowingly.

"Yeah, but you're not Al Capone. Lots of people forget to pay their taxes. Don't they?" She swiveled in the chair and focused on the gun again quizzically as if she had no idea what it was.

"It's a little more serious than that."

Her face came to life and she looked at him. "Jesus Johnny. If you have to run away because of taxes, imagine what's going to happen to me? I killed someone!"

"I told you, I'm going to help you take care of that. Let's go over some of the particulars, and I'll call the fellow I know." Johnny whistled softly through his teeth shaking his head. "You know, I still can't believe a peanut like you killed a guy. How big was he?"

"I don't know exactly. He was big—five-ten and maybe one-sixty. I can't believe it either. I feel really bad."

The odor of low tide permeated the kitchen. Johnny looked down at her legs and bare feet. There was a small pool of blood under the kitchen chair where her feet were tucked. "You're bleeding and you need a bath." He bent over, picked up her leg and examined her heel. "The way that's bleeding it must be deep. Better get it cleaned and bandaged before it gets infected. Come on." He walked out of the kitchen toward the stairs. She followed him but stopped where the carpet began. A trail of mud and blood stained the cream-colored tile floor.

"What about your carpet? I don't want to get it all dirty and bloody."

He walked over, picked her up in a fireman's carry, held onto the banister, went up the stairs and set her down in the bathroom. While she was in the shower, he called Markie.

RILEY CRADLED her body in the steaming shower till the chill was gone. Her muscles relaxed, but her skin tingled as the water rinsed the mud and dirt from an intricate patchwork of scratches all over her feet, hands and face. She soaped and shampooed, sat down in the tub and rubbed the mud from her feet with a bar of Irish Spring. A steady stream of blood from her heel swirled down the drain. Even after she shut the water off, it flowed bright and fast. She grabbed a towel, dried off, and wrapped it around herself. From the tub she leaned over and opened the medicine cabinet. She couldn't find anything to wrap around her foot to stop the bleeding. She wondered where Johnny kept his giant first aid kit. She didn't want to be such a bother. But the blood would not stop. She hopped over, sat on the toilet and wrapped almost a whole roll of toilet paper around her foot.

She crept into the hallway and opened a closet door, hoping to find some bandages or the big first aid kit. She froze. It was not a closet. It was Johnny's bedroom. On the bed, guns and knives were lined up, organized by size, looking sleek, yet creepy, like a pile of black polished bones. She took a few steps into the bedroom and looked closer. Next to weapons, lay a suitcase filled with money, stacks of bills—one-hundred dollar bills!

She heard a rustling noise behind her. She jumped and turned around. Johnny stood there glaring at her. He looked angry. That face she'd seen when she rang the bell was back.

"What are you doing? This door was closed." He looked at the stuff on the bed and back at her.

"I was...I was looking for the closet, for some bandages, because my foot is bleeding. I didn't want to bother you or get your rug bloody." She looked down at her foot and tried to ignore the stuff on the bed. Pretend it was what everyone packed when they were going out of town.

"No, this is my room. Not a closet." His whole body seemed tense now, coiled like a spring. He looked at her foot and knitted his brow at the bright blood that had already soaked through the toilet paper. He took her by the elbow and led her into the hall. She walked awkwardly on the side of her foot trying not to get blood on his carpet or drop her towel. "I wish you hadn't gone in there," he said firmly. "I happen to be a gun collector, that's all. I'm going to put those in storage before I go." His voice sounded oddly formal. She could tell he was trying to control himself and it scared her.

He looked at her and sighed. "You don't have clean clothes do you? Let me see if I can find some for you." He went into his room, rummaged around, came back and handed her a t-shirt and some women's leggings. "My girlfriend Jean left these here."

Riley hopped into the bathroom and put on the clothes. When she came out, he was holding the first aid kit. "I almost forgot to pack this. Come on. Can you make it down the stairs?"

She nodded, held the railing, hopped down the stairs back into the kitchen and sat at the table again. He set the first aid kit down, turned on the light, sat in a chair in front of her and motioned for her to lift her leg. She lifted it and he held it in his hands.

He wrinkled his nose as he unraveled the toilet paper. "Never put toilet paper on a cut. Even clean, it's not sterile." He lifted and twisted her foot so he could examine the bottom under the light. He raised his eyebrows then squinted. "There's still glass in there. It's pretty deep. You got lots of cuts on your foot, probably the other one too. Not a good place to be barefoot, out there at Squaw Rock."

"Yeah," she said. "I would have preferred a beach in the Bahamas, but what're you gonna do?"

As he inspected her foot, she glanced again at the gun on the table. He reached into the first aid kit, pulled out some tweezers, sterilized them and started picking the glass from her sole. He bit his tongue while he did it. But this time she did not laugh.

"Listen dear, I have some bad news. While you were in the shower, I called that guy on the phone. He's an old friend who's got some connections around town. I asked him if he knew anything about your father."

Johnny shook his head and focused on removing the glass from her foot. "I'm sorry to tell you this, but the fellow said he heard your father has been taken out."

He looked up and cringed at her expression. She looked as if she had been slapped. "What does that mean?" She pulled her foot away, set it on the floor and leaned toward him. "Murdered?"

He nodded. "God only knows why. It could have been in a bar fight, over a gambling debt, anything. But in light of that information, I think you should get out of town for a while too. Why don't you come with me? We'll go on a little trip, until everything blows over with that boy you killed."

She leaned back in the chair and stared at him. He looked down and motioned for her to give back her foot. "I'm not done. You're still bleeding."

"I don't believe you."

"Look."

"I don't believe you about my father." Her eyes narrowed. "I have a funny feeling that you're lying to me. There's something you're not telling me."

He stared at her. His jaw hardened, he sucked on his teeth and finally sighed. "You know, sometimes the truth isn't what's good for you. Sometimes the truth is dangerous. A lot of people get killed, seeking the truth."

She gave another sideways glance at the gun on the kitchen table and then her eyes ran around the room, seemed to run up the stairs to his bedroom back to what was spread out on his bed. She knew too much. Her suspicion, her sudden hostility, and her challenge to his authority did not sit well right now.

"So, it's better to live a lie than seek the truth?" she asked.

"It's better to live, to keep breathing. Every day above ground is a good day, dear. Now give me your foot."

She raised her foot, set it in his waiting hands and leaned back in her chair.

"Who is this guy who said my dad has been 'taken out'? And come on, what's with all that stuff on your bed? Nobody packs like that, even if they're dodging the IRS. Who are you, Johnny?"

"Jesus, look at that!" He held a long, sharp, sliver of glass in the tweezers up to the light. "That was in your foot."

She leaned in to see what he held. Then she grabbed his wrist, the hand that held the tweezers, looked into his eyes and pleaded. "Tell me. Just tell me what's really going on. I need to know."

He leaned closer, stared straight into her eyes. "The LSD that guy slipped you has poisoned your brain. That's what's going on. So just... just do what I tell ya and try not to think too much."

"How would you know...have you done LSD? You don't seem like the type of guy to experiment—"

"I didn't. They gave it to me, all right. They put it in my food, in my water. I thought I was going crazy. Believe me I know what it's like."

"Who? Who did this to you?"

"The government. I was in prison. It was some kind of experimental research. I got an early release, but I don't know... what they did to me with the LSD...it seemed worse than the crime I'd committed."

"What were you in for?"

"Bank robbery."

"They gave you LSD while you were in prison? That's messed up."

They were both lost now. Johnny in the past, in those unfathomable years he'd spent in prison. The memories, the terrifying thought that he might be locked up again.

RILEY'S MIND was caught in the twisted reality that the government would give prisoners LSD. She had believed there was some kind of higher order in the world. That authority, as much as she shunned and distrusted it, was at least beyond evil.

"You can't trust anyone or anything when that stuff is poisoning your perception," said Johnny.

Riley smiled and her voice filled with sarcasm. "Come on. You can't mean that stuff—the guns and knives and money I saw on your bed was all an illusion?" She looked toward the stairs, "That stuff is there, and you are not who I thought you were. I might see things that aren't there, but I see what's really there too. I don't know what's true. I always thought underneath, everyone was good. I thought I could meet a nice old guy on a bench—a gentleman. I thought a guy like you was solid gold, Johnny. I never even questioned…but now I know I was wrong, to trust you, and think you actually cared about me. You're a criminal aren't you?"

JOHNNY'S FACE was soft but serious. He spoke in a low intense whisper. "Listen, I admit my business activities are mostly criminal. It's a rough game. You play it and lose, then you're either going to die or do a lot of time. You have to play to win, and that means you got to kill other people before they kill you. You got to drop a dime on them before they rat you out. In my line of work, all human decency, forgiveness, and mercy, must disappear if you want to survive. But when you're sitting on a bench in the morning, you're not working then. You're watching the sunrise. You see a beautiful young girl, trying to be strong, to keep her chin up when the world is dragging her down and the last thing you want to do is hurt her. The way things turned out—I did hurt you. Your father… Riley, he was stealing. It was one of my associates who killed him. We're not teachers. We can't give a rap on the knuckles and keep the kids after school. It's a war, and sometimes there's collateral damage. But I never meant to hurt you. From the sounds of it, your father was no good. If you were my daughter, I'd have protected you from all this."

Tears streamed down her face. "I know that all I ever did was to complain about him to you. But he was my father, and he was good once, before he started drinking again." She narrowed her eyes on his. "What are you going to do now, Johnny? Are you going to kill me too?"

He reached out and cupped her jaw in his hand. "Katie, no matter what else I've done, I would never harm you."

She blinked and searched his face. "Who the hell's Katie?" she yelled.

Johnny's hand slid down to her shoulder, his palm on the side of her neck. Anger coursed through his body. His fingers became stiff and hard around that slender, ropey neck. How easy it would be to snap.

Riley pressed him. "Johnny, who the hell is Katie?"

Caesar walked into the kitchen, let out a yelpy yawn and settled on the floor by her feet. The old dog, purchased to fill Katie's void, was almost sixteen. This was their last night together. He watched as the dog licked blood from the floor and then started on Riley's heel. Johnny closed his eyes and pulled his hand from her neck.

A long time ago, before he'd learned self control, he might have let his anger take over his hand, but now he contained it. He did not know how to make it right. This situation, a job gone bad, that had come back to haunt him. He could give her anything she wanted that money could buy. But he could never give back her parents or any semblance of a normal life.

"Katie was my daughter." He stared into the past remembering carrying her lifeless body, light as a pile of linen, down the hospital corridor.

"What happened to her?"

"She died," he mumbled.

"Did you kill her too?"

He looked at Riley with the hatred he reserved for those he killed. He stood up and hovered over her, picked up the juice glass from the table and threw it at the wall. He breathed deeply through his nose and tried to reign himself in before he did something he would regret. He fell back into the chair, his chest heaving from the adrenaline and anger pumping through his veins. He closed his eyes, shook and hung his head. "No. I didn't. God killed her. Maybe he took her to punish me. But if that's the kind of God he is, then damn him—damn him!"

Fifty-one

RILEY SLID her hand across the kitchen table toward the gun. A rush of anger and loss hit her stomach and tingled in her veins. She had to kill Johnny for what he did to her father. In a flash, the force of Johnny's strong old hand descended upon hers and flattened it to the table. With his other hand, he picked up the gun and tucked it behind him. Her body shuddered from the inevitable defeat. Her anger drained out of her and was replaced by sadness—not only for herself—but everything. She sighed and shook her head. "Johnny, have you been pissed off at God your whole life or just since your daughter died?" she asked.

He didn't answer. There was no anger in his eyes now. He just stared sadly at his loyal, old dog who'd come over to lick her foot. She could not kill Johnny. She could not hurt him with her small fists or the kicks she'd learned in Taekwondo. The darkness in him seemed as ancient and indestructible as the universe itself.

She'd been attracted to his quiet stealth, to the power and confidence that emanated from him. He seemed in control of the cruel world, which victimized her. Now she saw what his power was based on. He was a man who would kill to win and then somehow justify it. If he could do that, he could kill her too, no matter how much she might remind him of his dead daughter.

Yet there was something else about him, something she'd felt that first time she'd met him and squeezed his bicep when he was sitting on the bench. It was his basest instinct—maybe a weakness. If she could play to it, at least for a little while, she might win.

She closed her eyes and tried to replace her anger with a sorrowful but seductive look. She licked her lips, leaned toward him and spoke in a low whisper. "Johnny, I'm sorry to hear about your daughter. You would've been a great father. You would've given Katie everything." She shook her head and tilted it. "But I'm glad you're not my father." She moved closer and looked into his eyes. "Even now, knowing all that I do…" She looked at the floor. "I still have feelings for you."

He looked at her with narrowed eyes. She looked at the floor again. "The kind I shouldn't have." She gauged his reaction. Except for three quick blinks, he was absolutely still.

"In your own twisted way you were trying to protect me from my father's recklessness. Weren't you?" She moved closer, her face just inches from his, her eyes focused on his lips. It was easier than she had anticipated, playing a young seductress. After all, most everything she'd ever watched on TV or movies—from Shirley Temple to Madonna—had prepared her for this role.

Speechless, he nodded and stared at her, his eyes drifted down from her face. She felt his gaze on her body, a vulnerable yet powerful instrument, which she slithered onto his lap. She kissed him, long and hard on the mouth. He was quiet. His hands caressed her hips and back.

She stopped kissing him, grasped his jaw in her hand and put her face close to his scolding him like a child. "Part of me will always hate you. You know that don't you?"

His eyes searched the kitchen floor. He nodded, swallowed, sighed and looked at her suspiciously. She held his gaze. Her voice broke. "I don't care who you are, or what you've done. I don't want to be alone."

"You'll come with me then?"

She nodded and looked around. "I need some things from my apartment, but I don't want to go back there. I'm afraid if I do, I'll change my mind. "

"I'll go." He rose, grabbed his keys from the bowl and looked down at Caesar. "It's time to say good-bye to this poor old chap and drop him off at Mrs. O'Leary's. Let's make a list of what you need. While I'm gone I want you to try and get some sleep."

He grabbed a prescription bottle from the first aid kit and started back up the stairs. "Come on," he said.

She held onto the banister and hopped after him. He went into his room, grabbed a big army duffel bag from the closet and piled the guns and knives into it. He closed the suitcase, put it on the floor and turned down the blankets of his bed. "Lie down."

With her throat dry and tight, she swallowed. The saliva felt sharp, prickly, infused with fear. She did as he told her and got into the bed. He twisted the cap off the prescription bottle, went into the bathroom, came back, and handed her a glass of water with two pills.

"Take these. They'll help you calm down and get some rest. I'll be back in a couple of hours."

The pills, two chalk white angels of death, sat in her sweaty palm. She looked up at Johnny. "I better not. I could have an allergic reaction or something." She lifted her hand to give them back.

He grabbed her hand and closed her fingers around the pills. "That's very rare. Just take them."

Terrified, she put the pills into her mouth and took a swallow of water. The bitter, chalky substance dissolved under her tongue and made her want to vomit. She forced herself to stay calm as she watched him zip the duffel bag. He came over to the bed and put his hand on her back. "Shoes, clothes, a couple of books. Anything else?"

She shook her head. He bent and kissed her. She kept tight lipped. The chalky substance disintegrated and slid down her throat.

"Sleep," he said and guided her down until her head rested on the soft pillow.

The sheets felt so clean and crisp that they almost hurt her skin.

"I'll be right back." He lifted the duffel bag, heaved it over his shoulder and hurried down the stairs, forgetting the suitcase.

Fifty-two

THE FRONT DOOR squeaked open and thudded shut. Riley ran to the bathroom and spit what was left of the pills into the toilet. She turned on the sink and drank the running water, drinking and spitting three times. She turned the water off and pulled at her hair from the scalp as if trying to activate her brain. She stuck her fingers down her throat but nothing came up. How long would it take for the pills to put her to sleep?

She looked at her image in the mirror and gathered her will. She'd fallen for Johnny. Yet somewhere inside her was a fighter—who had killed rather than be hurt again. Her poor father was dead. What had they done to him? She'd gone through too much to give up and give in to Johnny. Yet even now that she knew who he was, and what he'd done, there was still something dangerously alluring about him. She fought a strange urge within her to succumb to his power.

In a confused panic, she ran back into the bedroom and rummaged through the closet. She found a gym bag, opened the suitcase, and stuffed as much money as she could into it. She looked under the bed—for what she didn't know. She just felt the overwhelming impulse to keep searching. A small revolver gleamed up at her from inside the drawer of the bedside table. She picked it up, surprised how well it fit into her hand. Was this what she'd been searching for? Who was directing her actions? She shoved the gun into the bag with the money.

In the kitchen, a brown phone hung from the wall. She stared at it, tried to calm down and figure out exactly what she was going to say. The policeman wanted her name, but she refused to give it. At the core of her being she felt the police weren't trustworthy. She wondered if they could trace the call, if she'd soon hear sirens and pounding on the door. She gave them the address of her apartment building, and told them they better hurry if they wanted to catch him. She replaced the phone on the receiver, grabbed the gym bag and flew out the door.

The cold sidewalk shocked her feet, and she remembered that she needed shoes. Her bike was still there, even though she had neglected to lock it. She positioned the duffel bag backpack style on her back, swung her leg over the bike and began to ride back to Squaw Rock.

Dawn was breaking all around in soft pinks and blues, the colors of newborns. The rusty white sedan was the only car in the parking lot. She needed that car now, and she had to hurry before the sleeping pills took effect. The keys weren't in the door. She searched the front seat and the ground. The only place left to look was his pocket.

She crept up the gravelly, uneven path, watching her step for glass. A lump lay in the distance looking like nothing more than a sandbag or some trash. But she knew it was him. The cattails and sumac covered his face. She placed the gym bag next to her and knelt over him. Her fingers fumbled then slid into his pocket and grasped the keys.

Tired now, her eyelids like heavy doors begging to be closed, she stumbled down the walkway and got into the car. She needed to get somewhere safe where she could sleep. She drove the Squantum causeway—Dorchester Bay on the north side, Quincy Bay on the south, dawn breaking to the east, spilling like a runny yoke into the water.

At the intersection of Quincy Shore Drive, she stopped at a red light. Dunkin Donuts was on the left, girls in pink and orange polyester uniforms stacked trays of donuts on the shelves. Out of the silence, sirens screamed. White and blue cop cars, flashing red, raced by and turned into the parking lot of Lewisburg Square. She stared as they passed.

Right down the street, the Quincy Bay Inn rose up and seemed to almost lean out over the Neponset River. The fact that some of the pink neon letters of the sign had been missing for years gave her hope that they might rent her a room—barefoot and too young. She grabbed two hundred-dollar bills from the gym bag and went into the lobby.

Fifty-three

HER FIRST KISS had blown his mind. The passion—he couldn't believe it had come from her. Yet the second kiss had been tight lipped and weird. Doubt kept him alert and cautious. He dropped off Caesar as fast as he could—no time for a drawn-out, tear-jerking goodbye. He'd deal with the loss of his constant companion later, when he could finally catch his breath.

He drove to her apartment on automatic pilot. With his mind free floating, he replayed the strange night. He saw the pills in her hand, and the words "allergic reaction" echoed in his mind. Then he was back at the hospital the night his daughter had died. "Allergic reaction—very rare"—the Doctor's somber voice had sounded hollow, bass. He stepped on the gas, not wanting to leave Riley alone for too long. He'd given her the pills to calm her down, but what if they reacted with the LSD, or she had an allergic reaction, and he returned to find her dead?

Even though he was in a hurry, he still parked a good three blocks away from her apartment. Once inside her apartment, he hurriedly scooped shoes and a pair of jeans from the floor of her bedroom. A picture on her bedside table caught his eye. It was Riley with her father and mother at a restaurant or something, all smiling, their heads together. Chilling recognition—her mother looked exactly like the woman from his nightmare. Yet he'd never seen her. How could he know what she looked like?

In the distance, he heard a siren scream. It grew louder. He dropped the picture. The frame shattered on the floor. Her cat meowed, jumped up on the windowsill, squeezed under the half open window and disappeared.

Johnny followed the cat's instincts. He dropped Riley's belongings, pushed the window all the way open and climbed out onto the fire escape. With careful quick steps, he descended the black mechanical vine until he reached the alley behind her apartment. He took the back streets to his car. He'd been dodging cops in this neighborhood since 1940 and not much had changed about it. As he drove down the street, he passed police cars zooming down the block toward Riley's apartment. She had betrayed him.

ALONE, driving north on I-93, Johnny remembered the last time he had left town by himself. It was almost forty years ago, his first exile, when he had hopped the circus train. Back then, he was content to be alone, but this time he wanted a companion. He felt like he had lost his daughter for a second time. But Riley wasn't Katie. She was Donavan's daughter. Had been Donavan's daughter, that is.

When she slid her hard young body onto his lap and looked at him with those seductive eyes, his rational mind had disintegrated. All thoughts of Riley as a daughter were lost to a strong lusty feeling and an overwhelming desire to screw her. But she had tricked him, and he had fallen for her. It had almost led to disaster.

The radio played a familiar song about blue eyes. He had heard it over the years, but had never really listened to the words. He glanced in the rearview mirror and looked briefly at his own blue eyes. His dreams felt empty. He had guns and money stashed both with him and around the world. He had fake I.D.'s, and a strong healthy body. He looked like any other middle-aged white guy in America. He could disappear and live in relative freedom. Yet he was alone and Riley had no one to protect her. At least the bag of money he had left might keep her off the streets.

SHE WAS ALONE. From the screened porch of the weather-shingled house on Grand Street in Falmouth, she could see the vast ocean. Steel blue stretched to the horizon dotted with passing sails and ships. In the parking lot across the street, a man removed chairs and umbrellas from his trunk. He was attempting to transform himself into a human cart when a little girl escaped from his car. She toddled across the parking lot toward the steep stairs that led to the beach. A woman emerged from the passenger side and started running after the toddler, but the contents of her beach bag spilled. She yelled to the man. He dropped his load, chased after the toddler, and scooped her into his arms. The world was a dangerous place for little girls. She was lucky to have her parents to protect her.

Riley turned from the screened porch window. They had been happy, that summer when she was four or five, in the house on Grand Street, overlooking Falmouth Heights Beach. With the missing money from her father's sock drawer, her mother had rented the very same house for the whole month of July. Maybe she had just wanted to be happy again, and had thought that renting the house might bring back a better time. Yet she had always said, "The road to hell was paved with good intentions." Riley closed her eyes and conjured her mother's presence. Her voice came on the sea breeze, soft but salty—full of regret. Was it the money that had started all this trouble, or the lack of it?

The Sunday Boston Globe lay scattered on the white wicker furniture. A half eaten piece of toast sat next to Johnny's picture and the headline "The Camel's Narrow Escape." He stared up at her from the paper. She zipped her sweatshirt and hugged off a chill, even though it was eighty-one degrees. A two-and-a-half page article had been written about Johnny, the anonymous tip, and how they had *almost* caught him. When she cooked an egg, watched the sunrise, or saw an old man with a dog, his image haunted her. He was not safely locked away. He was out there somewhere.

"Beyond all notions of right doing and wrong doing, there is a field. I'll meet you there. For when the soul lays down in that grass, there is nothing left to talk about." Rumi 12th Century

About the Author

Alison (Johnson) McLennan currently lives in Ogden, Utah with her son and husband. When not writing, she enjoys rock-climbing, skiing, snowboarding, mountain biking and yoga. Falling for Johnny is her first novel.

Look for her short stories, children's interactive series, and second novel, Ophelia's War, (available late 2013). Find her on FB and Twitter or ask questions and give her feedback through twistedrootspublishing.com

32583519R00121

Made in the USA
Lexington, KY
25 May 2014